MURDER IN SAVANNAH

(The Feminist with the Golden Balls)

William Breedlove Martin

W & B Publishers
USA

For information:
W & B Publishers
9001 Ridge Hill Street
Kernersville, NC 27284

www.a-argusbooks.com

ISBN: 9781942981770

Book Cover designed by Dubya

Printed in the United States of America

This book is for

my wife,

Frances,

my daughters,

Baynard and Rachel,

and my grandchildren,

Malley, Bubby and Mimi.

For sweetest things turn sourest by their deeds:
Lilies that fester smell far worse than weeds.

William Shakespeare
Sonnet #94

Chapter 1

Around 1:30 a.m. on that second Wednesday in January, The Other End was not as rowdy as it had been an hour earlier when Christian Peters and I'd had to break up a fight between two Marines and three Army Rangers. Even so, when my cell phone vibrated and I saw on the little screen that the call was from Detective Sergeant Lou Ackerman, my partner and mentor, I told Peters I'd be right back and stepped outside.

Flipping the phone open and covering my other ear with my free hand, I said, "What's up, Lou?"

"Sorry to butt in on your moonlighting, Slick, but we got you a body. You be ready in about ten minutes?" Lou asked in his gruff, gravelly old voice.

"I'll be outside," I said, my pulse speeding up almost as much as it had years before when I had been about to make my first jump as a paratrooper. The reason for this was that back in December I had been promoted to Detective with the Savannah Police Department and this would be my baptismal investigation of what I knew from Lou's "got you a body" was a homicide or a death that looked suspiciously like one.

The night was cold for Savannah, 28 degrees and windy, but I was hardly out of the club when the unmarked white Crown Vick rounded the corner and eased to a stop beside the curb in front of me. Less than a minute later, with my heart again pounding as I buckled myself in across from him on the bench-type seat, Lou hit the gas and we were off.

The scrawny little guy was wearing a pea-green tie and the cheap brown corduroy jacket that looked as old as I was. The usual unfiltered Camel protruded from his virtually lipless mouth.

"So tell me what we got, Lou?" I said, as we rounded one of the oak-shaded squares in the historic district of downtown Savannah.

"You went out there to school, didn't you, Slick?" Lou asked, the Camel twitching.

He was referring to the State University at Savannah, or SUS, which was about five miles west of downtown, not far from the hookup with I-16.

"Yes, I did. I finally graduated, too. Last summer," I said.

"What'd you take up?"

"My major was English, if that's what you mean."

"English? What the hell for?"

"I had to major in something. And I like to read. So tell me about this body."

"You're gonna love this, Slick."

"What?"

"It's out there."

"What's out where?"

"The body. At your school. And it's an English professor."

"What's his name?"

"I don't know, but it ain't a him. It's a her. The guy in campus security, Beeson, Benson or something, I think the dispatcher said his name was..."

"Baldwin. Tom Baldwin. He's retired Army Airborne. He's a good guy," I said.

"Anyway, he said one of the clean-up crew found her in her office about an hour ago. Strangled. Said there ain't no doubt. You know where Hampton Hall is?"

"Sure. That's where most of my classes were."

"Well, that's where we're going. The Lab Boys'll be there in a little while."

The campus looked much as it had on those many nights when I'd had to hurry to get to my classes on time. The sidewalks, the parking lots, the main quad, and the red-brick, generally barn-shaped building were all brightly lit. There were no people, though, or at least none that I could see, and the only car, aside from ours, was one of the SUS police cars. Parked sideways up on the grass and sidewalk, blocking the entrance to Hampton Hall, it was a sure sign that something was amiss.

We were met at that entrance by a campus policeman, a well-built black guy about my age, spit-polished and immaculate in his iron-gray uniform. He led us up the stairs to the second floor, then pointed toward the middle of the hall and said, "The last office on the right, in the cul-de-sac across from the display case." Leaving us, he went back down the stairs, presumably to wait for the Lab Boys.

As Lou and I headed down the hall, I knew that his laser-beam eyes were taking in everything from the trash cans to the wall postings, the intentness of his wrinkled old face reminding me of a computer with the mouse on Save.

When we got to the display case and made the right turn into the cul-de-sac, we saw two men standing outside the last office on the right, the door of which was ajar. One of them was the retired paratrooper I knew, Tom Baldwin, who had dropped from six stripes as a Sergeant First Class in the Army to three stripes as a shift supervisor at SUS. He was about my height, six-one, but much heavier, with a belly that overhung his pistol belt but was as solid as a bag of cement. His face was every bit as lined as Lou's and he walked with a bad leftward list, the result, he said, "Of too damn low a jump over Grenada back about a million years ago."

Standing next to him was a bald, wizened little white man of at least seventy. In old, shabby clothes and scuffed white sneakers with Velcro straps, he was staring at Lou and me through a pair of bifocals patched with duct tape.

I heard Sarge say that the old man's name was Johnny White, that he was a member of the janitorial crew, and that it was he who had found and reported the body. My eyes, however, and most of my attention, were not on Sarge and Johnny but on the door beside them.

Taped or pinned on it was an array of political statements. The centerpiece and obvious star was a ten-by-twelve color photograph of a fading but still pretty woman with brown hair much too long for her age whom I would have recognized, even without the autograph, as Gloria Steinem. Nearby, along with a scattering of brochures announcing conferences on women's literature and feminist studies, was a gallery of black and white New Yorker-type cartoons characterizing men as tyrants and idiots. Up near the top of the door and arranged in the shape of an arch over everything else were the words, in huge black fonts, A WOMAN NEEDS A MAN LIKE A FISH NEEDS A BICYCLE.

What really got me, though, was in the center of the door and inconspicuous, all but drowned out by the visual stridence of everything else. It was a simple black nameplate, cut into which, in white letters, was DR. MILDRED MARGULIS.

My jaw of course did not literally drop, but Sarge, seeing the look on my face, said only "Yeah" with his mouth but a great deal more with his eyes.

Lou, who seemed never to miss a thing, said, "Y'all know something I don't?"

"I'll tell you later," I said.

Back in December, when I had been assigned to Lou, he had made it clear that I was to be what he called "the alpha dog" in our investigations. In the dozen or so cases we had been together on thus far, he seemed to have been more or less pleased with my work, because he had said mostly good things. But this, as I said earlier, would be my first homicide and I was, to be crude about it, scared shitless of having those death ray eyes see me do something dumb.

Again reminding myself of my long-ago vow always to remain calm and to be as country-boy polite and un-cop like as possible, I turned to the old man and said, "You discovered the body, Mr. White? Is that correct?"

"I did, yeah," he said in a weak, raspy voice.

"When was that?"

"When I was getting ready to mop."

"Can you remember exactly what time that was?" I asked, noting that he had a watch on his shrunken little wrist.

"Right before I told him," he said, looking at Sarge.

"Allowing five or so minutes for him to get from here to the guard shack, that would have been about 1:15, give or take maybe five minutes," Sarge said.

"When you were getting ready to mop, was the door open or what?" I asked.

"No, but the light was on because I saw it underneath. Underneath the door."

"What did you do then?"

"I knocked and when didn't nobody answer I went in."

"The door was unlocked?"

He shook his head. "I got a key."

"A pass key?"

"Yeah. It'll open near about every door out here."

"When you opened the door, did you turn the knob with just your key or did you use your hand too?"

"The key. Just the key."

I nodded, then said, "And what you saw when you went into the office is exactly what's in there now? Is that correct, Mr. White?"

"I didn't touch nothing. I hightailed it over to security."

"Did you see anybody in the building or on your way over to security?"

"I didn't see nobody."

"Did you leave the professor's door open or did you close it and lock it behind you?"

"Closed it and locked it."

"Did you touch the knob when you did so?"

He shook his head. "Just with my key. Like before."

"So the office was locked between the time you left it and the time when you and Sergeant Baldwin came back to it? Is that correct?"

"Yeah, it is."

"And of course you, Sergeant Baldwin, when you went into the office you used just your key and didn't touch anything either?" I said.

"That's correct. I assessed the situation, then made some phone calls. I've been outside the door, with Johnny here, ever since," Sarge said.

I nodded, then said to both Sarge and Johnny, "Thank you, gentlemen. I think we can take it from here. If you think of anything that you think might be of help to us, give me a call at either of these numbers."

I handed each of them one of my business cards, which had come from the printer's only three days before. Much as I had at my college diploma when I finally got it, I had stared at my cards with both pride and a certain amount of disbelief. Like my new badge, they were proof positive that I was really and truly a detective.

When Sarge and Johnny were out of the cul-de-sac, Lou looked at me with his death ray eyes and with a little grin said, "It's later, Slick."

"Later?" I asked, then remembered and said, "I had a class under Dr. Margulis about a year ago. I hated her guts. Just about everybody in the class did. Sarge did too. He had several run-ins with her."

"What was her problem?"

Jerking my head toward the door, I said, "That tell you anything?"

"Ball busting fem libber?"

"You got it, buddy. World class."

"Well, let's see if we can't get us a good look-see before the Lab Boys get here," Lou said, slipping on his latex gloves, then taking a ball point pen out of his jacket pocket and using it to ease the ajar door completely open.

The office was a perfect square, maybe twelve feet by twelve feet, and the desk, facing the door, was about two-thirds of the way in. Dr. Mildred Margulis was behind it. Her arms limp by her sides, she was slouched in her chair, with her head stretched back to the limit of her neck, her long brown hair hanging halfway to the floor, her mouth agape, and her lightless brown eyes gazing up at the ceiling. On her face was a look of pure terror and around her neck, stark against the white of her blouse, was a shiny purple ribbon about an inch wide. At the end of the ribbon, hanging between the swells of her smallish breasts, was a round bronze medal embossed with a runner in full stride. From the lobe of her left ear, on a delicate chain about an inch long, dangled a pair of little golden balls that could have been testicles or maybe just figs. The lobe of the right ear was torn and several flecks of blood were on the collar of her blouse.

After we'd snooped for about fifteen minutes, Lou nodded and said, "Okay, Slick, what we got so far?"

As I always did at that point in an investigation, I felt like a schoolboy called upon to recite. I said, "It's a homicide. No doubt about it."

"How so?"

"The neck. The marks on the neck. The look in the eyes. The lamp knocked off the desk and still on. The pens and pencils, and the mug that had held them, scattered on the floor around the desk. The papers on the floor, also scattered and in contrast to the footlocker neatness of everything else. The rip in the right ear lob, from where the earring was yanked out."

Nodding, Lou said, "Where is it?"

"That's a good question," I said. "I looked under the desk and everywhere else I could without touching anything."

"What else?"

"She knew the assailant and wasn't afraid of him. Or her."

"Oh?"

"There was no forced entry and she was strangled from behind. The weapon, the ribbon on the medal, probably had been hanging with the other medals, four of them, that are still on the coat rack, which is several feet behind the desk."

"How do you know she wasn't strangled somewhere else and then put in the chair?" Lou asked, a challenge in his eyes.

"If that had been the case, the desk lamp and the other stuff wouldn't be all over the floor. Unless, of course, the assailant put them there to mislead us. But I don't think so. I'm sure, or sure enough to bet on it, that she was killed right where she is now."

A moment later I said, "There's something else too."

"What?"

"I think the assailant, standing behind her, garroted her with both strands of the ribbon, pulled her hair out of the way, then placed the ribbon around her neck. He could've slipped it over her head first, before he killed her, but she was a runner and a pretty strong woman and the ribbon was kind of thin, probably too thin for a single strand to have worked. So he strangled her and then ripped off the earring. He gave her an award and made off with a souvenir."

"You're saying the killer was making a statement, Slick? Is that what you're saying?" Lou said with one of his wry little grins.

"That's exactly what I'm saying. He wasn't content just to kill her. He had to desecrate her body, too."

Lou and I continued our own snooping even after the Lab Boys got there. I went through the handbag that was in the bottom drawer of the desk and found, along with the usual female items, a wallet containing a driver's license, several credit cards, a SUS ID, and $52 in assorted bills. Also in the wallet was a school picture of a pretty little girl, six or so, who had grown into the even better looking young woman, maybe eighteen, in the framed picture on the desk.

"Her daughter?" Lou asked.

"Probably. She talked about having one in that class I took from her."

"Was she married?"

"Not when I had that class."

Beneath the phone, on top of the Savannah telephone book, was a directory that listed by department the contact information for all SUS employees. Because of the latex gloves I was wearing, I had some difficulty in turning the pages, but eventually I got to THE DEPARTMENT OF ENGLISH and found MARGULIS, MILDRED. Beside the name of each professor was a parenthesis, in almost all of which was a first name, female for the males and male for the females. Seeing no name in the parenthesis beside Margulis, I said, "If I'm reading this right, she wasn't married."

"Can't imagine why," Lou said with a smirk that no doubt referred to the women's lib pictures, posters, and slogans that were also on the inside of the office door.

***

At 6:55 Lou eased the Crown Vick to a stop in front of a small, one-story house that, like the rest of the houses in the neighborhood, was well-kept and very middle-class looking. In front of the house was a late model white Chevy Blazer with huge tires on shiny rims, a Georgia Bulldogs decal on the rear window, and several splashes of mud on the rocker panel behind both the front and the rear wheels. Not in the carport but beside it on the grass sat a silver Honda Accord that looked about ten years old.

We were met at the front door by a young man, twenty or so, in faded jeans and a red flannel shirt. He was as tall as I was and had the thick, strong look of a well-fed construction worker. In his good, almost handsome face were intelligent blue eyes, and covering most of his longish black hair was a red and black Bulldogs cap with the bill forward.

"Y'all come on in. I'm Bryan," he said in a thick, very Southern voice as he shook hands with Lou, then with me, his hand bigger and harder than mine and probably as strong.

"She's still pretty upset, seeing her mama like that and all," he said, ushering us into a living room that looked much as I would have imagined. It had the usual furnishings of a sofa, a coffee table, chairs, bric-a-brac, etc. but something gave it a severe, uninviting look. Maybe it was the absence of rugs and family photographs or just the way I felt about Professor Margulis.

Standing in front of the sofa, in jeans and a white Bulldogs sweat shirt, was Gloria Margulis, who was even better-looking in person than in the photograph back at the crime scene. Around 5'7", she had blue eyes, sculpted cheeks, full, beautifully shaped lips, and a slender but nicely fleshed body. The only resemblance I could see between her and her mother was the light brown, shoulder-length hair.

After introductions, everyone sat down, Gloria and Bryan on the sofa and Lou and I in chairs on the other side of the coffee table.

I extended my and Lou's sympathy, then said, "Ms. Margulis..."

"Wills. Gloria Wills. Call me Gloria, please."

I nodded. "Gloria, your parents were divorced. Is that correct?"

"Yes."

"Does your father live in or near Savannah?"

"No. He lives in Colorado, in Denver. I called him this morning right after I got back from...from identifying my mother."

"Do you have any family in Savannah?"

She shook her head. "The closest is in Kentucky, my Aunt Jane. She's my mother's older sister."

"Does she or any other member of your family know about your mother?"

"Nobody but my father and my grandfather. My mother's father. I called him too."

"Where does he live?"

"Also in Denver."

"Were you at home all last night?" I asked.

"Yes."

"Your mother had a night class this quarter, on Tuesday and Thursday, from six until eight-thirty. Is that correct?"

"Yes."

"What time did she get home from it? Generally?"

"Between nine-thirty and ten. Sometimes a little later."

"What time did you go to bed last night?"

"Eleven, maybe eleven-thirty."

"You didn't think anything amiss when your mother wasn't home by then?"

"No."

"Why not?"

Gloria looked at Bryan, then said, "She didn't always come home after class."

"She stayed out?"

"Yes."

"All night?"

"Sometimes."

"Where?"

Gloria's shrug was barely perceptible. "With friends."

"Were they men friends?"

"Yes."

"Do you know their names?"

"Some of them."

"How many were there?"

"I don't know."

"Do you know if she was on bad terms with any of them? Any of them who might wish her harm?"

Gloria again glanced at Bryan, then said, "No, not really."

"What do you mean?" I asked, aware that Lou, as always, was taking it all in.

"There was this one guy. He got upset when she dum...when she stopped seeing him."

"What's his name?"

"Nigel. Nigel Helton. He's a professor out at SUS. In the biology department."

"Your mother dumped him and he got upset about it? Is that what you're saying?"

Gloria nodded. "But he wouldn't hurt her. I know he wouldn't. He wanted to marry her."

"When did your mother break up with him?"

"Last summer. I don't remember exactly when."

"Do you know of anyone else who had any kind of conflict, romantic or otherwise, with your mother?" I asked.

After a deep sigh and another glance at Bryan, Gloria said, "Detective....What did you say your name was again?"

"Loomis. T.J. Loomis."

"Detective Loomis, my mother had conflicts with a lot of people."

"Her students?"

"Yes."

"What about her fellow professors, her colleagues?"

"Them too."

"Were these conflicts serious?"

"Some were."

"How serious?"

"Serious enough to make my mother cry."

"Your mother didn't cry easily? Is that what you're saying?"

"My mother prided herself on being strong. She'd almost rather die than cry."

Reminding me of a snake in the way that he suddenly came alive and struck, Lou said, "What was your conflict with your mother about, Gloria?"

"I loved my mother very much, Detective," Gloria said in an aggrieved tone, her red eyes getting moist as she turned toward him.

"I'm sure you did, but most daughters have conflicts with their mothers. What were yours? What were they about?"

Closing her eyes as tears spilled down her cheeks, Gloria said, "Everything. Just everything."

Shifting his eyes from Gloria to Lou and me, Bryan said "Y'all mind if I say something?"

Lou shook his head and I said, "Not at all. Please do."

"What it mainly was, when you get right down to it, was that Gloria's mama, Dr. Margulis, just flat out hated being down here," Bryan said, slowly shaking his head.

"In the South, you mean?"

"Yes, sir. She was from Colorado, from Denver, and she didn't like anything down here—the weather, the gnats, people saying ma'am to her, nothing."

"Did she like you?" I asked.

"No, sir."

"What about you? Did you like her?"

"I tried to."

"But you didn't?" Lou said.

Bryan shook his head. "No, sir. I didn't. I didn't like her at all."

I said, "What do you do for a living, Mr...."

"Doyle. Bryan Doyle. I work for my daddy."

"Doing what?"

"Building houses. Doyle Construction."

I nodded. "I've heard of it."

"I go to school too," Bryan said.

"To UGA?" I asked, referring to his Bulldogs cap.

"No, sir. To SUS."

"When are your classes?"

"I'm not taking but one this quarter. It's on Tuesday and Thursday nights."

"What time?"

"Six to eight-thirty."

"What's the class?"

"Western Civ 112."

"What building's it in?"

"Hampton. Hampton Hall."

"Did you go to your class last night, Bryan?" Lou snapped, his death rays blazing.

"Yes, sir, I did."

"What about afterwards? What'd you do afterwards?"

"I went home."

"Do you have your own place or do you live with your parents?" Lou continued.

"With my parents."

"Where is that?"

"In Wilshire Woods."

"What time did you get home last night?"

"About nine."

"Were your parents there then?"

"No, sir. They weren't."

"Where were they?"

"At the hospital. My grandmama—my mama's mama—she's got cancer."

Lou said, "I'm sorry," then "Was anybody there when you got there?"

"No, sir. Nobody was," Bryan said with a nervous look in his eyes as he shook his head.

***

C. Edward DiFong, III, also known as Mr. Showboat, was the Assistant District Attorney assigned to the case. I'm not sure how long he'd been one of our twenty or so ADA's, but it was long enough, when we first heard we were stuck with him, for me to groan "Oh, shit!" and for Lou to shrug his boney little shoulders and say "Don't sweat it, Slick. He ain't gonna fuck with us."

Behind my reaction, first of all, was that DiFong, 30 and no more than 5'6", was one of those runty little men with a compelling need to one-up or put down any man more than two or three inches taller than he was. He couldn't do this physically, being pudgy and about as athletic as an overfed lapdog, so he did it, or tried to do it, in other ways, mainly with the power that being an ADA temporarily gave him over defendants and the cops on his cases.

A native of Atlanta and a graduate of the University of Georgia law school, DiFong was also something of an updated scalawag, which is to say the kind of Southerner who, when it suited him, could be so politically correct as to make even Jesse Jackson and Gloria Steinem take note. This was most evident in the courtroom. He seemed blind to color, gender, and class when the crime involved only the same general demographic, such as white-on-white, black-on-black, female-on-female, or poor-on-poor. But woe be unto the accused if, say, he were a white male and his victim had been a black of either gender or a female of any color. In such cases DiFong pulled out all of the stops in representing himself as an avenging angel and the guy in the dock as more evil than Hitler.

Lou, naturally, saw through this a lot better than I did. He said there was "none of that social conscience bullshit" behind it, just ambition, pure ambition, and that DiFong was like most young ADA's in that he would play the race card, the gender card, or any other such card if he thought he could use it as an ace. Further, all of our prosecutors, from the Big Boss DA on down, knew that Lou was the department's ace investigator and did his best work when he was left alone, especially during the initial stages of an investigation.

There were two other reasons for Lou's assurances that we wouldn't be messed with. One was that, despite his ambition, DiFong was at bottom very lazy and comfort-loving. The other was that he had seen enough of those death ray eyes to be just flat out scared of Lou.

So, rather than joining us at the crime scene at 2 a.m., C. Edward DiFong, III had clicked off his cell phone and gone back to sleep. He had also declined to go with us back out to SUS later that morning for the next stage of our investigation.

Chapter 2

At 9:52, having made arrangements with Dr. Steve Harrison, the Head of the Department of English at SUS, Lou and I were standing by the chalkboard with Carla Wells, our fingerprinter, in a classroom in Hampton Hall. Most of the desks in front of us were filled with members of the English department, and, our meeting set to begin at ten, we were waiting for the rest of the department to arrive. All English classes for that day had been cancelled, and Dr. Harrison had assured me that his entire staff would be present.

Lou was his usual bored-looking but hyper-alert self, and Carla was quite composed, but I was in a dither that I had to struggle to control. I had been on the go, without even a minute of sleep, for the past thirty hours; I had added two more cups of coffee to the three I had at breakfast; and I was about to make a speech to a room full of English professors, thirty-two in all, Dr. Harrison said, ten of whom, including Dr. Harrison, had been my teachers.

At 10:02, immediately after the last vacant seat was taken by a bespectacled, runner-skinny professor whom I recognized as Mr. Flanagan, Dr. Harrison, who was standing beside the door, gave Lou and me a solemn nod that abruptly ended the low buzz of nervous chitchat. Seconds later, after closing the door, he was the focus of every eye in the room as he stood behind the lectern a few feet to my left.

In his mid-to-late fifties, Dr. Harrison was a badly overweight man, 5'10" or so and at least 250 pounds, and I remembered from my two classes under him that he suffered from bad knees, frequent shortness of breath, and probably a number of other health problems. He had a fine head of black hair combed straight back and a face that was unlined, gentle, and, despite the extra chins and the beginnings of a wattle, still quite handsome.

In his soft but richly resonant voice, Dr. Harrison said, "Early this morning, around 1:30, a member of the cleaning crew found Mildred Margulis dead in her office. She apparently—perhaps I should say definitely-- had been murdered, strangled. The story was on the front page of the Savannah Morning News this morning and was the lead item on all four local channels. So I assume that we all are aware of this?"

When no one said otherwise, Dr. Harrison said, "I called this meeting at the request of the two officers who will be handling the case, Detective Lou Ackerman and Detective T.J. Loomis. Detective Loomis, I'm sure some of you will remember, was one of our majors. I know you'll join me, Dean Thomas, the President, and the entire SUS community in cooperating in every possible way with these officers." Looking over at me and nodding, he said, "Detective Loomis."

Dr. Harrison stepped away from the lectern, but I remained where I was. My heart picking up speed, I looked back at the thirty-two pairs of eyes boring holes in me and said, "Detective Ackerman and I want to thank you for coming here on such short notice. We know that this is a very difficult, very painful time for you, and we don't want to make it any more difficult or painful than it already is. In investigations such as this one, however, the first twenty-four hours are the most crucial, so we're going to have to take certain steps that will require your patience and your understanding."

"What, if I may ask, is the reality behind what you euphemistically refer to as 'steps', Detective Loomis?"

From the voice alone, so deep and rich, so much an actor's voice that it had always made me think of Darth Vader's without the hiss, I knew that the speaker was my favorite professor, Dr. C. Clarkson "Chuck" Wagner.

Turning toward him and seeing the old twinkle in his tragically dark eyes, I said, "For one thing, Dr. Wagner, Detective Ackerman and I will need to question each of you as soon as possible. We'll need to start as soon as this meeting is over."

"Are we to infer, then, that we all are suspects?" Chuck Wagner asked.

"More like sources of potentially valuable information," I said with a painful little smile.

"Suspects," Chuck snorted. "We're all suspects. And no doubt we'll all be fingerprinted too."

"Yes. We'd like to do that too."

"This is intolerable! Just intolerable!"

The voice that made this outburst was as rasping as Chuck's was resonant. It belonged to a rail-thin, freckled woman with sunken cheeks, rattlesnake eyes, and a butch cut of carrot-orange hair starting to whiten. Though I never had had her for a class, I knew that she was Dr. Julia Kerns, the second of the department's firebrand feminists, unmarried and reputedly a lesbian.

"I'm sorry, Professor, but fingerprints are an essential part of our investigation routine. We're going to make it as convenient as possible. Ms. Wells here"—I glanced over at Carla—"will do it in your offices. We won't ask you to come downtown."

"Well, it's demeaning and insulting to all of us but especially to me and I refuse, absolutely refuse to submit to it!" Dr. Kerns said.

Becoming every inch the Bad Cop as he turned his death rays on her, Lou said in a low growl, "You saying you don't want to cooperate with us, Professor?"

"For your information, Detective, Mildred Margulis was my very, very close friend and colleague and I very much resent the implication that I could have had anything to do with her death," Dr. Kerns fired back, spitting out 'Detective' as if it were synonymous with scumbag.

"We need your prints, Professor. You can give them to us out here, in your office, or you might want to take a little ride with us downtown. It don't matter which to us," Lou said with a slight shrug of his scrawny little shoulders, his growl and eyes, especially his eyes, enough to scare even a hardened street punk, let alone a gaggle of English professors.

On the face of most of them was the look of someone whose sphincter had just bitten through underwear and into the wood of the desk beneath it.

***

In his office after the meeting, Dr. Harrison didn't take official refuge behind his desk. Instead he sat across from me in one of the chairs in the little reception area over by the tightly stuffed bookshelves. As it had during my classes with him, his breathing seemed labored, even at rest.

Fixing his eyes on mine, he said, "The Department, as you saw and as I'm sure you can understand, is quite upset by this, but let me again assure you that you'll have our complete cooperation. So, tell me, T.J., how can I help you? I'm sure you have some questions."

"Yes, sir, I do," I said, taking out my pen and pad. "How long has Dr. Margulis been a member of your faculty?"

"She came here in the fall of 1988, from Penn State."

"Penn State? She left Penn State to come to SUS?"

"Yes. We offered her a tenure-track position, which she didn't have there. She had only a series of one–year appointments."

"She was divorced and had one daughter, Gloria, around eighteen, who lives with her. Is that correct?"

"It is."

"Did she have any gentlemen callers that you know of?"

"I think she'd had several since she's been here, but I know of only one. That is, I saw her with only one."

"Do you know his name?"

"Yes. Nigel Helton. He's on the faculty out here, in the biology department."

"When did you last see them together?"

"I can't say exactly, but it wasn't too long ago. Six months maybe."

"Do you know if she was seeing him at the time of her death?"

"I don't think so, but I'm not sure."

After looking for a long moment into his relaxed, very gentle eyes, I said, "Dr. Harrison, do you know of anyone who might have a reason for killing Dr. Margulis?"

After another long moment, Dr. Harrison said, "Not for killing her, no."

"What about for disliking her?"

"You had a class under her, if I remember correctly."

"Yes, sir. I did."

"Then you know that she was—how shall we say it?—controversial? Provocative?"

"Yes, sir, but I think that would be putting it mildly. Most of the people in that class hated her, really hated her."

"Yes, and the ones who didn't, loved her," Dr. Harrison said with a nod. "That was the way she was with students. They either hated her or loved her."

"What about you?"

"I?"

"How did you feel about her?"

Dr. Harrison thought for a moment, then said, "I respected her for her energy and work ethic, and for the passion and strength of her commitments. And I had no serious problems in working with her."

"But?"

"She could be....well, difficult," Dr. Harrison said with a little smile.

"In what ways?"

"She could be a bit overbearing."

"About what?"

"Various departmental matters, mostly."

"Such as?"

"Hiring. Promotions. Class schedules. Curri-culum. That sort of thing."

"What about the other members of your department? How did she get along with them?" I asked.

"Not all that well, really."

"She had enemies? Colleagues who hated her?"

"Hated may be too strong a word."

"Disliked then. Colleagues who disliked her?"

"Actually, I don't think that Dr. Margulis had but one actual friend in the department."

"Dr. Kerns, the one who got so upset at the meeting?"

Dr. Harrison nodded. "She had a few allies but only one friend. I could be wrong."

"Allies?"

"Colleagues who made common cause with her on certain issues but otherwise had little to do with her."

Nodding, I glanced at my pad, then said, "Dr. Harrison, can you recall when you last saw Dr. Margulis alive?"

"Yes. Yesterday morning, a little after ten, I think it was."

"Where did you see her?"

"Here, in this building. She had just come in and was on her way to her office."

"Just come in? She didn't have an early class?"

"She never had an early class. She was a runner and liked to run in the morning."

"What was her class schedule this quarter? Do you know it offhand?"

"I knew you'd want to know, so I checked it. On Monday through Friday she had a class at eleven and another one at one. On Tuesday and Thursday evenings she had a class from six to eight-thirty. That was the one she had last night, English 3220, which is a survey of Modern American Literature."

"I'm going to need a roll for that class and for the two others."

Dr. Harrison nodded. "I'll see that you get one."

"We don't yet have the medical examiner's report, but at this point we think she died somewhere between nine and midnight. Can you tell me where you were during those hours?"

"Yes, I can. I left my office at 5:30, my usual time, and went home and walked my dog."

"Where do you live, Dr. Harrison?"

"About a mile from here, in Sherwood Forest."

"How long did it take for you to walk your dog?"

"Twenty minutes. Maybe thirty."

"Then what did you do?"

"My wife and I went out to dinner."

"Where?"

"At Luigi's."

"That's over in The University Shopping Plaza, isn't it?"

"Yes."

"What time did y'all get there?"

"Seven, maybe a little after."

"What time did y'all leave?"

"Around 8:15, 8:30."

"Did y'all go straight home from there?"

"Yes, we did."

"And you were at home the rest of the night?"

"Yes, I was. I was at my computer, working on a poem, when the Dean called me about Dr. Margulis."

"What time was that?"

"Around 1:30 a.m."

"Do you generally stay up that late?"

Dr. Harrison gave me a rueful little grin. "Unfortunately, I do. I don't sleep well."

I reviewed my notes for several seconds, then said, "Let me ask you again if you can think of anyone who had a quarrel with, or a grudge against, Dr. Margulis. Faculty, student, anyone you can think of."

"Well, as you know from your class with her, her students either loved or hated her, and many of her student evaluations are scathing. I've also had, in the time she's been here, more students come to me to complain about her than for any two or three other members of my staff combined. There've been a good many females, many of them quite vocal, but most have been males."

"Do you know if she ever received any threats from students?" I asked.

"No, not as such. At least they weren't overt threats. But she did have two run-ins that upset her and are a matter of record."

"What were they?"

"She was stalked, but only on campus as far as I know, by a student, a black male, who had a grade appeal against her. She assigned him a D and he thought he deserved at least a B."

"Did he win his appeal?"

"No, he didn't. The committee unanimously upheld the original grade."

"Did the stalking occur before or after the hearing?"

"Before."

"But not after?"

Dr. Harrison shook his head. "Not as far as I know."

"I'll need the name of that student."

"I'll see that you get it."

"What about the other run-in? You said there were two."

"Yes. The other one was with a basketball player she accused of plagiarism and took before the Honor Council. The charges didn't stick—he didn't put quotation marks around some of his verbatim citations--but he was quite incensed about it. He said, among a great many things, that she was a racist."

"He too was black?"

'No. White. He claimed another basketball player in the same class, a black kid—his roommate in fact—had the same sort of problems with documentation that he did but she ignored them and came down just on him."

"Was his claim investigated?"

Dr. Harrison shook his head. "He didn't make it officially, just face-to-face with Dr. Margulis in her office. He said she was a fucking liberal bitch and everything else. It's all in the account she wrote."

"He frightened her? Is that what you're saying?"

"She says he didn't, but he did. He's a huge guy, about 6'8" and 250 pounds, maybe more. And mean. He can't shoot but he's a one-man demolition squad under the baskets. He has elbows like scythes."

"I'll need his name too."

"I can give it to you now. Jason Harper."

***

When I had been working on my degree, I had seen Professor Jack Flanagan many times but had never taken a class under him. What I had seen of him, and heard about him, was consistent with what I concluded within a minute or two of entering his office that Wednesday, shortly after Leaving Dr. Harrison's. The guy was a character.

In his mid-fifties, he was of medium height and, except for a little extra around the middle, runner-skinny, with thinning gray hair combed into a mild pompadour and a pinched, pointed little face that made me think of an ostrich staring through a pair of tortoise-shell glasses. His un-ironed blue button-down shirt was dressed up with a wide American flag tie and the cuffs of his faded jeans were badly frayed and short enough to reveal sky-blue socks with a bright yellow Tweety Bird on them. Each of his scuffed brown loafers had a bright penny in it.

But it was not so much Flanagan's appearance or the book-stuffed little windowless office that first struck me. It was the smell, the thick, locker room stench that, after I sat down, I saw the source of. Hanging out to dry on the coat rack in the corner were a singlet, a jockstrap, a pair of shorts, and a well-worn pair of New Balance running shoes.

"So, Detective Loomis, what do you think I know that might help you see that justice is done?" Professor Flanagan said as he cocked back in the chair behind his desk, his little mouth serious but his eyes flashing irony or Irish blarney or something, I could not have said what.

"How did you get along with Dr. Margulis? Were y'all on good terms?" I asked.

"Let's just say that my late colleague and I were not unlike Arabs and Jews or Red Sox fans and Yankee fans and let it go at that, shall we?" Flanagan said, his eyes even harder to read.

"These differences—were they personal or professional?"

"In this line of work, Detective Loomis, the two are generally the same. What we teach is what we read, and what we read is what we are."

"You and Dr. Margulis read different books? Is that what you're saying?"

"That's a big part of it, yes," Flanagan said. "The Doughboy said you were one of our majors."

"The Doughboy?" I asked.

"Yes, as in Pillsbury. My lard ass boss, Steve Harrison," Flanagan said with a smirk.

I nodded. "I finished back in 2005."

"Then you no doubt remember, from your readings in the eighteenth century, 'The Battle of the Books,' in which Swift defends the Ancients against the Moderns."

"Vaguely," I said.

"I am an Ancient of sorts, Detective Loomis, in the sense that I champion and teach only the best that has been and is being written. By best I refer only to a work's literary quality, not to its value as political propaganda or minority reparations, which, as you no doubt know, is a kind of literary compensation for female writers, black writers, etc. for their exclusion from more or less official reading lists in the past. The canon as it's called. My late colleague, on the other hand, was..."

"I understand," I said, heading off his lecture. "Can you tell me, Professor Flanagan, where you were last night between nine and midnight?"

He gave me a sharp, quizzical look. "Is this an interrogation, Detective Loomis?"

"No, sir. It's an interview. Just an interview."

Flanagan shrugged his narrow little shoulders. "I was here. On campus."

"The entire time?"

"I left around eleven."

"You were in your office until then? From nine until eleven?"

"I was in the library for a while. Then I took a run."

"What time was that?"

"Do you want the exact time?"

"Yes. If you can tell it to me."

"I started at exactly 8:21 and finished 58 minutes later, at 9:19."

"You timed yourself?"

"Over my eight-mile loop," he said, holding up the big watch on his left wrist. "I have a log entry if you want to see it."

I shook my head. "Did you run alone?"

"I did."

"Did anyone see you?"

"My loop, Detective Loomis, is through Sherwood Forest and I dare say I appeared in the headlights of everyone who drove in either direction past me," Flanagan said with a flash in his eyes.

"What did you do when you finished your run?"

"Thirty pushups."

"After that?"

"I got a Diet Pepsi out of the machine in Hampton, just down from my office."

"Did anyone see you then? In Hampton Hall, that is?"

"The last class of the night having ended at 8:30, I may have been seen by someone I didn't see, but I didn't see anyone. As far as I could tell, the building was empty. Except for me of course."

"After you got your Diet Pepsi, you came back to your office?"

"Yes. And I remained there until around eleven."

"Do you generally stay in your office so late?"

"I do."

"Why?"

"I have my reasons."

"What are they?"

With an edge in his voice, Flanagan said, "If you must know, Detective Loomis, I recently broke up with my live-in lady friend and I'm not exactly eager to return to a dark, empty, and rather sepulchral house. I'm sure you understand."

***

More than any I had had thus far I dreaded my interview with Dr. Julia Kerns. With her sunken cheeks, fading red butch-cut, and rattlesnake eyes, she was, in appearance alone, a singularly repellant little woman, and I had seen flashes of her anger, and heard her snarl, at the meeting of the English Department.

I therefore was completely surprised when, after knocking on her office door, I was politely, even graciously invited to come in and make myself comfortable.

"You said during the meeting a little while ago, Dr. Kerns, that you and Dr. Margulis were very close friends and colleagues," I said, my eyes taking in the wall-to-wall books, the big framed pictures of female writers (Virginia Woolf was the only one I recognized), the signed color photograph of Hillary Clinton, and a bottle of Perrier from which Dr. Kerns frequently took sips.

"We were. We were very close," she said, her voice far from pleasant but not exactly rasping either.

"I have a good idea of how painful this must be for you and I apol..."

"I understand. Ask me anything you like," she cut in.

Nodding, I said, "When was the last time you saw Dr. Margulis?"

"Yesterday, around one p.m."

"Where did you see her?"

"In her office."

"You went there to see her?"

"Yes. To chat. We'd both just gotten out of class."

"How did she seem to you? Did she seem worried or upset about anything? Anything unusual?"

"Yes and no."

"What do you mean?"

"Yes, she was upset, and no, not about anything unusual."

"What was it that she was upset about that wasn't unusual? Please be as specific as you can."

"Well, for one thing, she was upset about her daughter."

"Gloria?"

"Yes."

"What about Gloria?"

"She is, or was, very disappointed with Gloria."

"Why?"

With a wry little smile, Dr. Kerns said, "Gloria has, as Mildred used to put it, 'gone native.'"

"'Gone native'? I don't follow you."

"Gloria has embraced—and with much enthusiasm, I might add—the culture, if you can call it that, of the South. In other words, the child, although in the 99th percentile in intelligence tests, has little ambition beyond being barefooted and pregnant. I'm exaggerating of course but not by much. She does seem intent on throwing away her gifts."

"I suppose Gloria's boyfriend was included in Dr. Margulis's disappointment?"

"You've met him? Bryan?"

"Yes. He was with Gloria early this morning when my partner and I talked to her."

"What did you think of him?" she asked, her eyes looking more than ever like a rattlesnake's.

"He seemed a nice enough kid."

"He hated Mildred. Actually hated her."

"Enough to kill her, you think?"

"I don't know about that, but he hated her."

I nodded, then said, "You said Gloria was one thing Dr. Margulis was upset about. What else was there?"

"Steve, of course," Dr. Kerns said, sipping on her Perrier.

"Your Department Head, you mean? Dr. Harrison?"

"Yes."

"You said 'of course.' Do you mean by that he and Dr. Margulis had ongoing problems?"

"Yes."

"What were they?"

"Actually, there was only one."

"What was it?"

Taking another sip of Perrier, Dr. Kerns said, "Steve Harrison, pure and simple, cannot stand strong women."

"Such as Dr. Margulis?"

"Yes. Such as Dr. Margulis."

"Do you think he could have killed her?"

Dr. Kerns's laugh was rasping and bitter. "Not a chance."

"Why do you say that?"

"I wouldn't have said it if Mildred had been poisoned or killed in some other kind of sneaky, insidious way, but Steve Harrison, to put it in sexist terms, simply hasn't the balls to strangle anybody, let alone Mildred."

"Do you know of anyone who had and might have done it?"

Dr. Kerns laughed again. "In this department? You've got to be kidding."

"What about that biology professor Dr. Margulis recently stopped seeing? Nigel, I believe Gloria said his name was."

"Nigel Helton. Nigel doesn't impress me as being a violent man, but he was a man in love and rejected, so you never know."

"What about any other man or men Dr. Margulis was seeing?"

"I haven't met any others, so I can't say."

As if preparing for a dangerous plunge, I paused for a moment, then said, "Dr. Kerns, I'm sorry, but I have to ask you where you were last night between nine and midnight."

"I was at home."

"Where is that?"

"In Marshview Villas. I have an apartment there."

"Your schedule on your door indicates that you have a six to eight-thirty class on Tuesday and Thursday nights this quarter, so you must have gone straight home after it, Marshview Villas being only a couple of miles from here."

"I did."

"Was anybody there with you?"

"No. I live alone."

"You said that the last time you saw Dr. Margulis was around one yesterday afternoon."

"Yes."

"So you didn't see her before or after your class last night, which was at the same time hers was?"

"No, I didn't."

"Did you see anything in or around Hampton Hall last night that struck you as odd or out of the ordinary? Anything that might bear on this case?"

"Yes. Now that you mention it, I did see something."

"What was that?"

"After my class, on my way to my car, I saw a basketball player, Jason Harper, go into Hampton Hall. Jason Harper is..."

I nodded. "I know who he is. Dr. Margulis charged him with plagiarism and took him before the Honor Council."

"I suppose Steve Harrison told you that? And about the scene in her office? The things he called her?"

"He did. He said it was ugly."

"It was. It was very ugly."

"When you saw Jason Harper, was he alone?"

"Several classes had just let out, so I can't say for sure, but I think so."

"I have just one more question, Dr. Kerns."

"What is it?"

"You said you didn't think there was anyone in your department with 'balls' enough to have killed Dr. Margulis. Does that include Professor Flanagan? I understand that he and Dr. Margulis didn't get along."

With another bitter little laugh, Dr. Kerns said, "Professor Flanagan is a witless buffoon and a myriad of other things I despise, but he's not a killer. I'd be flattering him if I said he was."

***

Last on my list for that day was my all-time favorite professor, Dr. C. Clarkson "Chuck" Wagner, but since he wouldn't be available until 4:30 and I had an hour to kill, I took a chance. I walked across the quad from Hampton Hall to Gaston Hall and, after checking the directory on the first floor, went up to the second floor and to the office of Dr. Nigel Helton, hoping that he would be in. He was.

"Dr. Helton, I'm Detective T.J. Loomis of the Savannah Police Department and I wonder if I could ask you a few questions," I said.

"Why, yes. Sure. Please come in," he said, seeming not at all surprised as he opened the partially open door the rest of the way and gestured toward the chair in front of the desk. "Won't you sit down?"

As he went around his desk and settled in the chair behind it, I noted that his office, like those of the English professors, was filled with books and that Dr. Helton was a smallish man, maybe 5'9" and 170 pounds, in his late forties. He had a soft-looking, pleasant face, thinning brown hair pulled back in a pony tail, and bird-nervous blue eyes behind wire-framed granny glasses. He was wearing baggy jeans and a rumpled white button-down shirt, open at the collar.

"I assume you're here about the death of Mildred Margulis," he said, fixing his eyes on mine.

"Yes," I said. "I understand that you and she recently ended a relationship. Is that correct?"

"We did, yes."

"How long did this relationship last?"

"A little over a year."

"Did you end it or did she?"

"It was a mutual thing."

"When did it end?"

"Around the first of August. Six, maybe seven months ago."

"Were you upset about it?"

He shrugged slightly. "Not really."

"Was she?"

"As I said, it was a mutual thing. We'd grown apart."

"So she wasn't upset? Is that what you're saying?"

"I can't say for sure, because I had no further contact with her, but no, I don't think she was. She was a very strong woman."

I nodded, then said, "Was she seeing other men?"

"When?"

"When you were seeing her."

"Not to my knowledge, no."

"Were you seeing any other woman or women during that time?"

"No."

"So the breakup wasn't over another man or woman?"

"As I said, Detective Loomis, we had grown apart," he said with a slight edge in his voice.

"Do you know if she was seeing any man or men between the time of your breakup and the time she was killed?"

"No, I don't."

"So you haven't seen her since early August, when y'all broke up?"

"That's correct. I haven't seen her or talked to her or anything else since then."

"At this point we think that Dr. Margulis was killed sometime between nine p.m. and midnight last night. Can you tell me where you were during that time?"

"I was at home."

"Where is that?"

"In Westwood Forest."

"That's about a mile from here, isn't it?"

"My house is exactly 1.7 miles from here. I measured it on my car's odometer."

"Were you alone?"

"Except for my dog, yes, I was."

With my eyes hard on his, I paused for a long moment, then said, "Dr. Helton, do you have any idea who could've killed Dr. Margulis?"

"Mildred, as I said before, was a very strong, very independent woman, and not everyone on this campus appreciated her. Many, in fact disliked her. I don't know of anyone who disliked her that much, though," he said, obviously choosing his words with care.

"Not even that basketball player she took before the Honor Council?"

"I don't think so, no. He's a stupid goon, but not even he's that stupid," Nigel Helton said with a slow shaking of his head.

***

Dr. C. Clarkson "Chuck" Wagoner was the first English teacher I had when I started SUS about eight years ago. In his early fifties at the time, he seemed all that I, country hick that I was, had ever imagined an English professor should be.

Around 5'11" and a solid, even somewhat rugged looking 180 pounds or so, he had broad shoulders and massive hands, with fingers as big as small bananas and a handshake that could make me smile to keep from wincing. His jet black hair, as short as a skullcap, and his patrician-looking face belonged on an old Roman coin, and after I read Paradise Lost I never could see his dark eyes without thinking of a fallen angel. He had a bad knee and walked with a cane, but his limp, instead of making him look weak and vulnerable, merely added to the sense that I, and probably most other people too, had of him as a personage. He favored tweed jackets with suede elbow patches and striped silk ties on his blue or white oxford shirts. And there was of course the voice, Darth Vader's without the hiss, that enabled him to make even "Good evening, Mr. Loomis. I trust you are well?" sound as dramatic as "To be or not to be" or some other such line from Shakespeare.

As naïve—dumb is more like it—as I was back then, I never would have even suspected he was gay had it not been for a girl I was seeing at the time and who sat beside me in the second class I had under him. Quite taken by his looks, voice, and the always bulging front of his pants, she shook her head one day and lamented to me, "What a waste. What a sad waste." When I asked her what she meant, she hardly could believe I didn't know what she said was obvious to everyone else. She went on to say that Chuck had the hots for me and didn't like her because she was getting what he wanted.

If Chuck did indeed have a letch for me, he kept it entirely to himself and, as my faculty adviser as well as my teacher for four courses, was never other than a damn good guy in an avuncular sort of way. During our many chats in his office he told me, among countless other things, of his upbringing in rural North Carolina, of his two great-great uncles who fought in the Civil War, and of his failure to find a publisher for even one of the six novels he had written and whose boxed manuscripts were stacked like bricks on a shelf in his office.

He also told me about his dear friend Sammy Ray and of the two grown children Sammy had from his marriage, whom Chuck talked about as if they were his own. I eventually met Sammy, who was bald, pleasant, something of a Nervous Nellie, and totally dependent on Chuck, when a fellow iron-pumper and I moved them from their place downtown and into their condo not far from campus, which they christened "The Anchorage."

The last time I had seen Chuck, except at the department meeting that Wednesday, was at my graduation back in the summer of 2005, when, in full academic regalia, he had hugged me, crushed my hand, and made me promise to stay in touch.

So, although I was looking forward to seeing him at 4:30 that Wednesday afternoon, I was also a little uneasy about it because I knew I was going to get fussed at for not "keeping our friendship in good repair," as he himself probably would put it.

His office looked exactly as I remembered it. The wall-to-wall shelves behind the desk were neatly stuffed with books, and beside the filing cabinet hung a big color portrait of Stonewall Jackson and several small Matthew Brady-looking black-and-white photos of un-famous Confederate soldiers, two of whom I knew to be Chuck's great-great uncles. Both of them were little more than boys, and one of them looked much as Chuck must have looked at the same age. On a little bookcase below them, along with more books, were the boxed manuscripts, which Chuck, never less than theatrical, referred to as "The Rejected Oeuvres of C. Clarkson Wagner."

"T.J., my boy, no matter the sad event that occasioned our re-union, I am indeed delighted to see you again after so very long a time," Chuck said from behind his desk, his voice as resonant and powerful as ever. "And I must say, you're looking both well and good. I trust what I'm seeing is indeed what you are?"

"I'm doing fine, Chuck," I said with a grin.

"I read in the paper of your recent elevation from flatfoot to snoop and I felt, I confess, a certain quasi-paternal pride. I said to Sammy—I'm sure you remember Sammy—that one of Savannah's Finest is also one of my finest. I said that now you'll be ferreting out the Bad Guys instead of quite literally chasing them down. Do you like it or do you, at least a little bit, miss the thrill of the chase?"

"I like it fine so far, but it's early," I said. "But how're you doing? You look right well and good yourself."

"Except for feeling the increasingly cruel and insistent pinch of Time, I suppose I'm faring well enough," Chuck said with a little shrug.

"Still writing?"

"Of course. Despite my chronic inability to publish, I still both live to write and write to live."

"What are you working on now? Another novel?"

"Actually I just last week finished another one, something altogether new for me. My earlier oeuvres," he said, tilting his head toward his Rejecteds, "were neither au courant in their setting nor politically correct in their concerns. This new one isn't politically correct either, but it is indeed au courant. I do not exaggerate when I say it is as au courant as today's headlines. Quite literally. That I can assure you."

I knew I was in for a long lecture on the new novel if I didn't head it off, so I glanced at my watch and said, "Chuck, I really do hate to rush, but I have to meet my partner in about fifteen minutes."

"I understand perfectly," Chuck said, closing his eyes for a second as he nodded quickly. "How can I help you?"

"You can start by telling me how Dr. Margulis got along with her colleagues," I said.

"Campus wide or just in this department?"

"Both. Start with campus wide."

"Like all careerists, she was on every possible committee and I dare say she ruffled the feathers of many of her fellow servers. I can't give you any of their names because I myself avoid committees like the plague itself, but I have no doubt that Professor Flanagan can. Not much happens on this campus, at least in the way of gossip, that he doesn't know about or can't find out."

"What about in your department?"

"If you asked the question: 'Did you truly like Dr. Margulis?' to everyone in this department, and put them all under oath, on peril of their immortal souls, to tell the truth, I dare say not a single one of them would answer yes. Most of them, however, if not put under oath, would say 'Yes, I like her okay,' or words to that effect, because of the go-along-to-get-along ethos in academe. There is also the intimidation factor. Half of the department, and most of the women in it, are—or were—scared to death of her."

"You got along with her, though, if I remember correctly."

"Of course I did. I felt sorry for the poor thing," Chuck said, his dark eyes for a moment seeming even darker. "For all of her in-your-face fractiousness, she really was a lonely, rather pathetic creature."

"What about Dr. Kerns? They were close friends, weren't they?"

Chuck raised his left eyebrow and said, "With 'devotion's visage and pious action we do sugar o'er the devil himself.' Or herself in this case."

"You're saying they weren't friends? That it was just show, at least on Dr. Kerns's part?"

"What to me merely 'seems' may indeed be 'is'," Chuck said with a slight shrug.

"Why, though? Dr. Kerns is as much of a firebrand feminist and man-hater as Dr. Margulis was. Or so I heard when I was out here."

"Yes, and that might well be the rub. Professor Kerns was the department's reigning radical until Professor Margulis rushed in and usurped her noisy little throne. Why, the poor thing—Professor Margulis, that is—really was as dedicated as a hardshell missionary when it came to bringing light to the benighted."

"So I heard and so Dr. Harrison said, or at least implied."

"Yes, Steve definitely would."

"Why do you say that?"

"Steve Harrison is a very gentle man, a generous man, a good Department Head and, at his best, a quite impressive poet. And he's never been anything but a good friend to me." Pausing for moment, Chuck sighed as he shook his head. "He's not a healthy man, T.J. I worry about him."

I nodded. "I know what you mean. His breathing looks labored even at rest and his blood pressure, as much overweight as he is, has to be sky high."

"You don't know the half of it," Chuck said, his eyes darkening even more. "At least two mornings a week he sits in that very chair you're sitting in now and chats with me while he eats his breakfast. He'll be breathing so hard he can barely talk for two or three minutes after sitting down."

"From climbing the stairs?'

"Yes. Two little flights. His face'll be red and he'll sound as if he's on the very threshold of 'that undiscovered country'. I'll say, 'Steve, you are all right, aren't you?' and he'll insist he is and go on with his Mickey D sausage and biscuit, which he helps along with Diet Coke. He also has a bad knee and a worse back and I don't know what all else. And those, I regret to say, just his bodily infirmities."

"He has others?"

Chuck nodded. "He would have you believe, and I think most people out here do believe, that he's a Kutuzov the Imperturbable, but he's not. He most definitely is not a Kutuzov the Imperturbable."

"What's a Kutuzov the Imperturbable?" I asked, knowing I was asking for a lecture.

"Kutuzov was a Russian general during the Napoleonic wars—Tolstoy put him in 'War and Peace'— who, no matter how fiercely he was attacked, remained as stolid and unmoved, as unflappable as an anvil. The sleepy-eyed old fox was a master of tactical inactivity and let the French generals wear themselves out in their frenzies against him. Kind of like Muhammed Ali did George Foreman with his rope-a-dope tactic, which I'm sure you remember. Excuse me. Which I'm sure you've heard about. I sometimes forget how young you are, T.J."

"So you're saying that Dr. Harrison is not really as calm and collected as he seems?"

"Precisely. That beneath that unruffled surface is a maelstrom of conflicts. He takes everything, and I mean everything, personally and hard, very hard. That's one of the reasons, perhaps the main reason, that he's such a fine poet. And he is—or he thinks he is—a master of subtlety and outright obfuscation."

Pausing for a moment, Chuck grinned, then said, "But I digress. I was leading up to something."

"I think it had to do with Dr. Harrison's opinion of Dr. Margulis. I said that he said he admired her energy and dedication."

"Oh, yes. That. That's a perfect example of what I'm saying. Steve apparently would have you believe that he admired her just as I know for a fact that he would have me believe that he's as much of a conservative Republican as I am."

"But he didn't admire her and he's not a conservative Republican?"

"Hardly. The man voted twice for Bill Clinton, if that that tells you anything. Mildred of course was much further to the left, and quite noisy about it—downright vociferous at times—but that didn't bother Steve. It didn't bother him at all. In fact, I think he rather liked it."

"So what did she do that he didn't like?"

"It's a long story and you need to be getting on."

"Just the basics."

Chuck thought for a moment, then said, "Among Professor Margulis's many, and I mean many, offenses against Steve, she accused him of being a drunk and an incompetent and unfair Department Head and more or less forced him to submit to a ghastly week of so-called 'reconciliation talks' with her and the Vice-President. She also made very snide, very cruel remarks about Steve's wife Mahalia in an email that made the rounds on campus. Far, far worse to a poet, though, she made no secret of her opinion of his poetry. She said it was worse than drivel. She said it was logorrhea."

"This is embarrassing, Chuck, because I know I've seen and looked up the word, but I can't remember what it means," I said.

"Logorrhea, T.J.," Chuck said with an arching of his left eyebrow, "is a diffuse, undisciplined outpouring of words. It is, if you will, verbal diarrhea."

"She said his poetry was shit, in other words?"

"Yes, she said his poetry was shit. Loose shit at that."

I nodded, then rather sheepishly said, "Chuck, I hate like the very devil to ask you this, but..."

"You want to know where I was last night?"

"Yes. Between nine and midnight."

"I was at home, at The Anchorage."

"Were you alone?"

"As a matter of fact, I was. Sammy, for reasons known only to God, had gone to the theater to see that ghastly re-make of The Dukes of Hazard. He was addicted to it when it was on TV, you know," Chuck said, rolling his eyes in a combination of disbelief and disgust.

Chapter 3

There were no surprises in the medical examiner's report. Dr. Mildred Margulis, a Caucasian female of 46, died of strangulation sometime between 9 and 10 p.m. on Tuesday, January 18th. No drugs, legal or otherwise, were found in her system. She had not been raped or, aside from the strangulation and ripped earlobe, harmed in any way.

The crime scene was equally predictable. There had been no forcible entry and although there were definite signs of struggle, no blood or skin had been found beneath the deceased's short fingernails. There were no fingerprints on either doorknob, the inside or the outside, but twenty-two sets had been found in the office, along with eight identifiable and separate sets of footprints. There were no prints, however, on either the ribbon or on the medal attached to it. Both, obviously, had been wiped clean, even of all but a few flecks of neck skin that had come off during the strangling.

"What'd I tell you, Lou?" I said, trying not to sound too triumphant. "He got her from behind then cleaned off the weapon and awarded her with it. And for a souvenir he yanked off the testicles-looking earring and vamoosed."

"You say 'he.' You ruling out the dyke?" Lou asked.

"Not entirely, but I don't think she—or most women, really—would've been strong enough. There's no doubt in my mind, though, that Margulis knew who it was and wasn't afraid of him. Otherwise, she wouldn't have let him get behind her. That makes the jock, and maybe the daughter's boyfriend, a little less suspicious, wouldn't you say?"

Lou shrugged. "Maybe. Maybe not. You said she was a pretty ballsy broad."

"She was, but I doubt if she'd turn her back on this Harper guy, especially at night when the building's almost empty. Dr. Harrison said he was a huge thug and Margulis was scared of him even if she wouldn't admit it."

"We'll check him out and the daughter's boyfriend and the stalker, the black guy," Lou said with a quick nod.

On Thursday morning it took me from 7:12 until 7:21 to walk from Dr. Margulis's office in Hampton Hall over to the jock dorm on the other side of the campus. It took me another four minutes to get to the second floor and to find the right suite. Having learned the day before that the basketball team had a home game that night and that his first class was not until 9:30, I was all but sure that Jason Harper would be in and probably still asleep.

I was right. After opening the door, seeing my badge, and hearing my request, a tall, clean-cut black kid left me alone in the room. A minute later he reappeared and said, "He's coming," then said he had to get to breakfast and hurried out.

The living room or the common room, or whatever it was called, was a mess. The coffee table in front of the sofa was littered with textbooks, pizza boxes, and empty Coke cans, and a pile of dirty laundry lay in the center of the floor. A game show, with the sound muted, was on the big flat-screen TV, but before I could make out what it was, Jason Harper appeared.

Dr. Harrison had not exaggerated. At least 6'7" and a raw-boned 250 pounds or so, with a jutting jaw and mean eyes, he looked as menacing as a Bad Guy in a Bruce Willis movie. He was wearing gray gym shorts and a white, wife-beater undershirt, and he obviously was not happy to have had his sleep disturbed, especially by a cop.

"Mr. Harper, I'm Detective T.J. Loomis of the Savannah Police Department," I said, starting to offer my hand, then thinking better of it. "I need to ask you a few questions."

"What about?" he said, his mean eyes sizing me up and seeming to note the bulge of the 9mm Glock beneath the left shoulder of my jacket.

"I'm investigating the death of Dr. Mildred Margulis. She was murdered in her office last night."

"Yeah. Somebody told me," he said, utterly unfazed.

"Why don't we sit down?" I said.

"Whatever," he said with a shrug, then plopped down on a battered lounger and began watching the soundless TV.

Glaring at him, I said, "You need to turn that thing off, Mr. Harper."

Returning my glare for a moment, he reached down beside the chair and picked up a remote switch, then pointed it at the screen and killed the picture.

Seated on the sofa, I glanced at my pad and said, "I understand you had a class under Dr. Margulis last spring. Is that correct?"

"Yeah. I had one."

"I also understand you had a serious run-in with her."

"You understand right."

"Do you want to tell me about it?"

"You already know about it or you wouldn't be here."

"I want to hear your side of it."

His face filling with disgust, he said, "She started on me the first day of class."

"Got on your case, you mean?"

"Yeah. Big time."

"What about?"

"She made us all stand up and introduce ourselves and say where we were from and all. She asked me if I played basketball and when I said 'Yes, ma'am', she went all fucking ballistic."

"Because you said 'ma'am'?"

"Yeah. She said ma'am was sexist and demeaning and all that politically correct shit. I said it was just how my mama taught me and she said she didn't care, not to do it again, ever."

"Did you?"

"I slipped up once or twice, but it wasn't just that. It was me being a guy and white and Southern. And not gay. I mean, most of the stuff she made us read was about what shits straight guys, especially straight white Southern guys, are to women and blacks and gays. You had to agree with everything she said or she'd raise hell with you right in front of everybody."

"Did you ever disagree with her?"

"One time in her office."

"Was that before or after she charged you with plagiarism?"

"Before."

"What'd she say that you disagreed with?"

"Shit about me being a Southern male."

"Meaning?"

"Meaning that I hated blacks and gays. And women. That I wanted to keep them down."

"What'd you say to that?"

"I said she was doing the same thing she says I was doing."

"Stereotyping?"

"Yeah. Stereotyping. Stereotyping everybody in the class. Sucking up to blacks like you wouldn't believe, them and this one gay guy. And she hated white girly girls too. Half the white guys dropped the course and I would've too but Coach wouldn't let me."

"What about the plagiarism she charged you with? Dr. Harrison, I believe, said it was just some problems with documentation and that the Honor Council acquitted you. Is that correct?"

He nodded. "I listed my stuff, my sources and all, and put the page numbers in. I did all that, but I didn't put quotation marks around everything I needed to. She was just after my ass and looking for something, any damn little thing she could find."

"I believe Dr. Harrison also said a black basketball player in the same class, your roommate in fact, had the same problems and she didn't say a thing about them. Is that correct?"

A bitter little smile played across his face. "You know why they were the same?"

"No. Tell me."

"I did them."

"You mean you wrote his paper?"

"Just his quotes. I did them the same as mine. I thought I was doing them right."

"And you say Dr. Margulis didn't say a thing to your roommate about it?"

"Just what she wrote on the bottom. She said it was a good paper. She fixed the quotations marks where they belonged and gave him a B-."

"Dr. Harrison said you confronted her in her office and said she was 'a fucking racist bitch' and a few other things, but that you didn't make any official charges. Why didn't you?"

"No way I'm gonna rat out my roommate, man," he said with a fierce scowl.

"Your black roommate?"

"Yeah. The guy that let you in."

I let myself grin. "Do you think Dr. Margulis would've appreciated the irony if she'd known about it?"

"Say what?"

"That you, a white, Southern, straight male, would rather protect your black roommate and teammate than get her into trouble, which you probably could've done."

"Yeah, well, what goes around comes around, and she got hers, you know what I'm saying?" he said with a shrug.

"You don't care that she's dead, Mr. Harper? She was somebody's mother, somebody's daughter, somebody's loved one, and somebody went into her office and killed her in a very violent, very painful way. That doesn't bother you?" I said, giving him as hard a look as I could.

"You think it was me, don't you?" he said, matching my glare with one of his own.

"I'm not going to bullshit you. Of all the possible suspects I've talked to thus far, you had the strongest motive. You obviously hated the woman. You also had the opportunity."

"Opportunity? What opportunity?"

"The opportunity to have killed her. She was killed in her office in Hampton Hall around nine on Tuesday night and you entered Hampton Hall around 8:35 that same night. Didn't you?"

"I guess."

"Why? You didn't have a class."

"How do you know?"

"Two ways. One, I know your schedule. Your last class each day is at 1:30. Two, there are no classes at SUS after 8:30."

"I went to see this girl, okay? She had a class that got out."

"What's her name?"

"Jennifer."

"Jennifer what?"

"Tompkins. Jennifer Tompkins."

"Where does she live?"

"Blue Lion Apartments, 186, 187, something like that."

"What's her phone number?"

"I don't know. I ain't never called her."

"She's your girl friend and you've never called her?"

"She ain't my girlfriend, man. She's just a girl I know, okay?"

"You're saying that you met up with her in Hampton Hall, around 8:30, when her class got out? Is that correct?"

"Yeah."

"How long were you with her in Hampton Hall?"

"Couple of minutes. Long enough to talk to her."

"Then what'd you do?"

"Left."

"Was she with you?"

"Yeah."

"Where'd y'all go?"

"Out to her car."

"You told her goodbye then or what?"

"I went home with her, man. To her apartment."

"How long did you stay?"

"I stayed all night, man. Okay? You want all the fucking details?" he said, glaring at me as he no doubt had at Dr. Margulis that day in her office when he called her a string of choice epithets.

At that moment, as his eyes burned holes in my face, I dropped him from near the top to near the bottom on my list of suspects. Ballsy broad or not, Dr. Margulis, having once seen those eyes, was extremely unlikely to have let herself be alone in her office with Jason Harper, especially at night when classes were over and the building was almost empty. Even if she had been that daring or dumb, or whatever it was, she would not have let him get behind her. On that I would have been willing to bet my new badge.

***

As I typed in WOMYN and the screen came to life, I felt even more like a voyeur or a tomb robber than I had during the previous hour, which I had spent nosing among the countless books and other leavings, including a stack of grade books.

In the one for 2004-2005, for spring quarter, I found the night course I'd taken, Modern American Literature I, along with my name and grades—one B and the rest C's, with a course grade of C. The sight of the grades flooded me with memories, only one of which was good. This was of the blessed relief I had felt when the course ended and I knew that I never again would have to see, or hear, Dr. Mildred Margulis.

I went first to the email, which was over-whelming. The woman must not have deleted anything but spam during her entire time at SUS, the earliest entry being for August 1996. After scrolling interminably down to 2005-2006, I began to hunt for anything that might be of use. Most of the entries were memos from other professors, mainly committee people, about meetings, changes in policy and curriculum and the like, but there were also a large number from students. Along with excuses for missed classes and requests for makeup tests and extended time for papers due, there were letters from former students, some of them, to my amazement, from males thanking Dr. Margulis for being such a wonderful teacher and mentor.

There also were short notes and two or three long letters from professors at other schools, Duke, Cornell, and Rutgers among them, praising some of Margulis's scholarship and wishing her well. There being nothing from disgruntled students, I had to re-consider my notion that she had deleted only spam.

Of the most interest to me, however, were the emails from two SUS professors. One of them was Dr. Harrison, who, along with brain-numbing junk about various more or less impersonal departmental matters, had written her a total of ten items about the 'reconciliation sessions' that Chuck Wagner had cited as one of Margulis's many offenses against their boss. The earliest of these ten was almost a year ago and expressed Dr. Harrison's "hope that you and I can resolve our differences and get on with our work." Nothing came of this hope, apparently, because the rest of the series was riddled with phrases such as "my repeated efforts," "your insistence," "my disappoint-ment," and the like.

Even more interesting were the items from heltonni@SUSed.com, which I soon saw was the address of Nigel Helton, the biology professor whom Margulis, according not to him but to her daughter, had dumped back in the Summer. To get to the first of these I had to scroll all the way back to 2004, but from then until only about four months ago, August 2007, not a day had passed when Helton not been in touch with her at least once. Upbeat and increasingly familiar, even affectionate in places, the ones from the beginning up to June of 2007 were about matters ranging from the time Helton would pick her up for their date to his desire to play some more ping-pong.

In June, though, the tone changed and the theme, obviously, was the breakup. Time and again Helton said, "I just don't understand" and "Why won't you even talk to me?" and "I just can't believe, after what we had, that you can treat me this way." His last entry was for January 11, at 9:32 p.m., exactly one week before Margulis's death. It said "There was a song a long time ago that you might remember, Everybody's Somebody's Fool, by Connie Francis. I was your fool, completely your fool, and the sad thing is that I would give anything to be your fool again."

After reading and noting in my pad the time and essence of all the emails I thought were of interest, which took from 9 a.m. until 1:45 p.m., I left SUS and went to the Y to pump some iron. Three hours later, around 5 p.m., I was back at Margulis's computer mousing through her various files, which in volume were even greater than her emails.

I did not lock the door to her office and re-attach the yellow police tape until 1:45 a.m. At that point my eyes burned and my brain ached and I never again wanted to see another computer.

***

"You said it wasn't the daughter or the dyke who was lying and you were right, Slick," Lou said around eight the next morning as we sat over coffee in his office in the SPD building downtown.

I nodded. "He told me three times, Lou—I have it in my notes—that he'd had no contact whatsoever with her after they broke up back in August, but he was emailing her as late January 11, a week to the very day she was killed. And they were whiny, sick-puppy, why-don't-you-love-me-anymore? crap. I didn't print them but I've got notes on the day and time of every one of them."

"What about all that other shit you said you found? You said it was pretty rough," Lou said.

Shaking my head, I said, "After a dozen or so of her files, I started thinking it's a wonder somebody hadn't killed her long before now. I'm serious, Lou. She had something nasty to say about half the people at SUS, even Kerns, her so-called BFF."

"BFF?"

"Chick talk for Best Friend Forever."

"What?"

"For one thing, that Kerns's book on mother/daughter relationships in contemporary fiction is superficial and poorly written. She said that in a letter to some kind of committee when Kerns was up for promotion to full professor. She voted against Kerns's promotion too. She also said that Kerns was weak on teaching and community service. And that was mild relative to what she said about Flanagan."

"What?"

"She said he was a witless buffoon and ought to be fired. She said that his talk on Irish literature every year around St. Patrick's Day is a disgrace to the school. And Chuck Wagner. She said he was a 'pompous, pretentious fraud.' Those were her exact words. She said it was no wonder his novels were unpublished, that what she'd read of them was pure drivel and that he was no more qualified to teach creative writing than she was to teach nuclear physics or something like that."

"And the fat boy? Harrison?" Lou said with a shrug. "I bet she said some sweet things about him."

"I'll say. In all of her annual evaluations of him she said he was a lousy teacher and an even lousier department head. That he was insensitive, authoritarian, misogynistic..."

"Mis-sagh-o-what?"

"That he hated women and did everything to keep them in 'their place.' She said he was 'an absentee department head' and never available when she needed him. That he was guilty of gross favoritism. It apparently got so bad that the Vice-President spent about a week trying to make peace between her and Dr. Harrison. She wrote about twenty letters to the SUS President and Vice-President and Dean complaining about him. And then there was this file that looked like a running list of things he did or didn't do that she didn't like. I'm telling you, Lou, it was vicious, downright vicious."

"Tell me."

"She said he was an obese pig. A drunk. That his poetry was self-indulgent shit, that his wife was a falling-down drunk. She said that at a swank restaurant when she was interviewing for the job, she—Dr. Harrison's wife, that is—got so drunk that she passed out on the toilet in the women's room. She said it was mortifying at first, when a waitress came to the table and told Dr. Harrison, but now she can't tell it to anybody or even remember it without laughing."

Grimacing in disgust, I shook my head and said, "That woman was a piece of work, Lou, world-class and card-carrying. I thought I knew how awful she was when I had that class under her, but I didn't. I didn't know anything."

After a hard pull on his Camel, Lou grinned and said, "When we catch him, Slick, we won't throw him in the slammer. We'll give him a gold medal. We'll even put it around his goddamn neck for him."

Chapter 4

Later that morning I checked out two alibis. The first had been given to Lou the day before by the black student who had stalked Dr. Margulis and had lost his appeal for a change of his grade from a D to something better. The manager of Yamato, a Japanese restaurant just off one of the historic squares in downtown Savannah, confirmed that James Smalls was one of his cooks, then showed me a staff schedule and a time card that all but cleared Smalls from my list of suspects. Both records showed that on the night of Tuesday, January 11, at the very time that Dr. Mildred Margulis had been strangled in her office at SUS, Smalls had been sweating over a stove in the kitchen at Yamato, his time card showing that he had punched in at 3:02 and out at 11:12.

After leaving Yamato, I drove out to the Blue Lion apartment complex, which was about a mile from the SUS campus. From the SUS registrar I had gotten the apartment number and the class schedule for Jennifer Tompkins, the girl Jason Harper claimed he had been with on the night of January 11. Her first class was not until 10 and, counting on her to sleep for as long as possible, I knocked on the door of #186 at 8:47.

Several long moments later the door was opened by a tall, brown-haired woman, 19 or 20, in a white terrycloth robe and blue flip flops. She had nice calves, a pretty face, and a sleepy, annoyed look in her eyes.

"Ms. Tompkins? Ms. Jennifer Tompkins?" I asked.

"Yes? I'm Jennifer Tompkins," she said, eyeing me suspiciously.

"I'm Detective T. J. Loomis of the Savannah Police Department and I wonder if I could ask you a few questions," I said, showing her my badge and ID card.

Seconds later she was sitting on the couch in her living room and I, pad in hand, was in a chair in front of her, on the other side of a coffee table. In the background I could hear the sounds of someone taking a shower.

"Ms. Tompkins, do you have any idea of why I'm here?" I asked.

Completely awake now, she looked me defiantly in the eye and said, "I know exactly why you're here. You think Jason killed that professor the other night."

"Jason Harper?"

"Yes. Jason Harper."

"So you do indeed know Jason Harper?"

"Sure I know Jason Harper."

"Do you have a romantic relationship with him?"

She studied my eyes for moment, then said, "Did he tell you that?"

I shook my head. "No. He said you were 'just a girl.' That's an exact quote."

She didn't redden, bristle, or in any other way show the hurt or annoyance that I'd expected. Without even so much as a shrug, she said, "Whatever."

"He said he was with you from around 8:30 on Tuesday night, when your class in Hampton Hall got out, until the next morning. He said he stayed here. Did he?"

"Yes."

"The whole night?"

"Yes. The whole night."

"You were with him the entire time?"

"If you mean every single minute, no, I wasn't with him the entire time."

"He left your apartment for a while? Is that what you're saying?"

"No, Detective, he didn't leave my apartment. He went to the bathroom two or three times and I didn't go with him. And he didn't go with me when I went," she said with her eyes hard on mine.

Glancing at my pad, I said, "I'm particularly interested in the time that night between 8:35 or so and 9:30. Were you with him every minute of that time?"

"Yes, I was."

"Where?"

"In my car, on the drive from my class to here. Then on this sofa and then in my bedroom."

"You're sure of that?" I said, giving her my hardest cop look.

"Yes, Detective. I'm sure of that. Do you want the details?"

"Mr. Harper asked me the same question and I'll tell you the same thing I told him, Ms. Tompkins. No. I don't want the details. But I do want to know what your status with Mr. Harper is now. You obviously have been in touch with him since Tuesday night."

She nodded. "Yes, I have."

"Have you been with him again?"

"If you mean have we fucked again, yes, we have."

"But you say, and he says, that y'all don't have a relationship."

"Not what I'd call a relationship."

"Would you like to have what you'd call a relationship with him?" I asked, watching her closely.

"Maybe I would and maybe I wouldn't. It's none of your business."

"I just don't want to see you get into any trouble, Ms. Tompkins," I said as gently and uncoplike as I could. "What I mean is that you need to be telling me the exact truth and not in any way, or for any reason, trying to cover up for Mr. Harper."

Her face reddening as her eyes flashed, she said, "You just don't believe me, do you? You think Jason killed her. You think just because he's so big and tough and didn't like her that he killed her. Well, he didn't. He couldn't have. He couldn't have because he was with me. Like I said. Exactly like I said."

***

When I got to the Y that morning, which was around eleven, the weight room was just the way I like it. Only five other people being there, all of them strangers, I would have no waiting in line for equipment and little if any need to make polite chitchat.

Midway through my first exercise, which was 100 reps in the leg raise, I saw someone enter, fresh and obviously ready to begin his workout. He was Christian

Peters, my bouncer colleague at The Other End, and I said to myself "Oh, shit."

Peters was not just a loudmouth, bully, and consummate jerk. He was also the kind of weight-room egomaniac who wanted an audience in the form of a spotter for every exercise he did, not just for heavy stuff such as squats and bench presses but also for vanity stuff such as curls. If none of the regulars were available, he would pester guys he'd never even seen before.

When he saw me, he walked over to where I was and said, "What's up, Loomis?"

"Not my energy. That's for sure," I said, not looking at him as I counted my reps.

"I guess you're just getting started, huh?" he said.

"Yeah, and I've got to turn and burn. I need to see somebody at 1:30."

"Well, I got something you need to hear."

"What is it?"

"I'll tell you before you go," he said with a slight shrug of his massive shoulders.

Something in his eyes made me so curious that for the next hour and a half, as I did my own exercises and spotted him on his, I could think of little else.

"So what's this you think I need to hear?" I asked as, drying myself off, I entered the locker room after my shower and saw him sitting on a bench, obviously waiting for me.

Glancing around the room to ensure we were alone, he said in an unusually low voice, "You're on that professor's murder, right? That Margulis woman?"

I nodded. "Yes."

"I knew her, man."

"So did I. I had a class under her about two years ago."

"Yeah, well, I had her just the other night, Saturday, three days before she got it."

"Had her? What do you mean 'had her'?"

"What do you think I mean? I've been fucking her, man," Peters said with annoyance.

Wrapping the towel around my waist, I sat down beside him on the bench.

"You want to tell me about it?" I said.

"What do you want to know?"

"You can start by telling me where you were between 8:30 and midnight last Tuesday, the night she was killed."

"Jesus, man. You know damn well where I was. I was at the club. Same as you. We got into it with some Jarheads and Rangers."

Nodding, I said, "Right. I remember. So how'd you manage to hook up with her?"

"She came in the club one night."

"When was that?"

"Six, eight months ago. She just walked up to me and said she wanted to see me when I got off."

"What'd you say?"

"I didn't have anything lined up so I said 'What the hell?' and told her it'd be late, after two, and she said, 'All right. I'll see you then.'"

"And she did?"

"Yeah. We went to her place."

"Was her daughter there?"

"No."

"What about at other times?"

"Nah. She'd come over to my place if her daughter was going to be there. She was pretty serious about that."

"But you did meet the daughter, Gloria?"

"Oh, yeah. Her and Bryan. He's her boyfriend."

"She didn't like Bryan, did she? Margulis, I mean."

"It went both ways. He couldn't stand her either."

"Do you think he killed her?"

Peters shook his head. "No way. I know who killed her. I'd bet my ass on it."

"Who?"

"Some guy named Nigel. I can't remember his last name."

"Nigel Helton. He's a biology professor at SUS."

"Yeah. She called him Ping Pong."

My memory flashing back to the number of times I'd seen the word in Helton's emails to Margulis, I said, "Why? Why'd she call him that?"

"B & D., man. He had this thing about being spanked on the ass."

"With a ping pong paddle?"

"Yeah. He got off on it."

"And she got off on doing it to him?"

"Big time, man. Anything to humiliate him."

"What else?"

Peters shrugged. "Telling him what a little dick he had. Having him come to her house when I was fucking her and wanting me to slap him around. That kind of shit."

"Did you? Slap him around?"

"Hell, no. I didn't play any of her damn games."

"But Nigel did? Ping Pong."

"Oh, yeah. The meaner she was, the more he liked it. Or so she said."

"Did you believe her?"

"Sure, I did. She hated men."

Nodding, I said, "So you're saying Ping Pong is a masochist, right?"

"I didn't say it. She did."

"She also said that the worse she was to him the more he liked it? Right?"

"Yeah. That's what she said."

"Why, then, do you think he killed her? If she was giving him what he wanted?"

"Maybe she gave him some shit that even he couldn't eat."

"Such as denying him pain, like in the joke?"

"Joke? What joke?"

"The sadist/masochist joke. A sadist is whipping a masochist and the masochist says, 'Harder. Harder. Hit me harder' and the sadist thinks for a moment and says 'No' and stops whipping him. I mean, she did stop seeing him, didn't she?"

"Oh, yeah, back in the summer, but he didn't give up. She said he kept sending her emails and trying to call her, but she wouldn't talk to him or anything. So maybe that's what it was. I don't know. But he did it, Loomis. I'd bet my ass on it," he said, his eyes steady on mine.

Nodding, I said, "Peters, I really appreciate this. I owe you one. I might want to talk some more to you about it."

"Any time, man."

"There's one more thing. It's purely personal. It doesn't have anything to do with the case," I said.

"Let's hear it," Peters said.

"I know you said you didn't have anything lined up that night, but I still find it kind of hard to believe that you, pussy hound that you are, could've hooked up with such a ball buster as Margulis for even one night, let alone for six or eight months. I know there's no accounting for taste and all that, but I find her totally repellant, downright nauseating."

"I was curious, man. First time, anyway, her being a professor and all. After that, I just liked the way she loved my dick. I mean, she really got off on it, big time, but she hated herself for it."

"She told you that?"

He shook his head. "She didn't come right out and say it, but I could tell. One time right after I'd finished fucking her eyes out she gave me a funny little smile and said 'I guess maybe a fish does need a bicycle every now and then.' I said 'Say what?' and she said there was a saying by this woman, some famous fem libber..."

I nodded. "Gloria Steinem. 'A woman needs a man like a fish needs a bicycle.'"

"Yeah, that's it. How the hell'd you know that, Loomis?" he asked, obviously both impressed and annoyed that I could one-up him in such a way.

"Oh, I read a book every now and then, Peters," I said with a little grin.

Chapter 5

That Monday the memorial service for Dr. Margulis was scheduled for noon, but I arrived on campus at eleven for my appointment with Dr. Harrison. After shaking my hand and offering me coffee, which I declined, he led me over to the little reception area in the corner of his office, where we sat down.

He was not in his usual casual slacks and a knit or button-up shirt with an open collar. He was in a white shirt and a blue striped tie that went with his black wingtips and the pants of his navy blue suit, the coat to which was hanging beside the door. His breathing, seemingly as always, was not easy and the fat of his neck hid most of the knot of his tie. He said he had just finished working on the "eulogy of a sort," as he called it, that he was going to deliver at the service.

"I'd just like to ask you a few more questions, Dr. Harrison, if you don't mind," I said as deferentially as possible.

"Not at all," he said with a solemn little grin, his gentle eyes seeming to have gone on full alert the moment I entered his office.

"As you know, Dr. Harrison, I've been going through the contents of Dr. Margulis's files, those you gave me and what's on her computer, her email included."

He nodded. "Yes, and I'm sure that you're finding them quite interesting."

"Yes, sir. I am. I'm especially interested in what some of them suggest about your relationship with her."

"My relationship with her?" he said, raising his right eyebrow.

"Yes, sir. Your professional relationship with her."

"It was the only kind of relationship I had with her."

"Yes, sir. I'm not implying otherwise."

Whatever he had intended to say was suddenly headed off by a light knock on his door followed by the cracking of the door and the appearance of his secretary's head.

"Dr. Harrison, I'm so sorry to bother you, but Dr. Margulis's father is here," she said, her eyes and tone saying the rest.

With a surprised look, Dr. Harrison said to her, "Ask him to come in, please," then to me, "I'm sorry, T. J., but I'll have to see him."

"I understand," I said, rising from my chair.

By the time Dr. Harrison had struggled to his feet, Thomas Margulis and I were shaking hands and introducing ourselves to each other. In his early seventies and, as I later would learn, a retired fireman, he was as tall as I was and strongly built but slightly stooped, with a full head of iron-gray hair and sad blue eyes in a weathered face. His tie and white shirt looked new, but his brown suit was just this side of shabby. He was from Colorado, his accent reminding me of some of my old Western States buddies in the paratroopers.

In the crook of his left arm was something that, under the circumstances, struck me as odd if not downright bizarre. It was a brown paper Piggly Wiggly grocery bag, closed at the top and shaped as if it contained a gallon jug of milk or maybe of water.

I told Dr. Harrison I would see him later and started to leave, but Mr. Margulis said he'd like me to stay, if it was all right with Dr. Harrison.

When the three of us were seated, Dr. Harrison said, "Mr. Margulis, let me first say how deeply sorry I and the department and the university as a whole are about the death of Mildred. We're all still in a state of shock and disbelief."

Holding the Piggly Wiggly bag in his lap, with both of his hands on it, Mr. Margulis nodded and said, "Thank you," then turned to me. "My granddaughter says you haven't caught Mildred's killer, Detective."

"No, sir, we haven't, but we soon will."

"She says she's a suspect herself, her and her boyfriend."

"She's not really a suspect, sir, but at this point, unfortunately, we have no choice but to consider almost everybody—everybody, that is, who was close to your daughter and doesn't have a good alibi. I'm sure you understand our position," I said as gently as possible.

Slowly shaking his head, he said, "I haven't seen Mildred since just before she came down here, back in '96, I think it was, or maybe '97. Gloria was just a little thing then, just starting school."

"She came here in '96," Dr. Harrison said.

"Tell me the truth, Professor. What was your opinion of my daughter?"

His cheeks seeming to redden slightly, Dr. Harrison said, "Your daughter had many outstanding qualities."

Thomas Margulis nodded. "She was smart. Oh, she was smart, smart as they come, and she'd work herself sick too if she didn't watch out. But there was always something she'd get all mad and bothered about. I don't know. She never got along with her mother. She's dead now, her poor mother is, God rest her soul," he said, crossing himself in the hurried way of old, lifelong Catholics. "Her two sisters— they could be hellions too. I'm not saying they couldn't. But they could be sweet. They could be just the sweetest things. But Mildred ...I don't know. I just don't know. She had to have her way, didn't matter what. She just had this need to be the boss, always the boss," he said, the pain and bewilderment in his old face cutting me to the quick.

Nodding, Dr. Harrison said, "That need is not at all unusual in people as highly intelligent as Mildred was."

Mr. Margulis turned his sad old eyes on me and said, "It was a man, Detective. Some man she made unhappy. So unhappy he just couldn't stand it anymore."

"We'll get him, Mr. Margulis. I guarantee it," I said with an assured nod.

"I hope you do. And I hope he goes to the gas chamber or wherever you send them down here. Whoever he was, she made him miserable, and I'm sorry. I'm sorry she did. But she was my baby girl, Detective. A long time ago she was my baby girl and now all that's left of her is here, in here," he said, his old eyes flaring with anger as he patted the picture of the happy little pig on the bag.

***

Several minutes before noon Lou joined me in the crowd of 100 or so that had gathered at the foot of the library steps. After returning my "Say, Lou" with a grunt of "How 'bout it, Slick," he began doing what I was doing, which was looking for, and if I found them, making mental notes of various people.

Not far from us were Bryan, Gloria, and Mr. Margulis, all three downcast and grim but none, as least as far as I could tell, weepy or even wet–eyed. This of course did not surprise me in Bryan, but it did in Gloria, who was stunning in black. No matter their differences, the woman who now was nothing but ashes in an urn in a Piggly Wiggly bag had been her mother and, to my way of thinking, the daughter should have been tormented by guilt if not by the kind of grief from which many women never get completely over.

Maybe, though, it was just that Gloria, however different she was from her mother in being such a hot-looking number and in liking the South, was like her mother in hating to cry or in any other way to appear weak. Her grandfather's face, however, especially his inward-looking old eyes, showed what he felt and, as in Dr. Harrison's office only a few minutes before, cut through my tough-cop pose like steel through tissue.

Chuck Wagner was a few yards back from them, leaning on his cane between two of my former history professors. He had on his usual jacket and tie plus, because of the biting cold, a gorgeous beige cashmere overcoat and a matching snap-brim cap of the sort that Robert Redford wore in The Great Gatsby. When our eyes met, he gave me a slight nod, his handsome face remaining grim but his dark, fallen-angel eyes glinting with amusement.

I looked for but did not see, and had not really expected to see, Jason Harper or the less towering but even more hulking Christian Peters, the last man, unless he was lying, to have slept with Mildred Margulis. Nor did I see

Professor Tom Flanagan, which didn't exactly surprise me but did make me wonder. I guess I'd halfway expected to see him in the very front of the crowd, smug-faced and gloating over the remains of a woman he seemed to have loathed.

I saw several other professors I vaguely remembered, plus a gaggle of scruffy-looking students, then, off to himself in the rear of the crowd, Nigel Helton. The stricken, downright crucified look on his soft, pleasant face filled my head with pictures of things Peters had told me, and I again lost my detachment. Mildred Margulis had been the kind of woman whom even her own father had not really liked, and I wondered how any man, even such a masochist as Helton apparently was, could ever have sought her out, let alone have cared enough to send her sick-puppy emails and then, as Helton now was doing, to grieve over her death. Then again, I told myself, he could be suffering more from guilt and fear than from grief—if he had killed her.

Turning my attention back to the front of the library, I again considered the scene there. On the third step from the top, centered like a cross on an altar, was the urn, gray and about the size of a gallon jug, that Mr. Margulis had held in his lap and would be taking back to Colorado. On the top step, right behind the urn, was a brown wooden lectern, and behind that, between the two big white columns, was a row of five folding chairs in which sat Dean Thomas, Dr. Harrison, Dr. Kerns, a young woman I didn't know, and Dr. Thomas Gleeson, the silver-haired and very presidential–looking President of SUS.

Precisely at noon, Dr. Gleeson glanced at his watch, then rose from his chair and walked over to the lectern. As he stood behind it and raised the goose-necked microphone to suit his height, a hush settled on the crowd, on the campus, on the entire world, it seemed to me.

"Can everybody hear me?" Dr. Gleeson asked, leaning toward the microphone.

Several people said yes and Dr. Gleeson, after a solemn pause, said in his strong voice, "We have gathered here today not to mourn but to remember and to celebrate the all too short life of our colleague, teacher, and friend,

Dr. Mildred Margulis. She was a person of incomparable energy and dedication and we..."

As Dr. Gleeson orated, I thought again of something Chuck Wagner had confided to me a year or so ago when I had been his student. During one of their early morning chats Dr. Harrison had told him of the time Dr. Gleeson had called him into his office and demanded to know what was going on in his department. This was after a Chamber of Commerce luncheon downtown when Dr. Gleeson had been asked by several alumni, "What kind of crackpot liberals are you letting teach out there, Tom?" In short, word of the radical feminism that Professors Margulis and Kerns inflicted on their classes was out and Dr. Gleeson wanted to know what Dr. Harrison was going to do about it. "Academic freedom being what it is, not to mention political correctness, there's not much I can do about it," Dr. Harrison had said. Later, after his third meeting with Dr. Margulis herself, Dr. Gleeson had shaken his head and, losing his usual cool, said, "I don't know how you put up with that damn woman, Steve. I really don't."

Dr. Gleeson continued with his pro forma hypocrisy, or whatever it was, for three or four very long minutes, after which Dean Thomas took his turn. From what Lou had told me of his talks with the Dean, I was all but sure that he too, for the sake of the daughter and the father if for no other reason, was putting compassion above honesty in characterizing Dr. Margulis as "an exemplary professional in every aspect of her work."

Dr. Harrison surprised me with his restraint and apparent honesty, by which I mean that he did little more than elaborate on, although with much more solemnity, what he had said to me in his office about Margulis's energy, passion, and "tireless devotion to her ideals."

I was equally surprised by Dr. Kerns. Her voice, of course, was about as dulcet as a blown out muffler, and I knew from my class with Margulis that some of what she said was simply not true, but she seemed truly to believe what she said. She praised her former friend and colleague for her devotion to her work as a teacher and scholar and for "her longstanding, courageous commitment to the free and easy exchange of ideas, however unpopular they might be."

I said to myself, "Yeah, right, as long as your ideas agree exactly with hers."

When Dr. Kerns sat down, the last of the five eulogists, the woman I didn't know, rose from her chair. As she stepped up to the lectern, a short-haired-and mournful looking female student standing next to Lou said in a low voice, "That's Sandi Hayes. Mildred was her teacher. She was our teacher. Our mentor."

Twenty-five or so, Sandi Hayes was short and squatty, with a face that would have been pleasant if not pretty had there not been such an angry look in her eyes and around her mouth. She was in a dark gray pants suit and, as her mentor had, wore her brown hair long, down close to her shoulders in fact, ala Gloria Steinem. Sandi also, in further homage to her mentor, had on large dangly earrings. They reminded me of little pineapples or, better yet, of little hand grenades.

After a long moment of staring glassy-eyed out into the crowd, Sandi, in a strong, slightly hoarse voice, said into the microphone, "Just as surely as Dr. Martin Luther King, Jr. was murdered for his stand against tyranny and injustice, so Dr. Mildred Margulis was murdered for hers. And just as surely as Dr. King's dream did not die with him, so Dr. Margulis's dream will not die with her. It will live. It will live in my heart, in my thoughts, in my words, and in my actions, just as it will in the hearts, thoughts, words, and actions of all women, of all of our sorely oppressed sisters."

Sandi Hayes went on for what seemed to me an hour but was really no more than five or so minutes. Several in the crowd, all of them females, shot forth a resounding "Yes!" at certain points, such as when Sandi called the murder a "a hate crime," while others, all of them males, detached themselves from the crowd and slipped away.

In his chair behind and to the left of the lectern, Dr. Harrison had in his face the same kind of pained look that I knew was in mine as I wished that someone would use an old-timey vaudeville crook to yank Sandi off stage. I knew, though, just as I'm sure Dr. Harrison knew, that she would be allowed to rant on for as long as she damned well pleased. Had he or any other man dared to interrupt her, she no doubt would have played the gender card and claimed that she too, like her mentor, was being silenced for being a strong, outspoken woman.

Chapter 6

When the service finally was over, Lou and I followed Nigel Helton across the main quad and into the building where his office was. Being behind him, I could not be sure, but it seemed to me that he several times wiped a tear from his eyes. Certainly he had the look and walk of a beaten man as he climbed the stairs to his office on the second floor.

He had hardly entered his office and closed the door when Lou, with his hard little fist, knocked three times in rapid succession. The schedule on the door indicated what Lou and I already knew, which was that Helton had no more classes that day.

When he opened the door, his eyes, along with the rest of his face, told me that he knew what was coming.

"Come in, gentlemen," he said even before I could ask if we could talk to him.

After closing the door and having Lou and me sit in the two chairs in front of the desk, Helton went behind the desk and sat down. A moment later, with a weak little smile on his soft face, he said to me, "You want to know why I lied to you the other day, don't you, Detective Loomis?"

"I didn't know you lied. Did you?"

"Yes. I said that I'd not communicated with Mildred Margulis since we stopped seeing each other at the beginning of August. I also said that we had drifted apart, that our breakup was by mutual consent and amicable."

"It wasn't?"

"No. She dumped me."

"Why didn't you tell me that then?"

"The same reason I didn't tell you I attempted to call her and sent her numerous emails. I was afraid you would get the wrong idea."

"What idea is that?"

"That I had a motive for killing her."

"And what motive might that be?"

"The anger and pain of spurned love."

"Wasn't that what you felt? Your emails certainly suggested it."

"Let's just say that I indulged in some rather extreme exaggeration."

Turning his death rays on Helton, Lou said, "She called you Ping Pong, didn't she, Professor?"

Helton's face reddened. "Yes. She called me that. What about it?"

"Y'all had a little B & D going. With you on the receiving end."

"I don't know what you're talking about, Detective."

"You're a college professor and you don't know what B & D is?" Lou said with one of his sneers.

"I know what B & D is but I don't know how it relates to me and to your investigation," Helton said in a huff, his face even redder.

"You want me to tell you?"

"I wish you would."

Nodding, Lou said, "She used a ping pong paddle on your ass. And you liked it so much that she, being the sadist, stopped giving it to you. So you killed her."

"No. No. That's not true. That is not true," Helton said, shaking his head, his cheeks on fire and his eyes bright with fear.

"What's not true?" I asked gently.

"I didn't kill her. I swear I didn't."

"But you did have this B & D thing with her?"

Helton nodded. "It was just foreplay. That's all it was. Just a game."

"Was the other guy part of it?" Lou said.

"I don't know what you're talking about."

"Sure, you do, Professor. The young guy with all the muscles and a dick that made three of yours. The one she picked up downtown and dumped you for. After, that is, she had her fun breaking your balls about him."

"All right. I did know about him. I admit it. But I didn't kill her. I swear to God I didn't kill her," Helton said, closing his eyes for a moment, then opening them and staring beseechingly at both of us. "You've got to believe me. I didn't kill her."

"Let me see now, Professor," Lou said, again sneering. "You told Detective Loomis here that you'd not been in touch with Professor Margulis since y'all broke up back in August. Now you say you lied."

"Yes. I did lie."

"You also told Detective Loomis that you and Professor Margulis parted amicably. That was a lie too, right?"

"Yes. It was."

"Then you said you didn't know about Mr. Big Dick when in fact you did know about him. So why should we believe you when you say you didn't kill Professor Margulis? How do we know you're not lying about that too?"

"Because I loved her, that's why. I loved her," Helton said, his eyes getting moist.

"Professor," Lou said, his sneer getting even nastier, "if I had a nickel for every time some poor smuck's killed some broad he said he loved, I'd be living in a penthouse and driving a goddamn Mercedes."

"I didn't kill her. I didn't. I couldn't have. I just couldn't have," Helton said, his mouth trembling and his eyes starting to water.

"If you didn't, who did?" I asked.

"If I knew that, Detective Loomis, I'd kill him myself," Helton said, his wet eyes flashing.

***

About fifteen minutes later Dr. Harrison and I were again sitting across from each other in the reception area in his office. This time, though, Lou was in the chair next to mine, looking as if he could fall asleep in the next minute.

"I believe you were asking about my professional relationship with Dr. Margulis when we were interrupted," Dr. Harrison said to me.

"Yes, sir, we were. What I was leading up to is that there's a pretty big discrepancy between what Dr. Margulis's files suggest about your relationship with her and what you told me when we talked the first time, right after we met with your department," I said.

With a tense, questioning look in his gentle gray eyes, Dr. Harrison said, "What's the discrepancy?"

"You told me that Dr. Margulis could be 'overbearing' and 'difficult' but that you had 'no serious problems in working with her.'"

"Yes. I said that, or words to that effect."

Glancing at my little pad, I said, "In your annual evaluation of Dr. Margulis for the past six years, though, you gave her an excellent rating in scholarship and a satisfactory rating in teaching, but said that she 'continues to be a divisive force in the department' and needs 'major improvements in collegiality.' Those were your exact words: 'a divisive force' and needs 'major improvement in collegiality.' You do remember writing that, don't you?"

"Of course I remember, but what I wrote doesn't contradict what I said. I had no serious difficulties in working with her."

"Yes, sir, but didn't Dr. Margulis write an official challenge to those evaluations and charge you with 'gender bias'?"

"Yes, she did."

"And in her evaluations of you, didn't she charge you, along with gender bias, with absenteeism, laziness, favoritism, general incompetence and outright dishonesty?"

Dr. Harrison nodded. "She did."

"And didn't the Vice-President more or less force you to undergo 'reconciliation sessions' with her?"

"The Vice-President merely suggested it. He didn't insist on it."

"But it was an ordeal, wasn't it? Five straight days of two-hour sessions. You sweated, according to what Dr. Margulis had in her computer, 'like a hog' and lost your breath--hyperventilated--twice and had to leave the room."

"It was, as you said, an ordeal," Dr. Harrison said with a nod.

Lou suddenly came awake. "There were some other things in her computer, Professor, real nasty and personal."

Dr. Harrison shifted his eyes from me to Lou.

"You write poetry, don't you?" Lou asked.

"Yes, I do."

"Is it any good?"

"I'm not the best judge of it, but it's been published in over forty different journals, so it must not be too bad."

"Professor Margulis said it was ...What was that word she used in the email, Detective Loomis?"

"If it's the email I think it is, she called it 'logorrhea,'" Dr. Harrison said.

"That's kind of like diarrhea but with words, right?" Lou said.

"I think you could say that, yes."

"How'd you know about that email, Professor? She didn't send it to you, did she?" Lou asked, his death rays switching on.

"No, but it made the rounds."

"It made you mad, didn't it?"

"No."

"She called your poetry shit and it didn't make you mad?" Lou asked, making a face of disbelief.

"Not at all. That's just her opinion."

"But you respected her, at least professionally. I mean, you did say that, didn't you?"

"Detective Ackerman," Dr. Harrison said, sounding as if he were being patient with a very dull student, "H. L. Mencken, perhaps the most influential American literary critic of the 1920's, said that F. Scott Fitzgerald's The Great Gatsby was really little more than a glorified anecdote. T.S. Eliot, an equally if not even more influential critic of the same period, praised the same book extravagantly. In literature, there is plenty of room for widely differing opinions."

Lou nodded, then said to me, "You want to tell him about that other email, Detective Loomis, or you want me to?"

"You can do it," I said, with what I knew was an uneasy look in my face.

"There's another email she sent out that said the same thing that was in her computer files. She sent it to...Who'd she send it to, Detective Loomis?"

"Originally to a professor at Penn State. This was right after she came to SUS. Later she sent it to various professors here, including Dr. Kerns and Dr. Helton, in the biology department," I said, after glancing again at my little pad.

"The one about my wife, you mean?" Dr. Harrison asked, looking at me, then at Lou.

Lou nodded. "She said your wife was a drunk, that she got so drunk at some restaurant downtown that she passed out on the can in the ladies' room. She said— Professor Margulis did, not your wife—that it was the funniest thing she'd ever heard."

"Yes. That one made the rounds too," Dr. Harrison said, seeming unfazed.

"Yeah and I bet made you mad, didn't it?" Lou said.

Dr. Harrison nodded. "Yes, it did. It made me furious."

"What'd you do about it?"

With a barely perceptible shrug, Dr. Harrison said, "I didn't do anything about it other than consider the source."

"You didn't even confront Professor Margulis about it?"

"No."

Shaking his head, Lou again made face of disbelief. "I find that hard to believe, Professor."

"Hard to believe or not, it's true."

After a moment, I said, "But you still say, Dr. Harrison, that you and Dr. Margulis had no serious difficulties in working together?"

"Yes, I do. I have always been able to separate my personal feelings from my professional relation-ships."

"Even when somebody says shit like that about your wife?"

"Especially when someone says shit like that about my wife," Dr. Harrison said, with what seemed to me a touch of smugness.

***

When Lou and I left Dr. Harrison's office, we walked to the other end of the hall and turned into the cul de sac where Dr. Kerns's office was. I had called her that morning and made an appointment for four that afternoon and we were early, my watch saying 3:46.

Her door open and Dr. Kerns at her desk, she waved away my apologies for being early and invited us to come in and sit down. With her skinny hand, which was surprisingly strong, she shook hands with me, then with Lou, seeming not to resent him for having come down so hard on her last Wednesday at the English department meeting.

"We have a few more questions to ask you, Dr. Kerns, if you don't mind," I said, again struck by the contrast between her reputation for man-hating nastiness and the polite, even gracious way she was treating us.

"I just hope I can be of some help in bringing Mildred's killer to justice," she said, taking a quick pull from her seemingly ever-present Perrier.

"You told me earlier, and you said again today in your eulogy, that you and Dr. Margulis, in addition to being close friends, were also close colleagues. That is correct, is it not?" I asked.

"Yes, it is. We worked closely together on a number of projects and regularly acted as sounding boards for each other's scholarship. I also helped her quite a bit with her computer problems."

"What do you mean by 'sounding boards,' Professor?" Lou asked.

"Each of us acted as a critic for the other."

"You mean y'all criticized each other?"

"Not each other. Each other's scholarly articles and my book. And we didn't so much criticize as critique. That is, we read each other's work carefully and assessed it, pointing out its strengths and weaknesses and making suggestions, that sort of thing."

"Did you like her work?" Lou continued.

"Oh, yes. Very much."

"What about her? Did she like yours?"

"Yes, she did."

"Did you and her ever have any differences?"

"By 'differences' I assume you mean disagreements or quarrels."

"Right. Disagreements or quarrels."

"No, not on anything substantive."

"Does that mean personally as well as professionally?" I asked.

Her gray eyes suddenly becoming as mean as a rattlesnake's, Dr. Kerns looked at me and snapped, "Yes. That's exactly what it means."

"You're sure about that, Dr. Kerns?"

"Of course I'm sure about that, Detective Loomis. What is this? A goddamn inquisition?" Dr. Kerns flared, her eyes darting from me to Lou.

"Professor, what is a...What do you call that review thing, Detective Loomis?"

"A post-tenure review," I said.

"Right. A post-tenure review. What is a post-tenure review, Professor?"

Dr. Kerns glared at him. "It's a peer review that tenured faculty members undergo every five years."

"A poll of your fellow professors on how good a job they think you're doing? Is that what you're saying?"

"Yes, Detective Ackerman. Why do you want to know?"

"You had one recently, didn't you? Back in the spring?"

"Yes, I did."

"How was it? I mean, did your peers think you're doing a good job or what?"

"They did. Most of them. There are always several who, for purely personal reasons, non-professional reasons, always say and write negative things about me."

"What about promotions? Do other professors have any say in that?"

"Yes. They express their opinions. It's supposed to be purely professional."

"You were promoted from associate professor to full professor last fall, weren't you?"

"Yes, I was, but where in the hell are you going with this?" Dr. Kerns demanded, her eyes burning. "I don't see that it has any relevance to your investigation."

"Four of your fellow professors in the English department opposed your promotion. Did you know that?" Lou asked.

"Yes, I did. The voting was seventeen for, four against, and one abstention."

"Do you know who those four were?"

"The forms are confidential, but yes, I know."

"If the forms are confidential, how do you know?"

"Because it's always the same people, that's how."

"Who are these people? Name them."

"Flanagan. Wagner. Etheridge, and either White or Ford. I'm not sure which."

"You got three out of four, Professor, same as on your post post-tenure poll," Lou said with a slow nod.

"How do you know all of that?" Dr. Kerns demanded, her glare even meaner. "Has Steve Harrison been letting you see my folder? That's what it is, isn't it? He's been letting you see my folder, my confidential folder!"

"No, he hasn't."

"I don't believe you. You couldn't have gotten that information anywhere else."

"We could and we did. Would you like to tell the professor where, Detective Loomis?"

"In connection with our investigation, we've been through the personal folder, the student evaluations, the computer files and saved emails, the hard-copy memos— every document that we could find of Dr. Margulis's," I said, returning Dr. Kerns's glare.

"So what?" she said, her voice now a snarl.

"So this," Lou said. "The fourth professor who gave you a bad post-tenure review and opposed your promotion wasn't either one of the two you named. It was the close colleague and friend you say you never had any disagreements or quarrels with, the one who liked your work, your 'sounding board,' you called her."

For a long moment, Dr. Kerns just stared at him. Then she said, "I don't believe you."

"Read her some of those notes you took, Detective Loomis. They're...What'd you say they were? That big word?"

"Verbatim," I said, flipping my note pad to the marked place.

"Right. Word for word," Lou said.

Clearing my throat, Dr. Kerns's glare seeming as hot as a blow dryer on my face, I said, "I took these excerpts from Dr. Margulis's computer file named Journal. The first one is from last fall, 9-06, and it's about your promotion. It says, 'J. K. is sure to get it and I don't really mind—honestly, I don't—but I can't in good conscience favor it. Her teaching is uninspired, perhaps even lethargic, and her book and most of her articles, even at their best, are so superficial as to be better suited to a Sunday newspaper supplement such as Parade than to any scholarly journal worthy of the designation. I know that SUS isn't Harvard or even Penn State, but the rank of full professor is supposed to mean something, even at a dinky little fifth tier school, and I will do what I can to see that it does.'"

Looking up from my pad, I saw what I was sure was a combination of disbelief and pain in Dr. Kerns's face as she stared back at me, her scrawny little body now deathly still and so very frail looking.

Feeling a rush of pity, I said, "The entry on your post-tenure review says pretty much the same thing. Do you want me to read it?"

Dr. Kerns slowly shook her head. "No."

"We can get you a hard copy of the whole thing plus the other stuff if you have any doubts," Lou said, his eyes again reminding me of a computer saving data as they stared at Dr. Kerns.

A grim little smile playing on her lips, she shook her head and said, "No. That's Mildred. You couldn't have made it up."

A very long moment later, as her eyes shifted from me to Lou and back to me, Dr. Kerns said in a low, barely audible voice, "Do you gentlemen have any more questions?"

Thinking that we had a great many more, I was surprised, even touched when Lou rose from his chair and in a gentle voice said, "We may want to talk to you again later, Professor Kerns, but no, not right now. You've been very helpful and we appreciate it."

***

At 12:55 the next afternoon, a week to the day since the murder, I was back in Hampton Hall. Standing outside the office of Professor Jack Flanagan, I was waiting for him to keep his office hour, from one until two, which was indicated on the schedule posted on his door.

At 12:59 I saw him approaching. He was talking to a pretty female student, apparently about something amusing, but his thin, bird-alert face became grim the moment he saw me.

"Tomorrow. We'll meet again tomorrow," he said to the student, then to himself or to me or to some imaginary audience, "'Tomorrow and tomorrow and tomorrow creeps in this petty pace from day to day to the...'"

"'Last syllable of recorded time'," I said, proud of myself for knowing the line.

"'And all our yesterdays have lighted fools' way to dusty death,'" Flanagan continued. Then looking at me, he said, "So what can I do for you today, Detective Loomis, aside from bandy Macbeth about? Let me guess. You want to question me again about the dusty death of my late but unlamented colleague and perhaps her idiot's tale of a life as well? Eh?"

"Yes, sir. I do have a few more questions I'd like to ask you," I said with a little grin.

Flanagan unlocked his door and gestured for me to precede him into his office and to sit in the chair in front of his desk.

As before, I took in the wall-to-wall books and the smell of the running shorts, jock strap, and shoes hanging on the coat rack in the corner.

"All right, Torquemada, you may begin your inquisition," Flanagan said, cocking back in his chair and plopping his scuffed brown penny loafers on his desk. That day, instead of Tweety Bird socks, he had on a pair of faded red ones.

"I've been through a good many of Dr. Marguliss's files, computer as well as hardcopy, and she seems to have felt pretty much about you as you did about her," I said, watching him closely.

"Oh, yes. I'm a 'brainless buffoon,' a 'disgrace to academe,' among a thousand other such things," Flanagan said with a slight shrug of his boney little shoulders. "Even so, Margulis simply was not in my league when you get right down to it."

"Down to what?"

"Down to the thing, after writing, singing, and of course drinking, that we Irish do better than anyone else."

"What's that?" I asked.

"Hate our enemies."

I nodded, then said, "You're a pretty serious runner, aren't you, Professor Flanagan?"

"It depends on what you mean by 'serious.'"

"I understand that a few years ago you ran the Boston Marathon in well under three hours."

"Two hours, forty-two minutes, and thirty-one seconds, to be precise. But that, alas, was long ago and far away in the country of youth. They do things differently there, you know."

"You still do well in your age group in local races. In the Savannah Half Marathon last year, in the 50 to 55 group, you placed...What was it? Second? Third?"

"Third."

"The reason I know is that I regularly read the race results in the Savannah Morning News. Your time at the beach was around 1:50, if I remember correctly."

"One forty-eight, twenty–six," Flanagan corrected.

"I remember seeing another name that I recognized. In the results of that race, I mean."

"I don't suppose I need ask whose," Flanagan said with a look of disgust.

"She beat you. If I remember correctly, she beat you by only a few seconds."

"Three seconds. Her time was 1:48:23."

"How'd that happen?"

"She crossed the finish line three seconds before I did, Detective Loomis. How do you think it happened?"

"I know that, but how could she outrun you? I mean, as serious about running as you are, I wouldn't have thought she could come anywhere near you."

"She couldn't in a 5 or 10K, but she was quite dogged...All right, I'll give the devil her due. She was quite gutsy over the long haul. And she was, let me remind you, in the 40 to 45 age group."

"In her computer files, the one named Journal, she talks about that race. She said she sprinted past you in the final twenty yards. Is that correct?"

"I wouldn't call her heavy-legged clop trop a sprint, but yes, she did pass me near the end."

"You didn't like it either, did you?"

"Of course I didn't, but I had only myself to blame. I had no idea she was that close."

"Tell me about the English Department meeting the Monday following the race," I said.

"Why? You obviously already know about it?"

"I've read her version of it and I've heard versions from several other professors in your department. I'd like to hear yours."

Flanagan shrugged. "She took a bow for it, literally. Then again, as you may have heard, she took a bow, figuratively if not literally, for everything she did. She was a walking neon sign of self-advertisement."

"She said that she and Dr. Kerns planned it."

"Oh, yes. She and that nasty little toad were continually hatching schemes of malice and discord."

"Tell me about this one."

"At the end of the meeting that day, The Doughboy..."

"Dr. Harrison?"

"Yes. Lard ass, aka the Doughboy, as in Pillsbury. At the end of the meeting he asked if there were any announcements and Kerns popped up and said she had one. She said she was proud to announce that the Department's highest finisher in the Savannah Half Marathon the previous Saturday was none other than Mildred Margulis. Somebody—I can't remember who—said, 'Are you serious? She beat Flanagan?' And Kerns said, 'Yes. She beat Flanagan.' She started clapping and said, 'Take a bow, Mildred. Take a bow.' And Margulis did. She actually stood up, grinned like a shithouse rat, and bowed, not once or twice, but three times."

"What did you do?"

"I stared at her."

"What about the others? How'd they react?"

"Most of them did as I did, stared, but several of her fellow travelers clapped and one of them, that pluperfect nitwit Lori Andrews, said 'Bravo! Bravo! You go, girl!' Her subtext, of course was 'Score one against the patriarchy!'"

"What about Dr. Harrison? The Doughboy as you call him. How'd he react?" I asked.

A look of infinite disgust spread over Flanagan's face. "It was enough to gag a maggot."

"Why? What'd he do?"

"He clapped, the gutless rat fink."

Nodding, I said, "Do you know how Dr. Margulis was killed?"

"She was strangled."

"Yes, but do you know what with?"

"I assume it was with hands, somebody's hands."

"It was with somebody's hands, but they used something."

"What?"

"The purple ribbon on the third place medal that Dr. Margulis won in her age group in the Savannah Half Marathon, the race she beat you in. The killer stood behind her and used the ribbon as a garrote."

For a moment Flanagan just stared back at me. Then he broke into a wide grin and said, "That is priceless. Absolutely priceless."

"Do you know what else?"

"No, but if it's that good, I'm dying to hear it."

"I suppose, at least from where you stand, that it's even better, Professor Flanagan."

"As I said, Detective Loomis, I'm dying to hear," he said, his eyes as hard on mine as mine were on his.

"After she was dead, the ribbon was lowered over her head and around her neck so that the medal hung against her chest like the thing it is, an award. And her left earlobe had been split from the dangly earring, which looked like two figs or a pair of testicles, having been ripped out and taken, apparently as a souvenir. Somebody had hated her that much. Enough to strangle her and then to desecrate her dead body."

Continuing our staring match, Flanagan said nothing for several seconds. Then he grinned again and said, 'Nice, Detective Loomis. Very nice, your little syllogism."

"I don't know what you're talking about."

"Sure you do. The person who killed Mildred Margulis had to have been a runner who really and truly hated her. Jack Flanagan is a runner who really and truly hated her. Ergo, Jack Flanagan killed her."

"I didn't say that."

"No, but you implied it and you probably think it. And I can understand why you do. I hated Mildred Margulis and if I'm not glad she's dead, I sure as hell ain't grieving. I was on campus without an alibi at the very time she was killed. And the manner of her death—call it the style—is definitely of a piece with me. But all that's just circumstantial, syllogistic. You don't have a single shred of real evidence to implicate me."

"You're quite sure of that?" I said, raising my right eyebrow.

"You fingerprinted and footprinted everything in that woman's office, didn't you?"

"Yes, we did."

"And you fingerprinted me and footprinted my running shoes and my loafers, the ones I'm wearing now?"

I nodded.

"And you didn't find a single match, did you? Nothing, no evidence whatsoever that I was ever in that woman's office?"

I shook my head. "No, we didn't. Everything was clean, even the ribbon. The killer knew exactly what he was doing. Exactly."

Chapter 7

Around two that same afternoon I went to The University Shopping Plaza, to Luigi's, the Italian restaurant where Dr. Harrison said he and his wife had eaten dinner the night of the murder. Most of the lunch bunch having come and gone, only a few of the tables and booths were occupied and only three or four guys were at the bar. The bartender said that the manager wasn't there but the assistant manager was and she would get him for me.

Several minutes later, in the little office in back, I was sitting on a sagging old couch with a guy I recognized from the weight room at the Y, Brad Burkett, a well-built retired Ranger Staff Sergeant in his early forties. He had been in Desert Storm as well as Iraq and his eyes, even more than his limp, told me that he had seen more than his share of hell.

"I didn't know you worked here, Brad. I thought you were selling cars, Hondas," I said.

"I had to get out of that. My old lady said if I didn't, it'd be 'Adios!' So I'm here and going to school, to SUS, taking a couple of courses."

"Sounds good. Are you full time here?"

"Full and then some, forty-five, fifty hours a week. But, hey, it ain't forever and I'll tell you, buddy. It beats the hell out of standing around a goddamn car lot. I'd rather do a tour in graves registration than that. Believe me."

His eyes studying mine, he said, "I know you didn't come here to eat."

"I need some information, Brad."

"What can I tell you?"

"Last Tuesday night, the night that professor at SUS was killed, were you here, say between eight and nine-thirty?"

"I was here all day. From eleven until closing, a little after ten."

"I don't suppose you know a guy named Harrison, Dr. Steve Harrison, do you? He's the head of the SUS English department."

"Sure, I do. I know Steve. He comes here all the time. Him and his wife, Mahalia. They're real nice folks, both of them."

"Did they have dinner here last Tuesday night?"

"They sure did."

"What time did they come in?"

"Seven, maybe a little later."

"How long were they here?"

"They left right at 8:30."

"You're sure of that? Eight-thirty?"

He nodded. "I had to help Steve get Mahalia to the car."

I gave him a quizzical look. "Why? Was she sick?"

He shook his head. "Mahalia's got a little drinking problem, T.J."

"What about Dr. Harrison? Does he have one?"

"Nah. He can really hold his, big as he is."

"But his wife—Mahalia—you say she can't hold hers?"

Again shaking his head, Brad said, "The skinny little thing looks like she might have cancer or be anorexic or something. It's really sad too, because she's a real sweet lady."

"I understand Dr. Harrison's very protective of her," I said.

"He's just as gentle as he can be. Don't fuss or nothing when she needs help. Just gives me a signal and we get her out."

"It's that routine?"

"Every two or three weeks maybe. Sometimes she's fine. In fact, most of the time she's fine."

"How often do they come here?"

"Once, twice a week together, generally on Tuesdays. But he comes by himself too, just to drink and talk to anybody who'll halfway listen. Sometimes he'll still be here when we're getting ready to close and I'll just about have to run him out. But, hey, he's a nice guy. I guess he's just lonely, you know what I mean?"

Brad paused for a moment, then said, "He's not in good health either. The other night, Tuesday, after we got poor little Mahalia to the car, he was breathing so hard I thought I was going to have to call EMS."

"I know what you mean," I said, nodding.

"They say she's a real genius with computers."

"Who says?"

"You know The Geek Shop? Three or four doors down from here, right next to Books-a-Million?" Brad asked, jerking his head to the right.

"No, I don't. What kind of geek shop?"

"Computer geeks. They fix computers. You can bring yours in or they'll do it remote or come to you, whatever you need. The manager—he eats lunch here a lot—he says Mahalia's his go-to geek. He says she can fix stuff the others can't. Steve calls her Queen Geek. He showed me a funny little poem her wrote about her. She's his third wife. Did you know that?"

***

I went from Luigi's to the Geek Shop, but Mahalia Harrison, one of the other geeks said, worked mostly out of her house and didn't come in, as he put it, "unless we're slammed big time." So, already having the address, I drove straight to Sherwood Forest, which my unmarked cruiser's odometer said was 2.3 miles from Luigi's and 1.4 miles from the SUS campus.

The Harrisons' house was typical of the houses in the subdivision in being solidly middle-class, nicely kept, and looking as if it would list for around $200,000 in today's market. Dr. Harrison's car, a dark green Buick LeSabre, was nowhere to be seen, as I had hoped would be the case, but an old gray Honda Accord was in the driveway.

After five or six soundings of the chimes, just as I was about to give up, the door was opened by a woman I knew was Mahalia Harrison. She was around fifty, as frail and anorexic looking as Brad Burkett had said, and, although it was the middle of the afternoon, she was still in her nightgown and housecoat. Her graying black hair was uncombed and ratty and her face was unmade and extremely pale, not sheet-white but close.

"Mrs. Harrison?" I said.

"Yes. I'm Mrs. Harrison," she said with a guarded look in her dark eyes as she stared at me though the screen.

"I'm Detective T.J. Looms of the Savannah Police Department and I..."

"Oh yes. Yes. Steve told me about you," she said quickly, her eyes no longer suspicious. "You were his student. You're investigating Mildred Margulis's murder."

"Yes, ma'am, I am and I was wondering if you could give me a few minutes of your time," I said, replacing my identification in the inside pocket of my jacket.

"Why, yes. Of course. Yes. Please. Won't you come in?" she said, sounding almost eager as she unlatched then opened the screen door.

"You'll have to excuse me for one little minute, Detective Loomis. Won't you sit down? Please. I'll be right back," she said, leading me into the living room, then gesturing toward the sofa and hurrying out.

The room was spacious and comfortably furnished, but the sofa and chairs, though they didn't have a new smell, didn't look as if they'd ever been used. The piles of the cushions were still crisp and a fragment of the cellophane that once had covered the sofa was visible down by one of the back legs. From opposite sides of the room two big bookcases stuffed with books faced each other, and on the mantle above the gas logs was an array of framed photographs. Like the mantel itself, the photographs seemed not to have been dusted in quite a while, if ever.

Two of them caught my eye. One, to judge from the clothes and smiles, was of the Harrisons on their wedding day. Dr. Harrison looked at least ten years younger and fifty pounds lighter, and Mrs. Harrison looked only slender, not at all anorexic. She in fact looked rather pretty in a faded sort of way. She also, as did Dr. Harrison, looked very happy.

Beside two clean-cut guys in their late twenties or early thirties, obviously Dr. Harrison's sons, was the other photograph that struck me. It was of a female, twenty-five or so, who, at least to my eyes, was about as good-looking as women get. With her severe, elegant cheekbones and gorgeous, hungry-looking lips, she could have passed for a brunette clone of Nicolette Sheridan back when she was twenty-five.

"These are some really nice pictures, Mrs. Harrison," I said as she re-entered the room and walked over toward me.

She was still in her nightgown and housecoat, but she had brushed her hair and put on some bright red lipstick that, rather than helping, only made the rest of her face seem paler and closer to sheet white. She stood close enough for my nose to tell me that she had brushed her teeth and used Listerine. Naturally I wondered if she were trying to mask the smell of what she may have drunk the night before or earlier that day.

"Yes. Yes, they are nice, aren't they?" she said, the way she looked at me and then at the pictures making me understand why Dr. Harrison was so protective of her and why I had never heard Chuck Wagner say "Mahalia" without first putting "poor" in front of it. I thought of some lines from T.S. Eliot that went something like "An infinitely gentle, infinitely suffering thing."

"That's a very nice one of you and Dr. Harrison. Were y'all just married?"

With a wistful little smile, she nodded. "That's one of my most favorite. Doesn't Steve look handsome? Just so handsome?"

"Yes, ma'am, he does, and so happy too. And the sons. They look just like him. They are his sons, aren't they?"

"Yes, Stan and Eddie. They're like him too, just as sweet and smart and all as he is, bless their hearts."

"I'm sure he's proud of them. And of her. She's perfectly beautiful," I said, shifting my eyes to the Nicolette Sheridan look-alike.

"She's not his."

"She must be your daughter then?"

"No. She's me. She's me, believe it or not, a long time ago."

"Oh, I can believe it, Mrs. Harrison. I can definitely see the resemblance," I said quickly, nodding slowly and blushing as I felt a rush of pity for her mixed with embarrassment for myself for never being able to tell a convincing lie.

Touching me gently on the arm with her worm-veined little bird claw of a hand, Mahalia Harrison made me feel even worse by saying, "It's so sweet of you to say that, Detective Loomis. Steve said you weren't a bit like a cop. He said you were just too nice and sensitive."

After offering me coffee, iced tea, or a Pepsi, diet or regular, which I declined, Mrs. Harrison sat on the sofa and I sat in front of her, in one of the new-feeling chairs.

"So tell me, Detective Loomis, how can I help you?" she asked, her dark, very intelligent eyes seeming huge in her thin little face.

"I'm not sure, Mrs. Harrison. I was just wondering about your take on the situation. Do you have any idea who could've killed Dr. Margulis?"

"I don't like to say unkind things, however true they may be, about anyone, Detective Loomis."

"But?"

"Mildred Margulis was not a very nice person."

"So I gather. I don't think any of her fellow professors in your husband's department really liked her. Professor Flanagan, by his own admission, couldn't stand her."

"He can't stand Steve either."

"Can you tell me why? Everybody else in the department, at least the ones I've talked to, seem to hold Dr. Harrison in very high regard, personally as well as professionally."

"You must not have talked to Julia Kerns."

"She has problems with Dr. Harrison?"

Mrs. Harrison nodded. "She's always making trouble about something. And so was Mildred. They were partners, accomplices. And Tom Flanagan. They were about the only real problems Steve had, with his staff anyway."

"They—Flanagan, Kerns, and Margulis, I mean—weren't a team, though, were they? I mean, from what I've been able to gather, Professor Flanagan loathed, and was loathed by, both of them."

"Yes, and that's why he hates Steve. He thinks Steve lets them run the department. He doesn't understand that there's just so much Steve can do."

"What do you mean 'just so much', Mrs. Harrison?"

"I mean they're women and they play it for all it's worth. Or played it in Mildred's case," Mrs. Harrison said with a flash of anger in her huge dark eyes. "She made Steve miserable. Both of them did. And Tom Flanagan did. Does. He still does."

"I gather that Dr. Harrison talks a good bit with you about his department?"

"Actually, he doesn't, except in a very general way. When I ask for specifics, he always says 'I can't go there' and he won't, no matter how much I push. He's very professional."

"How do you know these things then if he won't talk about them?"

"People in the department tell me."

"Who tells you, if I may ask?"

"Chuck does. Chuck Wagner. Do you know him?"

"Yes, ma'am, I do. I took four courses under him."

"You must have liked him."

"I did. I liked him very much. I still do."

"Chuck's Steve's best friend at work and is the sweetest thing, just the sweetest, gentlest, most thoughtful man," Mrs. Harrison said, her face softening. "He worries so much about Steve. You do know that Steve's not in good health, don't you, Detective Loomis?"

"Yes, ma'am, I'm afraid I do. Is it his heart, if you don't mind telling me?"

"His heart's the main thing. He's so heavy, just so very heavy, and he worries. He worries about every little thing and has a terrible time sleeping. Chuck's afraid he's going to drop dead in the hall."

Nodding, I said as gently as possible, "How's Dr. Harrison doing now, Mrs. Harrison? I mean, with the investigation going on and all?"

"Is this just between us, Detective Loomis? You won't tell Steve?"

"No. ma'am, I won't. This is just between us."

She thought for a moment, then slowly shook her head and said, "He doesn't say much, you understand, just that the investigation is ongoing. But I know. He feels so guilty, so very guilty."

"Does he say this or do you just know it?" I asked.

"I just know it. I know him. I know the kind of man he is."

"Mrs. Harrison, surely you're not saying that Dr. Harrison killed Dr. Margulis, are you?"

"Oh, no. Of course not. Steve wouldn't hurt a fly."

"Why do you say he feels guilty then?"

"Mainly because of something she did—that Mildred Margulis did—not to him but to me a long time ago, when she first came here. Something very ugly."

"The email, you mean?"

Her pale face did not redden or in any other way show distress. "Yes. How'd you know about that?"

"I saw it when I went through Dr. Margulis's computer. And Dr. Harrison confirmed it when I asked him about it. He said he was furious but didn't do anything about it. He didn't even confront Dr. Margulis, he said. Obviously, though, he told you about it."

"Not at first. I knew something was eating at him, really hurting him, and I finally got it out of him."

"What was your reaction?"

"I didn't believe it. I thought she was making it up."

"You didn't remember the incident?"

"I could remember going into the restaurant and sitting down, but nothing beyond that. It was all a black hole." With a sad, self-reproachful little smile, she said, "That sometimes used to happen to me when I'd had too much to drink, Detective Loomis."

"I understand," I said as gently as I could.

"But I lost it. I totally lost it when Steve said she wasn't making it up," Mrs. Harrison said, closing her eyes for a moment as she slowly shook her head. "Steve, bless his heart—he was just too wonderful. He called in sick and waited on me hand and foot. He didn't let me out of his sight for three whole days and nights. But I got okay, more or less, at least about that. I mean, I stopped dwelling on it years ago, maybe because she's made so much other trouble for Steve."

"But this guilt you say you know Dr. Harrison's feeling—I think if I were in his place I'd feel more relief than anything else. I might not admit it, but I'd feel it. I think most people would. Wouldn't you?"

"I certainly would, and I do. I admit it," she said without hesitation. "I'm not at all sorry that Mildred Margulis is dead, except for her daughter's sake. But I'm not Steve. I'm not wired the way he is. He's a poet, as I'm sure you know, and he's very introspective, obsessively, morbidly so, in my opinion. What I mean is he has a tendency to attach as much meaning, especially moral meaning, to what he thinks as to what he does."

"He's told you this?"

"Yes, in his poems. In one of them he says—I can't remember exactly how it goes—but he says 'If I am anything, I am my thoughts.' Something like that."

"Let me see if I understand, Mrs. Harrison," I said, studying her eyes. "You're saying that Dr. Harrison, because of his extreme moral sensitivity, is suffering from a kind of vicarious guilt because somebody else did what he wanted to do and thought of doing but could never actually do?"

"Yes. I know my husband well and I know that, except to defend me or himself, he wouldn't be physically violent with anybody, especially a woman. I also know him well enough to bet you anything that in his fantasies for the past ten years he has murdered Mildred Margulis almost as many times as I have."

Her frail little jaw seeming to tighten as her sad eyes again flashed, Mrs. Harrison slowly shook her head and said, "And that, I can assure you, Detective Loomis, is more times than either of us would care to count."

A moment later, her eyes now pleading, she said, "If Steve ever asks, I know you'll have to tell him you talked to me, Detective Loomis, but ..."

"Don't worry, Mrs. Harrison," I cut in with a little smile. "I'll tell him he'll have to talk to you if he wants the details. And to be perfectly honest, you haven't told me anything that I didn't already know in a general way. You remember, I had two courses under Dr. Harrison and I have a pretty good sense of his basic wiring. He's a highly intelligent, highly sensitive man, a very decent man."

"Yes. Yes, he is," she said, looking for a moment as if she were about to cry.

"Before I go, just as part of the routine, I need to ask you one or two questions about what you and Dr. Harrison were doing last Tuesday night, the night Dr. Margulis was killed."

"Steve already told you about that, didn't he?"

"Yes, ma'am, he did, but I just need to be sure about a few things. Dr. Harrison left his office in Hampton Hall around 5:30, his usual time, and came home, which would've put him here around 5:45 at the latest. Is that correct?"

"Yes, give or take a few minutes."

"Then he walked y'all's dog, which took him, he said, between twenty and thirty minutes?"

"About that, yes, depending on how much sniffing he let her do."

"And a little while later, around 7, y'all went to Luigi's for dinner?"

"Yes, we did. We generally go there on Tuesdays."

"Do you remember how long y'all stayed?"

"No, not exactly. A little over an hour, maybe an hour and a half."

"So y'all left around 8:30. Is that correct?"

"Yes. Around then."

"Did y'all stop off anywhere or go straight home?"

"We went straight home."

"Luigi's being only a tad under two and a half miles from here, that would've put you home around 8:45, maybe a few minutes later?"

"That sounds about right."

"And both of y'all were at home the rest of the night?"

"Yes. We were."

"I have just one more question, Mrs. Harrison."

"What is it?"

"Can you think of anything unusual or out of the ordinary that happened at Luigi's or that you may have seen on the drive home?"

"Such as?"

"I don't know. I'm just fishing, hoping you may be able to tell me something that might shed a little new light on the case."

She thought for a long moment, then gave me an apologetic little smile and said, "I'm sorry, Detective Loomis, but I can't think of a thing. The evening was very nice and relaxing, very routine."

***

First thing the next morning, a little before seven, I met Lou for breakfast at the Huddle House near the SUS campus.

"So what we got, Slick?" he said as he sat across from me in a booth and took his first sip of coffee.

As always when he asked such a question, I knew I was on trial.

"I checked out Mahalia Harrison, Dr. Harrison's wife. She's a sad case," I said.

"How so?"

"Her health, for one thing. She looks sick, physically sick, as if she has cancer. She might weigh a hundred pounds. And she definitely has a drinking problem. I got confirmation of that from the assistant manager at Luigi's, a guy I know from the Y. He said that on a fairly regular basis she gets so drunk that he has to help Dr. Harrison get her to the car. He said she did last Tuesday night. He said she and Dr. Harrison got there around 7 and left around 8:30."

Lou nodded. "That's what Harrison told you too."

"Right, but there's a catch. Those booze blackouts she has, like the one in Margulis's email?"

"What about them?"

"Either she had a really bad one Tuesday night or she's lying."

"Tell me about it."

"I asked her point blank if anything unusual happened when they were at Luigi's. She said no, nothing, that it was a nice, relaxing evening."

"Maybe she was just talking like a goddamn lawyer, Slick. You said 'anything unusual' and your friend says it ain't unusual."

"My gut tells me she's lying."

"What's she got to gain?"

"You apparently don't think it makes any difference?"

"The guy at Luigi's said that Harrison and her were there from about 7 until about 8:30. What does it matter whether she was soused or sober?" Lou said with a shrug. "What else you got? You said you leaned on Flanagan again?"

"I did, but I got pretty much the same old same old. What about you?"

Taking a sip of coffee, Lou said, "I been coming down pretty hard on the daughter and the boyfriend, separately and together, and he just don't strike me as the kind of guy who'd choke a woman with a ribbon and then hang a goddamn medal around her neck. I just can't see it. Can you?"

"No, I can't. Shoot her maybe or use his hands, but not a ribbon and definitely not from behind. He's a good ole boy and that just ain't the way good ole boys do it. I know. I'm one of them. What about the daughter?"

"Nah. She was at home the whole time. The lady across the street called her on the phone and talked to her between 8:45 and 9. Plus the kid loved her mother. They fought like cats and dogs, but the kid loved her. There ain't no doubt about that."

"You also said you haven't been able to come up with anything on any of Margulis's students, past or present."

"I'm still looking at two or three of them, especially that basketball asshole, that Harper guy. I'd like to bust his balls just for the hell of it."

"What about his alibi?"

Lou scowled. "What about it?"

"You don't believe it, what that girl, Jennifer Tompkins, said about being in bed with him all night?"

"Let's just say I have my doubts," Lou said, then with a shrug added, "But he don't seem like a ribbon kind of guy either."

"What about all those prints of his we got in her office, off the chair in front of her desk and especially off some of the books behind her?"

"Yeah. His and twenty-two other people's. But, hey, I ain't counting him out. I'm gonna stay on his ass," Lou said as he started on the bacon and eggs the waitress had brought.

After making a start on my own, I said, "So that pretty much still leaves us with Flanagan as our most likely."

"He hated her guts. There ain't no doubt about that, and he was in or near the building when it happened. So we got us a motive and an opportunity, but that's all we got. We ain't got an eyewitness or any prints, not a single one."

"No, because hating Margulis as much as he did, he never would've been in her office except when he went there to kill her. And he covered, wiped off his tracks."

"So you think he's our perp, Slick?"

"To be honest, Lou, at this point I just flat out don't know what I think," I said with a mournful shaking of my head.

Chapter 8

I went from the Huddle House over to the SUS campus, to office 213 on the second floor of Hampton Hall. After removing the yellow crime scene tape, I went in, turned on the light, closed the door, and did as I had done two times before. I sat in the chair behind the desk, the last chair Mildred Margulis had ever sat in, and tried to imagine myself as her in the concluding countdown of her existence. As my eyes moved over the ceiling, the walls, the books, and the various trappings, I hoped, as before, to see something I had missed or maybe had seen but had not seen as important.

But, also as before, I could not see or think of anything new and I was again flooded with something I never thought I could feel at all, let alone so intensely. This strange something was pity for Mildred Margulis, partly of course because she was dead and had died so horribly but mainly because, as far as I could tell and no matter the reasons, she had been so soundly disliked if not actually hated by almost everyone who knew her—except, that is, for her little band of student disciples and fellow travelers.

After wasting almost an hour on such embarrassingly un-cop-like musings, I resealed the office, started out of the cul de sac, and, entering the hall, almost collided with Chuck Wagner.

He was in bright brown loafers with even brighter pennies in the slots, brown slacks, and a beige turtleneck sweater beneath a rust corduroy jacket with dark brown patches on the elbows. His slightly graying black hair was as close as a skullcap and brushed forward, which, with his strong jaw and beetling brows, made me think again of a Roman emperor on an old coin.

Leaning on his cane, his powerful, Darth Vader voice making even his simplest utterance sound Shakespearean, he said, "We twain having both fortuitously and fortunately converged, T.J., why don't you hang around for a chat? If, of course, your schedule will permit. I don't have to strut and fret on the pedagogical boards again until eleven."

"I will. I surely will," I said, flattered as always by Chuck's obvious fondness for me. That I might be the object of his sexual fantasies, as my old girlfriend used to say, didn't bother me in the least. I knew that Chuck knew just how "incorrigibly straight" I was, as I had heard him say of someone else.

"Splendid. My door's unlocked so just go on down and I'll join you after I've used the facility," Chuck said, nodding in the direction of the faculty men's restroom.

Down on the first floor, as I opened the door to his office and entered, I was, as I almost always was when I entered a professor's office, struck by the array of books. Behind the desk were floor-to-ceiling bookshelves stuffed with them, their spines varying in color, thickness, and height. I remembered the first time I had seen them when, awed country town boy that I had been, I had said, "How do you manage to read all those books, Professor Wagner?" and Chuck, with one of his sardonic grins, had said, "Slowly, I assure you, Mr. Loomis. Very slowly."

I also took in the portraits of Confederate soldiers on the wall to the left of the desk, right above the little bookcase containing the boxed manuscripts of Chuck's unpublished novels, "The Rejected Oeuvres of C. Clarkson Wagner," he called them.

The centerpiece and star was a big color print of Stonewall Jackson, but the ones that most interested me were the enlarged Matthew Brady-looking black-and-white photographs of two un-famous Rebels, one of whom was an ancestor of Chuck. I couldn't remember his name, but the boy—and that's all he was, a boy of maybe seventeen—looked much as I imagined Chuck had at the same age.

I was standing in front of the pictures when Chuck limped in.

"He was your...What was he?" I asked, pointing to the boy, then turning to Chuck.

"A very distant cousin, on my mother's side. Thomas Joseph Weatherly of the 61st Virginia Volunteers.

He fell at Gettysburg, during Pickett's Charge, as I believe I told you. A lad. A mere lad in the fratricide, the four years of bloody fratricide," Chuck said, his naturally dark face darkening even more. "And it needn't have been. That's what makes it so awful. It needn't have been."

Chuck gestured for me to sit in the chair in front of his desk, then eased himself into the one beside his desk, put his cane in his lap, and sighed deeply.

"Speaking of cides, T.J., i.e. the killing of, how goes your investigation into that of my erstwhile colleague?" he said. "I trust progress is being made?"

"Not according to the local media," I said with a frown.

"Yes, but all too often in such matters, as in war, the first casualty is truth, which is another way of saying that y'all probably know a lot more than y'all are telling. That is correct, is it not?"

"I'll be honest with you, Chuck. The media say we have several 'persons of interest,' and we do, but that's it."

"By 'persons of interest' you no doubt mean persons with both a motive and an opportunity? I believe they were known as 'suspects' before our hypersensitive, politically correct times."

I could hardly believe what happened next. I'd heard of such things from Lou and others, but I'd thought of them mainly as just cop stories, much as, when I read about them in novels or saw them on TV, I'd dismissed them as contrived plot devices.

Throughout our chat, my eyes had more or less alternated between looking at Chuck and, as before, glancing about the office, mainly at the books on the shelves behind the desk, many of which I could not have seen if Chuck had been sitting at his desk instead of beside it.

At the very moment when I finished saying "We're still hoping that a smoking gun of some sort will turn up," my eyes zeroed in on an object on top of a boxed edition of Shelby Foote's "The Civil War". The edition was on the third shelf, and the object was in the two-inch space between the top of the books and the bottom of the shelf above them.

My heart speeding up, I pointed to the object and said, "That, Chuck? What is that?"

"What is what?" he asked, his eyes following my finger.

Rising from his chair, his face full of curiosity, he limped on his cane over to the shelves, then leaned down so that he could see the object.

"I need to look at that," I said, my heart about to jump out of my chest.

He reached for the object, but I snapped, "No. Don't touch it. I'll get it."

Taking my ballpoint out of my jacket pocket, I went behind the desk, leaned down to the level of "The Civil War", and with the tip of my pen eased the object out.

Looking at it as if it were long sought and freshly unearthed jewel, I compared it with the one that hung like a glass slipper in my memory. The fit was perfect.

"Do you know what this is?" I said, turning to Chuck, who was standing beside the desk.

"It looks like an earring," he said, his dark eyes fixing on the object dangling from my ballpoint.

"Yes, an earring, the very same earring, unless I am badly mistaken, that the killer ripped out of Mildred Margulis's left ear lobe and took as a souvenir," I said, my face flushing as my head filled with the worst kind of mixed feelings.

Staring at the little golden testicles or figs or whatever they were supposed to be, Chuck said nothing for a long moment. Then with a little grin and a look of bewilderment in his dark eyes, he turned to me and said, "T.J., I have no earthly idea of how that thing got there. None whatsoever."

***

Two hours later I was in the office of C. Edward DiFong, III, aka Mr. Showboat, and DiFong, behind his desk, reminded me of a jeweler in the way he was appraising the little golden balls in the clear plastic bag he was holding before him.

"So tell me again exactly where you found this," he said, his eyes remaining on the earring.

"On top of some books on a back shelf in Professor Wagner's office. As I said, if he'd been sitting behind his desk rather than beside it, I never would've seen it."

"And it's a perfect match, you say?"

"It is. Perfect."

Letting the bag drop to his desk and shifting his eyes to mine, DiFong said, "What'd you say to Wagner about it? What exactly?"

"I told him what I thought—what I was all but sure—the earring was. He could see how interested I'd suddenly become and how I handled the earring, with my ballpoint. So I really didn't have much choice but to tell him."

"What was his reaction?"

"Complete ignorance. He said he'd never seen it before and had no idea how it got in his office."

"Do you believe him?"

"Yes, I do."

"Why?"

"Two reasons. One, I know him pretty well. I had him for four courses and he was my faculty adviser. He's a good guy and I just can't see him strangling a woman with a ribbon."

"What's the other reason?"

"He's not dumb."

"How do you know he didn't put the earring there so he could claim it was a plant and he was being set up?" DiFong asked, his eyes telling me he knew he was being absurd.

"Because if he's guilty, the last thing he'd do is call attention to himself, any kind of attention."

Leaning back in his chair and clasping his pudgy hands across his belly, DiFong said, "What's Detective Ackerman's take on this?"

"Same as mine. That somebody's probably trying to set Wagner up. That if we knew who, we'd have our killer."

"You could be right. You sure could, but I don't know. I've got this funny feeling about Wagner. I think he knows a lot more than he's telling. It's just a hunch, but I've had it from the start, more or less," DiFong said, his eyes seeming to challenge me as he nodded slowly.

I waited for a moment, then said, "So, what are we going to do? We can't arrest him on just the earring, can we?"

"I guess we could, but we're not. We're going to keep a close eye on him and see if maybe he goes into some kind of damage control mode," DiFong said with another slow nod.

The man had surprised me. I had more than halfway expected him, even on the basis of such flimsy evidence as the earring, to send me and Lou out to arrest Chuck that very day.

Despite my relief, however, I remained in a state of worry and puzzlement. I still had no doubt of Chuck's innocence, but I knew in my gut that his troubles were just beginning. I found myself waiting, as Lou might have put it, for the other shoe to drop.

***

The next morning around nine, as I sat in the squad room across from Lou and sipped my coffee, the phone on the table buzzed. Lou answered it, then said, "Yeah. He's right here" and handed the receiver to me.

"This is Detective Loomis. How may I help you?" I said, knowing from Lou's face that the call was from outside the force, from a civilian.

"Detective Loomis, this is Jim Alston. I'm the Rector of St. Anne's Episcopal Church," a resonant, educated male voice said. "Are you by any chance in charge of the Margulis murder case?"

"No, sir. I'm on the case, but I'm not in charge. My partner, Detective Lou Ackerman, is," I said. "Would you like to speak with him?"

"No. The person I'm calling for specified you," Jim Alston said.

"Who is this person?"

"He's one of my congregants and he has some information that he thinks might bear on your case. He came to me with it this morning, only an hour or so ago. He's quite upset about it."

"When and where can I see him?" I said, my eyes signaling to Lou that this might be something big.

"He's with me at the rectory. Do you know where St. Anne's is?" Jim Alston asked.

***

The Reverend Mr. James Alston greeted me at the front door of the rectory. In his mid-forties, he was of medium height and sleekly pudgy, with a head full of salt and pepper hair and large hands that, although capable of a good handshake, seemed as smooth as a woman's. His straight, white teeth seemed even whiter against his shirt, which was solid black except for the white collar of his calling.

"He says that you and he had a class together at SUS about two years ago," Jim Alston said in a voice that was even smoother and more resonant in person than over the phone. "He doesn't think you'll remember him. His name is David Allen."

I shook my head. "I don't recall the name, but I'll probably recognize him when I see him."

"I need to tell you that David is a very decent, very sensitive young man, Detective Loomis," Jim Alston said, his face darkening with concern. "After much painful struggle he came to me this morning with what, unless I'm mistaken, you'll agree is a very painful dilemma between his loyalty to a friend and his duty to justice."

"What is this dilemma?" I asked.

"I think it might be best if you heard it from David himself. Please, if you'll follow me," Jim Alston said, leading me from the front vestibule down a short hall and into an office.

I recognized David Allen the moment he stood up from the couch and our eyes met. Short and slight, with fair skin, delicate features, short blond hair, and nervous blue eyes, he was dressed in Nikes, khaki pants, and a blue oxford shirt with a button-down collar. He had been with me in a night class, on the American novel, as well as I could remember, that Chuck Wagner had taught. He had sat on the front row but had never said a word unless Chuck called on him. The invariably high quality of his responses was one of the reasons I remembered him so clearly. The other was the obvious awe in which he had held Chuck.

"I remember you, David, sure," I said as we shook hands.

After offering us coffee, which we both declined, Jim Alston sat behind his desk and David and I sat in the two chairs in front of it.

For a long moment no one spoke, David's eyes seeming to me as nervous and scared looking as a rabbit's.

Finally, Jim Alston said, "David, would you like for me to describe the situation for Detective Loomis?"

"Thank you, Father Jim, but I can do it," David said, looking at Jim Alston and nodding, then turning to me and saying, "I saw on the news and read in the morning paper about the murder of the SUS English professor, Dr. Margulis. The media said she was strangled in her office last Tuesday night. That is what happened, isn't it?"

I nodded. "Yes, it is."

"I hope I'm wrong and that what I'm about to tell you has no relevance whatsoever. I pray to God it doesn't," David said, his delicate face filling with distress.

He paused for a long moment, then, seeming to get control of himself, said, "I guess the best place to start would be the relationship that I had with Professor Wagner—with Chuck. We were very close. We became very close during the course you and I had with him, and we remain close, although not as close as we once were."

"When you say 'very close,' what exactly do you mean?" I asked. "Were y'all lovers?"

His eyes steady on mine, David said, "Yes, we were. We're not anymore, but we were then. But that wasn't the main thing. At least for me it wasn't. The main thing was the belief, the faith that Chuck had—and I hope still has—in my potential as a writer. He helped me to believe in myself. He was my 'timely utterance,' to borrow from Wordsworth, at a time when I needed it. In fact, if he hadn't come along when he did, I don't know what I might have done. I was that lost, that desperate, as Father Jim can tell you."

David inclined his head toward Jim Alston, who looked grimly back at him and nodded.

"You probably know, Detective Loomis, that Chuck was—excuse me—is a novelist?"

I nodded. "Yes. I've seen the manuscripts in his office, and he's told me about them, but he wouldn't let me read any of them. He said that if a novel can't get published, then it's obviously not worth reading."

"He's wrong about that, at least about his. I've read them, all five, and they all should be in print. One of them, the one about the Civil War, is fine, really fine. But what I'm saying is that Chuck took me into his confidence, into his writer's workshop, so to speak, and showed me how he did it—how and where, for example, he got the idea for this or that novel, how hard he'd worked on a scene or a sentence—that sort of thing. He talked with me writer to writer, and he valued my judgment, even to the extent of doing something he'd never done before and, like F. Scott Fitzgerald, didn't believe a novelist should ever do. I'm sure you remember what Fitzgerald said about first drafts?"

"No, I don't. Refresh me," I said, wondering if he'd ever get to the point.

"He said you should never let anyone read your first draft—of a novel, that is—until you've finished it."

"But he let you read his? An uncompleted first draft?" I said.

David nodded. "Yes, he did, and what I remember reading in that draft, combined with the news about Dr. Margulis, is why I haven't slept for the past three nights and came to Father Jim first thing this morning. And why, finally, I told him I knew you and consented for him to call you."

My heart speeding up, I waited, certain that a revelation was only a second away. But when none came, even after three or four seconds, I said, "I must be missing something, David."

"Tell him what was in the manuscript, David," Jim Alston said gently. "Tell him what you read."

"I already did, didn't I?" David said, looking dumbfounded.

Jim Alston shook his head. "No, David, you didn't."

Turning to me, David said, "The novel—Chuck didn't have a title for it, just WIP, for work in progress—it was about a radical feminist professor who was strangled one night at her desk in her office."

My heart picking up even more speed, I said, "How exactly was she strangled? Can you recall the details?"

Grimacing, David shook his head. "I can't forget them. She was choked to death from behind, very slowly and painfully, with the ribbon on a medal she'd won in a race. After she was dead, the killer lowered the ribbon around her neck and let the medal hang, like an award."

Nodding, my heart now at full gallop, I said, "When did you read this work in progress, David? Can you remember exactly?"

"No, not exactly, but it was after we had that class with Chuck and that was about two years ago, wasn't it?"

"We can check it out," I said. "In any case, you read the manuscript long before Dr. Margulis was murdered? Is that correct?"

"Yes, that's correct."

"I assume you read a hard copy of it?"

"No, it was on Chuck's computer in his office. He let me read it while he was in class. I wish he hadn't. Oh, God, I wish he hadn't!" David said, his eyes filling with tears.

Nodding, I said, "I understand. Chuck was—is—my all-time favorite professor."

***

Shortly after noon, with my pulse still in overdrive, I was again in Eddie DiFong's small one-window office. This time Lou was with me and we were in the hard-back chairs in front of the desk. DiFong was in his fake leather lounger behind it.

When I started my story he had been sprawled back with his wingtips on the desk, his hands across his belly, and a bored, long-suffering look on his overfed face. Now his chair was straight up and he was gazing at me with a look of gleeful disbelief.

"Now tell me again. You say you had a class with this Allen guy?" he said.

"Yes, I did."

"And you say he's gay? That he and Wagner used to have a thing? Right?"

I nodded. "That's what he said. Used to have."

"Did it go bad?"

"He didn't say, but he did say they were still close. Obviously I can't say for sure, but I don't think there's any bitterness or vengeance or anything like that behind it, if that's what you wondering. On the contrary, the little guy was either miserable or one hell of an actor."

"So you believe him is what you're saying?" DiFong continued.

"Yes, I do. I believe him."

"That it's his conscience, just his conscience behind it?"

"Yes. His pastor says he's that kind of guy and he seems that way to me."

"He's not making anything up? About what he says he read, I mean?" DiFong continued as if he still couldn't believe what he was hearing.

I shook my head. "He'd have to have known the details of what really happened and there's no way he could. No way."

DiFong leaned slightly back in his chair and for several seconds stared at the wall above my head. Then he sat erect and said, "Okay. This is what I'm going to do. I'm going after him. I'm going to bring him in and book him for Murder in the First. And I'm not going to waste time on any damn preliminary hearing either. I'm going straight to the indictment."

Lou frowned and cleared his throat but DiFong said "Yeah, I know. This is just circumstantial, like the earring, along with being just hearsay from an unofficial, unsworn witness. Yada, yada, yada. But it's enough for now. And by the time I get the indictment filed it won't be just hearsay. It'll be fact. I'll have it in black and white."

"It might not be there. He might have erased it," I said, knowing what I soon would be doing and dreading it.

"Ten to one it's there," DiFong said with a cocky nod. "And if it's not there, it's somewhere else because I know about writers. They always keep a copy. Always. And we'll find Wagner's. We'll find it if we have to cut open his mattress and take his whole damn house apart. But find it we will!"

Chapter 9

Caroline Curry didn't have the kind of looks that drew stares from many guys my age. She wasn't blonde, she wasn't tall, she didn't have any tattoos or piercings, and she never dressed like a porno queen, even when she went barhopping. Nevertheless, I hadn't been able to take my eyes off her that night about two years ago when she and two friends had come to The Other End and I had carded them at the door.

She was a good-looking girl, there's no question about that. She had long, naturally wavy brown hair, a strong but sweetly demure face like that of Katie Holmes, Tom Cruise's wife, and a truly choice little body, with as fine a butt as I have ever seen. Still, it was not just the physical aspects of her looks that struck me. It was also the intelligence, the caution, and the complete, utterly unflappable self-possession that I sensed in the way she held her head and carried herself and, most of all, in the way her eyes seemed to study everything and miss nothing.

Soon after that night she began spending a lot of time at my apartment, including two or three nights a week, depending on my schedule as a cop and hers as an ER nurse. Even better, at least from a woman so bluntly honest, she almost always responded in kind to the many times I told her I loved her. But no matter how much I begged and attempted to reason that cohabitation was fast becoming the norm rather than the exception, she refused to leave her apartment and move in with me. She said she didn't care what everybody else did or how hypocritical she might seem. She wasn't going to cheapen herself by shacking up with anybody, not even me.

Far from bothering me, this show of old-fashioned character only increased my respect and longing for her. What did bother me, though, was her response to my proposal.

"I'd love to marry you, T.J. I truly would, but I can't. I can't and I won't as long as you're a cop," she said, her beautiful little face grim with finality.

It wasn't the low pay or the bad hours or, for some people, the low-rent stigma of cop work, she insisted, but the high degree of probability that sooner or later, Savannah being Savannah, I would end up mangled and bloody on a gurney in one of the city's ERs, maybe even hers. Already, in only two years, she had seen this happen to more people than she could count, including three police officers, one of whom had died as she felt for his pulse. The ER at Memorial on some Saturday nights, as I well knew, resembled a triage unit in a combat zone.

For almost two years I promised I'd get into something else, teaching school maybe, when I finished my degree at SUS. I stopped talking about becoming a detective and said nothing about continuing to study for the exam. I passed the exam, the first time I took it too, but by then she had left me. That had been back in August, shortly after I got my diploma but did nothing about finding another job. In the half year since then, I had not seen her or heard from her or even anything about her. Caroline Curry, I insistently told myself, was gone, completely and forever erased from my life.

When I answered my phone a little before seven that Friday morning, however, I recognized her voice the instant she said, "T.J." She had not needed to say "This is Caroline," let alone to add "Curry. Caroline Curry."

"Yes, Caroline Curry. Sweet Caroline," I said, rather jauntily using the old pet name I had taken from the song by Neil Diamond. "How in the world are you?"

"I'm fine. Would you like to have lunch with me today?" she asked, seeming very much the Caroline I remembered in the way she got straight to the point.

"I sure would. What time and where?"

"Is one all right, at The Bread Company?"

"Perfect," I said.

When I entered the trendy little restaurant at 12:51 and surveyed the crowd, I didn't expect to see her yet, but I did. She waved to me from a booth in the far right corner, the very booth in fact that had been our favorite. She was in tight jeans, a navy turtleneck, and the neat little jacket of butternut corduroy I had always liked.

"Caroline, you look terrific. You really do," I said, after we had taken our seats across from each other.

"So do you," she said with a piquant little grin. "I guess being a celebrity agrees with you."

I had no doubt that she was referring to what on all four local channels had been the lead story on the news yesterday evening as well as that morning. It had also been splashed across the front page of that morning's Savannah Morning News in fonts almost as big as the ones for 9/11--- SUS PROFESSOR ARRESTED FOR MURDER.

I returned her grin. "Is that why you called? Because you think I'm a celebrity?"

"No. I'd been planning to anyway. But aren't you? A celebrity, I mean?"

"No, Caroline, I'm not," I said solemnly. "I'm a schmuck. I'm a poor schmuck awash in ambivalence."

Her grin fading, she said, "He was the one you liked so much, wasn't he? I remember you used to talk about him all the time."

"Yes, I did."

"Do you think he's guilty?"

"The circumstances say, or at least suggest, that he might be. My gut says something else."

"That's why you're ambivalent?"

I nodded. "One of the reasons."

"I bet I know what another one is."

"Tell me."

"The way you felt about Dr. Margulis. I remember you hated that woman, T.J. You really hated her."

"So much I wouldn't want to arrest her killer?"

"More or less."

"You know me, don't you? You've always known me," I said with a grin.

"Well, you were never exactly Mr. Subtle, you know," she said, her smile and the look in her eyes making me feel about ten years old, which, that day at least, was a welcome feeling.

The waitress took our order and while we waited for our food Caroline, in response to my questions, told me that her parents, her little brother, her roommates, and her Dachshund all were fine, that she herself was still doing pilates at home and weights at the gym, and that, as I had taught her to do, she regularly checked the oil in her old Nissan and kept its tires evenly inflated. She also told me that, having burned herself out in ERs, she was now working for a group of orthopedists. I didn't ask, and she didn't volunteer, anything about her love life.

When our food came and we started on it, I got back to my original question.

"So, tell me, Sweet Caroline, to what do I owe the honor of your call and our lunch date? You said it wasn't my sudden celebrity," I asked with another of my little grins.

With a barely perceptible shrug, she said, "I just wanted to see how you are. I read about your promotion to detective a while back and then yesterday, when I got home from the gym, Claire was watching the news and you were on it. You were helping that professor out of the car. He was in handcuffs and didn't look happy, but you...You looked miserable, absolutely miserable."

"I was miserable. I am miserable," I said, scowling as I shook my head.

"Do you want to talk about it?" she asked, her eyes telling me that she knew I did.

"You don't mind listening?"

"No, not if you need me to. And I can't help but be curious. I'm like everybody else in Savannah."

"You know of course that everything I might tell you, now as back when we were together, is highly privileged information. If it got out, I could lose my badge. I'm serious, Caroline. You can't breathe a word of it."

"I won't, T.J. I promise. I never have and I never will."

I told her the details of the garroting, of the medal, and of the earring, then of what David Allen said he read and of the unsettling new light in which I now saw such things as Chuck's keen interest in the investigation and the extreme uneasiness I had been seeing in his tragically dark but hitherto calm eyes.

And I told her of something I hadn't yet told even Lou, something from Chuck's course in the American novel that had risen in my memory like a corpse out of a lake.

"I know you said you were going to read Theodore Dreiser's 'An American Tragedy' back when I was ranting and raving about it, but did you ever get around to doing it?" I asked.

"No, but I still plan to," she said.

"Well, I hope you will because, except for Moby Dick, it's the greatest novel ever written by an American. That's what Chuck said and I don't doubt it. Anyway, Dreiser got the idea for it from what he'd read about an actual murder in upstate New York, which is pretty much the way his main character got the plan for murdering his pregnant girlfriend--from a story in a newspaper. Chuck called it 'crossfeedings—' the way that art so often imitates life and life returns the compliment in various kinds of copycatting."

Her eyes studying mine, Caroline said, "So you're saying he copycatted himself? That he imitated art, his art?"

I quickly shook my head. "I'm not saying that he did, Caroline, just that it might be possible. You have to remember, first of all, that we have no proof of David Allen's claim."

"But you believe him, don't you?"

"Yes, I do, but what I believe or don't believe isn't evidence."

"Maybe not, but it was enough for the District Attorney---What's his name?"

"C. Edward DiFong, III, aka Mr. Showboat. And he's not the D.A. He's the Assistant D.A. assigned to this case."

Caroline nodded. "He said he had compelling evidence. He said he had a smoking gun. He said it right after you brought Chuck in. I heard him say it."

"That guy. I can't tell you how much I despise that guy," I said, my face no doubt looking as if I had just bitten into something rotten.

"He looked very young and aggressive," Caroline said.

"He is. He's my age. This is just his second homicide case--he lost his first one—and he's just generally the kind of sawed-off little fat shit with something to prove. You saw that circus when we brought Chuck in. He had every TV and newspaper jackal in town there. It was The Eddie DiFong Ego Show. And it could've been worse. He wanted it worse."

"You mean for Chuck?"

I nodded. "He wanted us first thing this morning to go out to SUS and arrest Chuck in his classroom. And to be there himself with TV cameras. Lou—my partner, my senior partner and mentor. He can't stand DiFong and he knows I like Chuck and he said, 'No way, Counselor.' Assistant D.A.'s don't mess with Lou on stuff like that, so we did it our way. My way, actually."

"Tell me," Caroline said, now so engrossed in the story that, like me, she had stopped eating.

"On Thursday afternoon, right after DiFong said to bring Chuck in, I called him, as I'd promised. I told him what we had to do and asked where and when he thought would be best. He said at his condo, that afternoon around five. He said he wanted to go ahead and get it over. He said he'd have his lawyer meet him down at the station. So we did. We went to his condo—he calls it The Anchorage. Dr. Harrison---do you remember my telling you about him? Dr. Steve Harrison?"

"Vaguely. He was one of your professors?"

I nodded. "I took two courses under him. He's the Head of the English Department and he writes poetry and is a really good guy. Anyway, he was with Chuck. He told him not to worry about his classes, that he'd already made arrangements for them. He kept assuring Chuck there had to be some explanation and going on and on about what he called 'the utter illogic of the evidence.' He was referring to the earring. He didn't know about David Allen and I couldn't tell him."

"That's what I was thinking about the earring," Caroline said with a nod. "I mean, if Chuck did it and took the earring, he surely wouldn't have it in his office. Not where it could be seen, anyway. He'd have to be just plain stupid to do that."

"That's what Dr. Harrison kept saying. He seemed a lot more upset than Chuck did. He said the arrest was an act of desperation, a fishing expedition, a media stunt. He said that no grand jury would indict Chuck on such flimsy evidence. He went on and on. Anyway, Lou and I finally took Chuck down to DiFong's goddamn ego show."

"Where is he now? Out on bail?"

I nodded. "He got lucky on that. His lawyer had him out in a couple of hours. But DiFong wants to bypass the preliminary hearing and go straight to the indictment, the grandstanding little bastard."

"You obviously don't think he should."

"Caroline, I don't know what to think about any damn thing," I said, keeping my voice low because of the people all around us. "I mean, I had to do my duty, but I didn't want to do it at the same time that I did want to do it. This was my first homicide and I had cracked it. Not Lou, not my grizzled old senior partner, but I—I had cracked it. Me. T.J. Loomis, Rookie Detective, Boy Wonder. And it didn't matter that it was just by chance that I'd been in Chuck's office and seen the earring and got the call from David Allen. I'd gone from the minor leagues to the majors and hit a home run in my first game."

"But you said you didn't think Chuck was guilty. You said you had a gut feeling about it."

"I do have a gut feeling. But it might just be that I don't want him to be guilty. I don't want him to be guilty because he's my friend at the same time that I do want him to be guilty because he's my home run."

"You haven't changed a bit, T.J. Not one bit," she said with a little smile. "You used to agonize over having to give a speeding ticket to someone you knew was poor, even if he'd been doing 75 in a 25 zone."

"This is different. A man's life—my friend's life could be at stake."

"Well, whatever it is, it's out of your hands. You did your duty and now it's up to the courts. And you said yourself that the evidence suggests it. That Chuck might be guilty, I mean."

Grimacing as I shook my head, I said, "Speaking of evidence, do you know what I'm going to do when I leave here?"

"What?"

"I have another warrant and I'm going out to SUS to ransack Chuck's computer and office in search of the stuff David Allen read. DiFong's about to pee in his pants to have it so he can go ahead with the indictment. If I don't find it in the computer, or somewhere else in his office, I'm going to call Lou and we're going to Chuck's condo to ransack it too. SUS has suspended him because of the charge and he won't be in his office, but he'll be at home and that makes me both hope and fear I'll find what I'm looking for on the computer. Otherwise I'll have to face Chuck and see those ineffably sad, Et tu, Brute eyes again, the way I did when I had to arrest him. I'd rather eat glass, Caroline, I truly would."

Her eyes seeming to peer into my brain, she slowly shook her head and said, "I don't think you're as ambivalent as you think you are, T.J. I mean, about Chuck as your home run. I don't think you'd hesitate to put him above your career. I think you already have. I'm not saying you'd commit perjury or withhold evidence or anything like that, just that you'd much rather see the charges against him dropped than get any kind of credit. That's one of the things about you that make you such a good man but maybe not such a good cop. It's one of the things I loved about you."

My face no doubt being as red as it felt, I came close to asking if she used the right tense of her verb. But, as with my failure to ask about her love life, I was afraid of what she might say. So I just forced a shrug and said, "Yeah, well, you know what they say: you can take the boy out of the little country town, but you can't take the little country town out of the boy."

***

When I left The Bread Company, I was again awash in ambivalence, not about Chuck—Caroline was right, I had cleared that up—but about Caroline herself. Both glad and sorry she had called, I was at least as fearful as I was hopeful that she would indicate she wanted to see me again as a possible prelude to our getting back together. In addition to listening intently to everything I said about the case, she several times smiled and looked into my eyes as lovingly as she sometimes used to do. She also said at least three times that she was "just so happy and relieved, so very relieved" that I now was a detective and no longer, as I had been as a street cop, almost always in danger of getting shot.

As our conversation wound down, I told myself I would play it safe and say goodbye with only a noncommittal "It was nice seeing you, Caroline. You take care now, you hear?" But I couldn't do it. Feeling as if I were again about to jump out of an airplane, I looked her steadily in the eyes and said, "So maybe you wouldn't mind if I gave you a call sometime?" She thought for a moment, then said, "No, T.J. I wouldn't mind if you did. Sometime," and that was that.

Without a hug or a handshake or even a perfunctory smile she turned from me and walked away, her butt as fetching and her walk as neat and self-assured as ever.

Chapter 10

Shortly after arriving at SUS I was sitting across from Dr. Steve Harrison in the little reception area in his office, waiting for someone in Computer Services, in response to my warrant, to bring me the password to Chuck's computer.

I told Dr. Harrison as much as I could, which was that DiFong had decided to bypass the preliminary hearing and proceed straight to the indictment.

"Just on the basis of the earring and the absence of an alibi?" Dr. Harrison asked, his gentle gray eyes and hugely fat but still handsome face full of alarm.

"No, sir. There's more now," I said, wishing I could relieve some of my distress by confessing everything to my old teacher.

"Evidence, you mean?"

I nodded. "New developments."

"I don't suppose you can tell me about them, can you?"

"I'm sorry, Dr. Harrison, but I can't."

"Can you tell me what you'll be looking for in his computer?"

"No, sir. I can't tell you that either."

"Well, how about this," Dr. Harrison said with a grim little smile. "Can you tell when he'll be served with the indictment?"

"Yes, sir. That I can tell you, although not exactly. It'll be as soon as the A.D.A. can get it prepared and approved, which should be tomorrow or the next day."

Taking a deep, uneasy breath as he shook his head, Dr. Harrison said, "Good God, T.J., I hate this. I can't tell you how much I hate this."

"I know. I hate it too," I said.

"Do you think Chuck's guilty? I want your honest opinion."

"Dr. Harrison," I said, my emotions squirming even if my body stayed still, "I honestly don't know what to think, even with the new developments. Do you think he is?"

His gentle, deeply troubled eyes steady on mine, Dr. Harrison said, "No, I don't. I don't know what your new developments are, but for over ten years now, almost for as long as I've been here at SUS, Chuck and I've been having early morning talks in his office or mine, mainly about writing, our writing, his novels and my poetry, but about a great many other things too. And I know him. I know him well. And I know that Chuck Wagner is simply too kind and gentle, too tolerant and forgiving of human frailty to kill anybody, let alone Mildred Margulis."

"Why 'let alone' her?" I asked.

"Because he pitied her. He was the only person in the department, at least while she was alive, to look beneath her in-your-face abrasiveness and see her for the lonely, desperately unhappy creature that she really was."

"So you're saying he didn't have the character or the motive?"

"Yes. That's what I'm saying. That's what I believe."

"And the earring? You're still convinced it was a plant?"

He nodded. "More than ever. It was put on display. It was practically screaming 'Look at me! Look at me!'"

I wanted to tell him about David Allen, but of course I didn't. Nor, for similar reasons, did I ask him if, during their early morning talks, Chuck had ever said anything about his new novel, his work in progress that was "as au courant as today's headlines."

***

In Chuck's office a few minutes later I felt even more like a voyeur or a tomb robber that I had in Dr. Margulis's the previous week. Around me were certain objects that, because of my fears for Chuck, had become painfully evocative—the stack of unpublished novels, the pictures of Stonewall Jackson and the other, un-famous Confederates, and, most of all, the boxed edition of Shelby Foote's 'The Civil War', on top of which I had spotted the earring. When I used the password of CCWAG and got the computer fired up, there was also the screen saver of a Matthew Brady portrait of Robert E. Lee, the old general's eyes even sadder and more tragic looking than Chuck's had always seemed to me.

Chuck was the exact opposite of the cyber packrat that Mildred Margulis had been. Instead of enough items to keep me scrolling until I was half blind, he had saved, in his files as well as in his email, a total of only 86—not a single one of which, except for a notice about health insurance that Human Resources had sent that morning, was from anybody at SUS. This didn't surprise me, Chuck having made no secret of his aversion to "administrative effluvia," as I once had heard him call a memo from the Dean or some other campus bigwig. In fact, the only purely SUS items on file were the exams and quizzes that he used in his courses. I recognized several of them, including the final exam that I, and of course David Allen, had taken in his course on the American novel.

Everything else was, or related to, his personal writing. On his hard drive, each in its own file, were copies of, as he called them, 'The Rejected Oeuvres of C. Clarkson Wagner' and that in manuscript form were stacked on the shelves beneath the Confederates. But no matter how much I scrolled and re-scrolled, read and re-read, I couldn't find anything designated WIP or that, called by another name, could possibly be what I was both hoping and fearing I'd find.

Then I moused out of his files and back into his emails, all thirteen of which, except for the one from Human Resources, were from literary agents. Most of them said pretty much the same thing—that they'd read what he sent but after careful consideration had decided that it just wasn't right for their list at this time, etc. The one I wanted to see again was dated Oct. 8, only four months ago, and was from an agent in Atlanta, a woman named Doris Wilcox.

It said:

Chuck, it was so good to hear from you again. You are right. This is definitely a new departure for you, and I think we can do something with it if the rest of it is as good as the chapters you sent. That, as we both know, is a huge IF, but I'm very hopeful and eager, very eager to see the whole thing. Best, Doris

In response to my call, Lou in his unmarked Crown Vick met me in front of the SUS administration building and we drove out to Chuck's condo. During the drive, which the odometer said was exactly 2.6 miles, I filled Lou in on my ransacking of Chuck's office as well as on my conversation with Dr. Harrison.

With one of his sour little grins, Lou said, "Wagner ain't dumb, Slick. I mean, if this WIP thing ain't in his office, in his computer or printed out like his other stuff, it ain't going to be in his house either. Not now anyway. Not now that we're on him. It probably don't even exist anymore. That Allen kid, his ex-little sweetie, might've had another conscience attack and clued him in. But even if he don't know a thing about Allen, Wagner sure as hell knows what he wrote and how much DiFong'ud like to get his hands on it. So what does he do? He does what anybody who ain't brain dead would."

Shaking my head, I said, "No. DiFong's right. Writers, novelists, always keep a copy. And that agent in Atlanta probably has one. Chuck sent her some chapters back in October, and by now he's probably sent her some more, maybe even the whole thing. She didn't mention a title, as I said, but it's the WIP. I guarantee it. And if she has a copy, Chuck does too because that's what writers do. They always keep a copy."

"Sounds like he's in for a little surprise," Lou said.

"I didn't call him, if that's what you mean."

"Why not? I thought you were going to keep him up to speed."

"I don't know. Professional duty, I guess," I said uncomfortably.

"Don't bullshit me, Slick. You know damn well why you didn't. You knew you didn't need to. You knew Harrison would the minute you left his office," Lou said with something between a scowl and a grin. "But, hey, it don't matter. If he ever had it at home and was gonna stash it someplace else, he'd of done it a long time before any two or three hours ago. You can bet your sweet ass on that."

I knew the moment Chuck opened the door that Dr. Harrison had warned him. It was in his eyes and face, that same "Et tu, Brute" look of terrible betrayal that had set my cheeks afire when I, his friend and former student, had had to read him his rights and arrest him.

Several minutes later the four of us--Lou, Chuck, Sammy Ray, and I—were seated at the dining room table. Sammy, whom I had not seen in several years, still had the same look of a soft, sweet, baldheaded old uncle, except in the eyes, which were full of fear. I knew how helplessly dependent he was on Chuck, and I wished with all my heart that I could assure him, as if he were a little child, that neither I nor anyone else was going to take away his caregiver.

His Darth Vader voice filling the room, Chuck said, "My attorney, whom I talked with a little while ago, of course said I'd be cutting my own throat, but I can see no point in not continuing to cooperate in any and every way I can. I am, after all, innocent, and I'm confident that, as Sophocles said twenty-five centuries ago, 'Time, and time alone, will show the just man.' So, tell me, gentlemen, how can I help you?"

As calmly as my internal turmoil would permit, I said, "Chuck, I'm sure you remember a former student of yours, David Allen."

"Certainly I remember David. A very bright, very gifted young man," Chuck said with a brisk nod.

"I had an interesting and, I have to admit, a very disturbing meeting with him yesterday," I said.

"Did you now?" Chuck said, then added, "And no doubt this meeting, if I may indulge in a Dickensian double negative, was not entirely unrelated to me?"

"It was entirely about you."

"Did you arrange this meeting or did David do it, if I may ask?"

"He did, through his pastor."

His dark, hurt eyes steady on mine, Chuck said, "Given David's highly active and compelling conscience, I would've anticipated this-- had I remembered. But, alas, to put it bluntly, I flat out forgot."

"You know, then, what I'm talking about?" I said.

"I do. The portion of my new novel, which at the time was in progress, that I let David read."

Turning to Sammy, who seemed about to jump out of his skin, Chuck said, "We are referring, Samuel, to the murder in my new novel, 'Death in Savannah', as it's now titled, which closely prefigured the murder of my late but, poor thing, little lamented colleague, Mildred Margulis."

Sammy looked dumbfounded. "Prefigured? What do you mean prefigured?"

"I mean that just as the female professor in my novel was strangled with the ribbon on a runner's medal as she sat at the desk in her office, so was my late colleague."

"Jesus Christ!" Sammy exclaimed, the blood draining from his red, hypertensive face.

"Life did not completely imitate art, however," Chuck continued. "In my novel, the writing of which antedated the actual murder by over a year, the medal was awarded to the victim—that is, hung around her neck after she was killed—whereas in reality..."

"The medal was 'awarded to Dr. Margulis too, Chuck. It was just never made public," I said.

Even this did not seem to faze him. He said, "I suppose, then, that the earring is our only major discrepancy."

Again turning to Sammy, he said, "You know of course about the earring—the first of Prosecutor DiFong's 'smoking guns'—that T.J. found in my office and had been ripped from the ear of my late colleague. This is not the way it is in my novel. Both earrings are in place when the body is found."

With his Bad Cop persona in full force, Lou said, "So you admit it, Professor?"

Chuck said, "Of course not, if you mean the murder. But if you mean the manuscript, yes. I confess to the prefiguring. It was exactly as David said."

"You do have a copy of it somewhere, don't you?" I asked.

Chuck gave me a weary, hurt look. "Even had I not received a little advisory call from Steve Harrison a little while ago, I think I'd be correct in inferring from your use of the word 'somewhere', as well as from the look in your eyes, that you've been rummaging about in my office, T.J. Am I correct?"

"I'm afraid you are, Chuck," I said, feeling my cheeks redden.

"But you didn't find said manuscript, did you?"

"No, but I did find something."

"What, if I may ask?"

"On your computer, a letter from an agent in Atlanta, about some chapters you sent her. She said they were 'a new departure' for you. That's in keeping with what you told me last week about your new novel being 'as au courant as today's headlines.' We are, are we not, talking about 'Murder in Savannah'?"

Chuck nodded. "We are."

"But it's not on your computer under WIP or anything else, whereas your other five novels are. Why?" I asked.

"Essentially the same reason, T.J., that I didn't tell you about the prefiguring when we first talked. I didn't want you to get the wrong idea, which I fear you have now."

"You deleted it?"

"I did."

"When?"

"Right after you left my office after the earring turned up."

"You destroyed evidence, didn't you, Professor?" Lou said with a sneer.

"Hardly evidence, Detective, and I didn't destroy it. I merely removed it from my computer," Chuck said.

"But you have a copy of it, don't you?" I said, then added "Somewhere?"

"Of course I have a copy. I have several in fact. One in manuscript—actually two, when you include the one my agent has—plus one on a CD and two on those little punch-in gizmos."

"Floppy disks," I said.

"Yes, although I have no earthly idea why they're called that, there being nothing floppy about them."

"Where are they, Professor? These copies of yours?" Lou asked.

"They're here."

"Here? In this condo?" Lou said, glancing about the room.

"Yes. They're in a closet, in my old army duffel bag. Would you like me to get them for you?" Chuck said as casually as if he were offering Lou a drink.

***

Twenty minutes later the Crown Vick was on its way back to town, a boxed copy of 'Murder in Savannah' was in my lap, and I, having just finished a call to DiFong, was again wishing I had never become a cop, let alone a homicide detective.

"I just don't know what to make of him, Lou. I swear to God I don't," I lamented as I shook my head.

"Sure you do, Slick. The ambitious little shit's a showboat. He wants to be on TV again."

"Not DiFong. Chuck. The way he's acting. The way he's been acting from day one."

"The guy ought to be in the movies. He ought to be playing some hoity-toity English guy or something."

"I don't mean that. I mean the way he's taking it. I'd be going out of my skull. Wouldn't you?"

"Yeah, knowing what I know. But he don't know what I know and you know. He's a college professor. He don't live in the real world."

"Here he is about to be indicted for murder in the first degree what does he do? He quotes from Sophocles. 'Time and time alone will show the innocent man' or however the hell it goes."

Lou nodded. "Yeah, and even when you get lucky and it does, if you get indicted and go to trial, you're gonna go through some real shit, don't matter if you do win. Lawyer fees alone'll break your ass."

"I just wish he wouldn't look at me the way he does."

"Yeah, like you ratted him out and stole his baby, just up and snatched the poor little thing right outa his arms," Lou said referring to the box in my lap. "What does he expect you to do? Look the other fucking way?"

"Recuse myself from the case, I guess."

"Don't sweat it so much, Slick. If it hadn't been you, it'd of been somebody else. And you been pretty soft on to him. A hell of a lot softer than I'd of been without you. I can tell you that. I ain't never liked college professors. They're assholes, every last one of them."

"I guess," I sighed. Then I shook my head and said, "And now, to top it off, we're going to have to listen to that damned DiFong gloat. 'Didn't I tell you? Didn't I? Didn't I tell you he had a copy?' The way he sounded on the phone, he's already peeing in his pants."

"You ain't gonna like this, Slick," Lou said with one of his ominous little smirks.

I studied his boney, Camel-browned old face for a moment, then said, "You're going to wimp out on me, aren't you?"

"Let's just say, to be high-faluting about it, that I'm gonna avail myself of one of the prerogatives of rank and let it go at that. Besides, a young guy like you needs the experience," Lou said, his smirk becoming a grin.

Chapter 11

I'd halfway expected DiFong to ask where Lou was, but he didn't. As I entered his office he seemed too excited, too downright gleeful to wonder about anything other than the typing paper box that he saw in my hands.

Dressed in a white shirt, blue tie, and bright red suspenders, he quickly sat erect in his lounger and motioned for me to have a seat in one of the chairs in front of his desk.

"That's it?" he asked, his eyes riveted on the box.

I nodded. "Yes."

"Okay. Get it out and turn to"—he glanced at a document on his desk—"turn to page sixteen."

I turned to page sixteen.

"Okay. Start at the top. Read me the first line."

"'invited me to sit down and I said, "Thank you, Professor, but I need to stand up. I've been sitting down all day,"' I read, recognizing the beginning of the murder scene, which Chuck, with obvious pride, had shown me hardly an hour ago. "'And she, again looking down at...'"

"'the essay she had been grading, said, "Give me just a minute and I'll be right with you,"' DiFong read, picking up where the first line ended and the second began. "'And I knew then that I would do it.' Is that what yours says?"

"Exactly," I said.

"How about this?" DiFong said, reading the rest of the page, where the killer tells of seeing the runner's medals hanging on the coat rack behind and to the left of the professor, of asking if she had won them and being told she had, and of walking behind her and, as if to admire it, taking off the rack the bronze medal on the purple ribbon.

"You got that too?" DiFong asked, looking up from his document and back at me, so pleased with himself that I wanted to gag.

"Word for word," I said, leaning forward and seeing that he'd been reading from the first page of what looked like a fax of five or six pages. "Where'd you get that?" I asked.

Cocking back in his lounger as he eased his black wingtips up on his desk and clasped his hands across his belly, he shook his head and said, "It's the damnedest thing I ever saw. I mean, I'd barely put the phone down after talking with you when Jeanne buzzed me and says there's a woman, a woman in Atlanta..."

"Doris Wilcox," I said.

"Yeah," he said, surprised. "How'd you know?"

"She's Professor Wagner's literary agent. I saw an email from her on his computer and he said he'd sent her a copy of his novel."

"That's right. That's what she said," DiFong said, nodding. "She said a friend of hers who used to live here gets the Savannah Morning News and saw the story. She didn't think too much about it at first and then she remembered Wilcox telling her she had a client down here. Said he was an English professor and he'd recently sent her a novel about another English professor, a radical feminist, being murdered in her office, choked to death at her desk. Wilcox said she really liked the novel, and Wagner too, and told herself over and over it was just some kind of bizarre coincidence. But it kept on bothering her, so she called me. Just to check, she said. This was right after you called and I was already going bananas, but I played it cool. I told her there might be something to it and asked, if she wouldn't mind, to send me a fax of whatever she thought I ought to see. And it came through, just a minute before you got here. The damn pages are still warm."

***

That Saturday night at the club I had moments when I felt so good about Chuck's chances that I'd catch myself looking forward to resuming the investigation and finding the answer to the question that was never far from my mind: Who had planted the earring in Chuck's office? If Lou and I could answer that question, I had little doubt that we'd have our man. Or woman, Dr. Julia Kerns being still on my list.

Such moments were rare. Most of the time I was too busy checking ID's and, along with Peters and the other three bouncers, keeping an eye out for trouble. We headed off four or five fights and broke up two, including one between two women. Much to Peters's annoyance I was flirted with, in one case blatantly propositioned by, three middling hot numbers who had seen me on the news when we'd brought Chuck in.

All four local news programs had run that footage again that Saturday, once in the morning and again in the evening, along with the indictment that DiFong had announced in his news conference Friday afternoon, hardly an hour after I had turned 'Murder in Savannah' over to him and left his office. And of course the indictment, including a picture of DiFong and a rehash of the case, was splashed across the front page of the Saturday edition of the Savannah Morning News.

Around midnight my hopes for Chuck, as if out of the blue, got the first of the two boosts they would get between then and noon on Monday. When David Allen had come forward, Lou, in response to my amazement, had said that such gratuitous contributions or confessions are not all that unusual in murder cases, even at the risk of serious involvement for those who make them. "They just do it, Slick. I don't know why, but they do. The thought of some poor fuck headed for Death Row gets to 'em, I guess," he said with a shrug of his boney little shoulders.

Maybe it was because she had her long brown hair down instead of up and was in bar-hopping clothes instead of a bathrobe. Or maybe it was because the light at the door was not good and I was in a hurry. In any case, I couldn't place her even after I read Jennifer Tompkins on her driver's license and compared the picture with her face. This was both professionally and personally embarrassing, the latter because I've always prided myself on remembering the face, and the name if I ever knew it, of women as good looking as she was.

"You don't remember me, do you?" she asked, then added "Detective Loomis" as I returned her license.

Aware that Peters, who was beside me checking other ID's, had pricked up his ears, I was tempted to respond with something suitably cheesy, but I didn't.

"You look familiar. Did I give you a speeding ticket or something?" I asked with a little grin as I studied her face, which, with hardly any makeup, bespoke a kind of wholesome sensuality that I've always liked in women.

"Do you remember Jason Harper?" she asked, her eyes steady on mine.

"Yes. Yes, I do," I said, the name flashing it all back. "I woke you up one morning a couple of weeks ago at your apartment to ask you some questions about him. You were in flipflops and white terrycloth robe."

Nodding, her face not just serious but downright grim, she said, "Can I talk to you for a minute?"

"Sure," I said, looking at Peters, whose nod meant he'd heard and would cover for me.

Several minutes later we were seated on one of the benches in the fine old square across the street, her face visible to me, as I'm sure mine was to her, in the glow and splash of light from cars, the club, and the bright bulbs hung in the limbs of the massive oaks nearby.

"So what can I do for you, Miss Tompkins?" I asked, all but sure not just from her face but from her having addressed me as Detective Loomis that she had come on serious business rather than, as Peters no doubt assumed, to hit on me.

"I'm so scared," she said in a low voice.

"What of?"

"I lied to you the other day and I shouldn't have. I knew I shouldn't lie to a police officer."

My interest even further quickened, I said, "What did you lie about, Miss Tompkins? Jason Harper?"

"Yes," she said sounding as if she were about to cry.

"So he didn't in fact stay with you all night the night Professor Margulis was murdered?"

She shook her head and said, "He didn't stay with me at all. He didn't even go home with me. He walked with me from my class out to my car and I left him. I left him at school."

After a long moment, I said, "Why, Miss Tompkins? Why did you lie to me about him?"

"We used to be close. We used to be very close."

"But you're not anymore?"

"No."

"You want to tell me how it came about?"

"You mean about us not being close anymore?"

"You can start with that."

"He can be so sweet. You wouldn't believe how sweet he can be. Not from the way he looks, I mean, as huge as he is and rough and so mean looking."

"But?"

"He can be mean too. Very mean."

"Did he ever abuse you? Hit you or anything?"

"He never hit me."

"What did he do?" I asked, her voice saying there was more.

"He choked me one time."

"With his hands?"

"No. With a towel. He slipped up on me from behind."

"With a towel? He slipped up on you from behind?" I repeated, my alarm system going on red alert.

She nodded. "I was always a little afraid of him, but after that I was terrified. He said he was just playing and was sorry and all, and I think he really was. He could be so sweet, like I said."

"Did you stop seeing him after he choked you?" I asked.

"Not right after, but soon after. I was too scared to right after."

"All right, Miss Tompkins," I said abruptly. "You'd stopped seeing Jason Harper because you were scared of him, but you lied to a police officer for him. And you said he walked with you from your class out to your car on the night Professor Margulis was killed. Why'd he do that? Why'd you let him do that?"

"He said he missed me and wanted to get back with me. He wanted to go home with me."

"What did you say?"

"I said no, not tonight."

"But you'd let him go at some other time? Is that what you implied?"

"That's what I wanted him to think, but I wasn't, not ever."

""Because you were scared of him?"

She nodded. "Yes. Because I was scared of him."

"So how was it, if you felt that way about him, that you went to bat and lied for him?"

"He came to my apartment the other morning all..."

"What morning? Be specific."

"It was the morning you went to see him. Right afterwards."

"That was the Thursday after the murder."

She nodded. "He said he needed me to help him. He said he told you he was with me all night Tuesday, from when I got out of class till the next morning, and if I didn't back him up he'd be in trouble, big time."

"Where did he go Tuesday night after you left him? Did you ask him?"

"He said he went to his apartment and watched TV. He said his roommate didn't come in till late, so he didn't have any proof and he knew you'd be talking to me. He was scared. I could tell he was scared."

"Did he threaten you?"

"He didn't actually say he'd hurt me."

"Yes, but you thought he would? Is that correct?"

She nodded. "From the look in his eyes and what he said about having to go to jail if I didn't. Yes, I did think he'd hurt me. Or might."

Trying in the shadows to read her face, I said, "Be honest with me, Miss Tompkins. Do you think Jason Harper killed Professor Margulis? I want your opinion."

"He hated her. He hated her for picking on him in class about being a Southerner and saying he plagiarized. He called her all kinds of names."

"Yes, but do you think he killed her? Yes or no?"

After a long, very tense moment, she shook her head and said, "I don't really know if I think it or not, Detective Loomis. Honest, I don't."

"Let me put it this way then. Do you think it's possible that he killed her? Just possible, given what you know about him?"

Slowly, her eyes fixed on mine, she said, "I wouldn't have come down here and told you all this if I didn't think that. Plus, I just feel so sorry and scared for Professor Wagner. I had him for two classes and he's just too sweet to kill anybody."

"That pretty much answers the other question I wanted to ask," I said, already planning my pitch to DiFong.

***

On Monday morning at 8:27 the office door of Professor Jack Flanagan was open and he was cocked back in his chair with his feet on his desk. His pinched little face again reminding me of a bespectacled ostrich, this time one deep in thought, he was in what I had come to think of as his uniform of a wrinkled oxford shirt with a flea-market tie, faded Levis with frayed cuffs, and cartoon character socks—Mickey Mouse this time—in scuffed brown loafers.

His tiny, windowless office was stuffed with books and, apparently also as always, smelled like a locker room from the New Balances, jockstrap, and other running gear on the coat rack. Seeming equally uniform, at least for so early in the day, was the closed door of the office diagonally across the cul de sac's narrow little hall, that of Dr. Julia Kerns, whose first class was never before eleven.

When I knocked once on the door and said, "Professor Flanagan?" he jumped up from his deep thoughts and motioned for me to come in and sit in the chair beside his desk. As I did so, he rose from his chair, looked out his door in both directions, then closed his door and locked it.

He sat back down in his chair and stared at me for several seconds before saying, "I guess you were surprised to get a call from me last night."

Unlike during my two previous visits to his office, he didn't seem hostile or whimsically literary or anything other than down-to-earth and worried, maybe even desperate.

"Yes, I was. I was very surprised. I was almost as surprised then as I am curious now," I said.

"There're some things you need to know, Detective Loomis. Some things I didn't tell you before."

"By 'before' I assume you mean before Professor Wagner was indicted?"

"Yes. Before that. Before that premature, downright criminal rush to judgment."

"What do you think I need to know, Professor? Tell me," I said, watching him closely.

With one quick nod he said, "One of my former students, who is also one of Chuck Wagner's former students, told me something a few months ago. We were talking about writing—he wants to be a writer, a novelist, and he's bright, very bright—and he said that Chuck had let him read on his computer a portion of the novel that he, Chuck, was working on at the time. It was about the murder of a radical feminist college professor, a real ball buster, and the details of her death—the choking with the ribbon on a runner's medal and so forth—were exactly those that you told me about when you, with what I called your 'syllogistic reasoning,' all but accused me of killing Margulis. You do remember that, don't you?"

"Yes, I do. I remember it well. In telling you so much, I told you things that only I and several others, all cop people, knew about. I shouldn't have told you."

"You did, though, and I immediately made the connection."

"That there was some kind of pre-figuring or copycatting going on? Is that what you're saying?"

"That's exactly what I'm saying."

"But you don't think, obviously, that Professor Wagner killed Professor Margulis?"

"I know he didn't do it. Chuck Wagner, for all of his interest in war and other manly matters, is a very gentle, utterly nonviolent man."

"So who did then? This former student of y'all's?" I asked.

"I don't know, but I think it's possible."

"That he killed Professor Margulis by the book, so to speak, and then planted the earring in Professor's Wagner's office?"

Flanagan nodded. "It's possible. I think it's possible."

"All right then. Why? Why, first, would he kill Professor Margulis? And why, second, would he try to frame Professor Wagner?"

"Do you know Sammy Ray? Chuck's friend? His 'significant other' or 'life partner' or whatever the hell is politically correct?"

"I met him once, yes."

"Well, he got very upset about Chuck and this student. He was afraid it was a lot more than literary mentoring or just another of Chuck's many pick-ups or ongoing letches. And it was more, a lot more, at least for this student."

"Who told you this?"

"Chuck and the student. At different times of course and in different ways, but the essential facts were the same. Sammy didn't give Chuck an ultimatum or anything, but Chuck knew how much he was hurting Sammy, so he stopped seeing this student. Dumped him, to be blunt about it."

"Dropped him completely, you're saying?"

Flanagan nodded. "Chuck said he'd never lied to Sammy in the past about his dalliances and wasn't about to start. So, yes, dropped him completely."

"And you believe him?"

"Yes, I do, and I would even if the student, with great wailing and gnashing of teeth as well as with words, and in this very office, had not corroborated it. I could feel his pain, if I may use a Clintonism."

Pain, like a pop-up on a computer, flashed in his eyes and I remembered what he'd said about his recent split from his live-in girlfriend—that his house had become "sepulchral."

I said, "All right. Vengeance, the spurned lover's payback could answer the second why. But what about the first? Why Professor Margulis? Why not somebody else? Why not Professor Wagner himself?"

"This student of course didn't loathe Mildred Margulis as much as I did, Detective Loomis. He's not Irish enough for that. But he did loathe her. He loathed her very much."

"He had a class under her?"

"He had two. And he couldn't stand the way she used her classes to propagandize her radical feminism and to exalt critical theory, radical feminist theory, over literature. He simply couldn't stand it, that and the way she patronized him as a gay."

"So this student killed two birds with one ribbon, if I may mix some metaphors?" I asked, eyeing him steadily.

"I'm not saying he did. I'm just saying it's possible and that this rat bastard DiFong needs to know about it."

"He does know about it. He's seen the relevant section of Professor Wagner's novel and has a sworn statement from the student. From David Allen. It's the main basis for the indictment," I said with a nod.

Looking more than ever like a perplexed ostrich, Flanagan stared at me through his tortoise-shell glasses and said, "How? How does he know about David Allen?"

"David Allen, in what apparently was a crisis of conscience, called me the other morning. He remembered me from a class we had together under Professor Wagner. He said, and later swore to, just about everything you've been telling me, except about being dumped. He just said that he and Professor Wagner weren't as close as they had been."

Flanagan stared at me for a very long moment, then said, "Yes, exactly, and that could be part of it."

"Part of what?"

"Part of his scheme. How else were you to know about the scene in Chuck's book if he didn't come forward and tell you?"

"We didn't really need David Allen for that, as it turns out. Professor Wagner's literary agent, a woman in Atlanta, heard about the case, got suspicious, and sent DiFong a fax of the murder scene in the novel. That was Friday afternoon, not long before DiFong's news conference."

"Yes, that was on Friday, but David Allen called you, you said, a week before that. He didn't know a thing about the agent. He..."

"Professor Flanagan," I interrupted as I studied his eyes, "there's one little fact that invalidates your very interesting hypothesis. Completely and irrefutably invalidates it."

He stared at me, waiting, his eyes as steady on mine as mine were on his.

I said, "On the night Professor Margulis was killed, David Allen was nowhere near Savannah. He was in Durham, North Carolina, looking into graduate school at Duke University. We have three independent confirmations of this."

Flanagan said, "Oh" and for a moment, but only for a moment, looked deflated. Then he said, "All right. Scratch David Allen. There's something else I didn't tell you before."

"Let's hear it."

"That toad across the hall," he said, his face filling with disgust as he shot his bird finger toward his door.

"Professor Kerns?" I said.

"Yes. That nasty little toad. She generally keeps her door open. Just to annoy me, she used to keep it open back when she smoked and smoking was permitted in the buildings, but that's another matter. Anyway, one afternoon last spring, not long after she was promoted to Full Professor, she was sitting in front of her computer, reading something on it, and suddenly she began saying, all but screaming, 'That bitch! That bitch! That goddamn bitch!' I guess she knew, my own door being open, that I was listening because she got up and slammed her door so hard the picture of Hillary Clinton fell off. Shortly after that, a minute or two maybe, I heard her doing something so totally out of character that I thought I was hearing things. I'm serious, Detective Loomis. I thought I was having some kind of auditory hallucinations."

"What was it?"

"That little toad, that certified, ball-busting, hard-as-nails little bunch-backed toad was not just crying. She was sobbing. She was sobbing like an abandoned child. I kid you not. Like an abandoned child. I didn't feel sorry for her, but I almost did. It was that bad. She was crying her eyes out."

"Because of something she saw on her computer? Something to do with another woman? One she called a bitch?" I asked, a light bulb beginning to glow in my head.

"I don't see what else it could've been. She doesn't call men bitches. She calls us jerks, bastards, shits and other such. I've heard her. Believe me, I've heard her."

"All right. Who was the bitch? Professor Margulis? An email from her maybe?"

Flanagan nodded. "I don't think it was an email. I think it was something else."

"What?"

Shaking his head as if I were rushing things, he said, "About a week after the little toad's sob session, I was having coffee with a friend in biology. He was on the promotions committee and I was breaking his balls about the committee's approval of the toad's promotion. He looked around to see if anybody was listening, then said sotto voce, 'You wanna hear something interesting?' I said, 'Sure, shoot,' and he said that four of the toad's colleagues in the English Department opposed her promotion and the one who opposed it the most, and wrote a scathing account of her scholarly and pedagogical shortcomings, one even more scathing than mine, was..."

"Professor Margulis?"

"You got it, buddy. Mildred Margulis, the toad's bosom chum and colleague, her scholarly collaborator. Judas herself. The guy in biology couldn't believe it. He thought they were tight as a frog's ass, comrades, blood sisters to the end, all that."

Nodding, I said, "I see where you're going, but how would Professor Kerns have known this? I mean, would she have had access to y'all's promotion ballots or whatever they're called?"

"Not to the ballots themselves, but to the numbers. The Doughboy—Harrison, our fearless leader—put them in a memo. For her there were 17 for, 4 against."

"So she would've known that 4 of her colleagues in your department were opposed to her promotion to Full Professor? Is that correct?"

"That's correct. She would've known the numbers."

"When? When would she have known? Before or after the sob-session, as you call it?"

Flanagan grinned in triumph. "The Doughboy's memo was in our mailboxes first thing in the morning of that same day, April 12, the date on the memo. The toad doesn't come in until around eleven, so she probably wouldn't have gotten hers until her last class was over, around four, about an hour before she went ballistic."

"You're sure of that date and time? Absolutely sure?"

"No doubt about it."

I nodded. "Go back to what made her go ballistic, what she saw on her computer. Are you saying it was something Professor Margulis said or wrote about her? About her promotion?"

"I can't think of anything else setting her off like that. 'That bitch! That bitch! That goddamn bitch!' And then all that sobbing. She lost it, Detective. Totally lost it. You should've heard her."

"How, though? I mean, Professor Margulis wouldn't have put that kind of stuff in an email. I heard about the one about Dr. Harrison's wife getting drunk at the restaurant, but this is different. This is very different."

"The toad's a geek, a cyber geek."

"Meaning?"

"Meaning she broke into Margulis's computer. They collaborated on their feminist rant—excuse me, scholarship, their precious scholarly agenda--and Margulis was continually coming to her for help. She'd sit in front of the toad's computer and the toad would walk her through all kinds of interfacing and formatting and whatever the hell else you do. And she'd give Margulis instructions over the phone about pushing G7 and mousing FXY12, all that."

"Hacked into Professor Margulis's computer and read her files," I said more to myself than to Flanagan, the light bulb in my head not glowing now but shining.

"You got it. Plus, she was out here that night. She had a class at the same time as Margulis's. She had the motive and the opportunity."

"Okay. What about the earring in Professor Wagner's office? She and Professor Wagner, as I understand it, weren't exactly on visiting terms, so how'd she manage that?"

"Piece of cake. Chuck's never here in the afternoon and she could've gotten the pass key from the secretary. All she'd have had to do was say she'd locked her keys in her office. I've done it plenty of times."

"Yes, but why Professor Wagner's office? They weren't, as I said, on visiting terms, but everybody I've talked to says he got along all right with her. Why not your office? Why not, to go back to my mixed metaphor, strangle two enemies with one ribbon?"

"Simple. If she could break into Margulis's computer, she could break into Chuck's too. That's probably where she got the idea. Do it the way he did it in his novel, plant the earring in his office, and count on something like what actually happened—on you seeing the earring and going into Chuck's computer or in some other way finding out about the novel."

"Yes, but why, though? Why Professor Wagner's computer in the first place? Why would she even bother to go into it? If she did?"

"That venomous little toad probably breaks into other people's computers and invades their privacy the way other geeks cruise the net or surf it or navigate it or whatever the hell you call it. She probably knows what's in every computer on campus, for Christ's sake," Flanagan said with a look of infinite disgust.

Nodding, watching him closely, I said, "I don't suppose I need ask why you're telling me all this, do I, Professor Flanagan?"

He shook his head. "No, but Chuck Wagner's a lot more than just a colleague and good friend. He's a man being framed and falsely accused. He's a man being railroaded. Justice is being sacrificed on the high altar of that rat bastard DiFong's ego and ambition. And I think you know this as well as I do, or at least think it every bit as strongly as I do. Don't you? Don't you think it, Detective Loomis?"

I shrugged. "Let's forget about what I might or might not think and assume for a moment that DiFong, after I present your two hypotheses, drops the charges against Professor Wagner and re-opens the investigations. That is what you think he should do, is it not?"

"It is."

"All right. Let's assume he does that. I'm not saying that he will. Far from it. The chances are about a thousand to one he'll laugh in my face. But just for the sake of argument, let's assume he puts me and my partner back on the case. We wouldn't look at David Allen again. His alibi is unassailable. But we would look again at Professor Kerns. You know who else we'd take another look at?"

"Of course I do. Me."

"That wouldn't bother you? You might end up hoisting yourself on your own petard, you know."

Flanagan shook his head. "That metaphor doesn't apply here. I'm not attempting to blow up anybody."

"What about Professor Kerns?" I asked, inclining my head toward her office across the little hall. "You'd like to see her blown to the moon, wouldn't you?"

"If she's guilty and goes to The Big House, I certainly wouldn't grieve, Detective Loomis. I'd bear it with great equanimity, I assure you. But I also assure you, despite what you no doubt think, that I wouldn't want to see even her railroaded."

Again leaning back in his chair and putting his Mickey Mouse feet on his desk, Flanagan looked me defiantly in the eye and said, "And as for taking another look at me, all I can say is 'Be my guest.' You can probe as deeply as Leviathan swims, and all you'll come up with is the syllogism you already have, which, as you well know, is so circumstantial as to be absolutely nothing. Zero. Nada. One-hundred per cent zilch."

Chapter 12

DiFong had been out of town all weekend but had gotten the message I'd left on his home phone Sunday morning around seven, which was as soon as decency would allow after my park bench talk with Jennifer Tompkins a few hours before. I said I'd come to his office at 1:30 p.m. on Monday unless I heard from him beforehand. I hadn't heard and he looked eager to see me, his smug face slightly aglow, probably from the two martinis that he almost always had at lunch.

Coming erect in his lounger as he motioned me to one of the chairs in front of his desk, he said, "So what you got for me, T.J.? To get you up and at 'em so early on a Sunday, it must be some pretty heavy stuff."

"Lou and I think it might be," I said, sitting down. "But I've got a couple of other things before I get to that. This morning, in response to his phone call last night, I talked to Professor Jack Flanagan in his office out at SUS. He's the Irishman, remember, who was so high on my original list?"

"Oh, yeah, I remember. He's not even a real Irishman, I think you said."

"He's from Boston, but he's more Irish than the real thing, at least with the blarney and all. Anyway, he was dead serious this morning. He knew about David Allen reading the murder scene in Professor Wagner's novel."

"How?" DiFong asked, tilting his head like the RCA dog.

"David Allen told him. Allen was kind of his protégée too, just in writing, though. Flanagan is straight, at least sexually. He also said, contrary to what David Allen told me, that Professor Wagner dumped Allen and Allen got all bent out of shape about it. And Allen also, he said, had some serious grievances against Professor Margulis."

"So he thinks he killed her, huh?" DiFong said with a little smirk.

"He said he thought it was possible and worth our looking into until I told him we already had and Allen was clean."

"And that's it? That's your heavy stuff?"

I shook my head. "No, just ambience, just a little SUS English Department ambience. Here's some more. I'm sure you remember what Lou and I told you about Professor Kerns, Professor Julia Kerns?"

"Basically. That she thought she and Margulis were Best Friends Forever until you read her what was in Margulis's computer about her uninspired teaching and all. And about Margulis being against her promotion. You said in your report that it came as a total shock and knocked her on her ass."

"I was sure it did and Lou was too, but Flanagan implies otherwise. Kerns is a computer geek and he thinks she hacked into Margulis's computer last spring, right after her promotion. His office is right down a narrow little hall from hers and he saw her read something on her computer that made her go ballistic and scream 'That bitch! That goddamn bitch!' He thinks she was referring to Margulis and what she read about herself in Margulis's computer."

Smirking again as he nodded, DiFong said, "So she sucked it up and bided her time, hoping something would turn up, which something did when, purely by chance, she hacked into Wagner's computer and, also purely by chance, she clicked to the murder scene in his novel and found herself a nice little plan. I think Professor Flanagan ought to start writing a little fiction himself."

"Well, as you know, Professor Kerns did have a class at the same time that night as Margulis did and no alibi. And you may also remember what I told you Professor Wagner himself said ---that he thought Kerns merely pretended to be BFFs with Margulis and in fact hated her for having come in and usurped her throne as SUS's Queen Leftist and Ball Buster."

"I remember. I also remember what you said about Wagner and Flanagan—that they were good friends and allies in the English Department's squabbles. Flanagan's just trying to kick a little ass and cover for his buddy, that's all it is," DiFong said, frowning as he shook his head.

Nodding, I said, "I'm inclined to agree with you on that. At least generally. Flanagan's not a liar, though."

"I'm not saying he is. I'm just saying he's trying to make a case out of nothing but a highly creative and very self-serving interpretation of some circumstances that most likely don't mean a thing. He's reaching for straws is what he's doing."

I wanted to say "Exactly. He's doing what you're doing," but I didn't. I told him about my Saturday night visit from Jennifer Tompkins, which, seeming to me and Lou a lot more than mere ambience, was the reason I had called him. I told him of Jennifer's lie and why she had told it and of her claim that Jason Harper had choked her from behind with a towel, and I reminded him of what a fearsome creature Harper was and of his ready, even proud admission of hatred for Mildred Margulis.

DiFong listened intently, his eyes never leaving mine as he nodded several times and, to my surprise, let me finish without a single interruption.

"You're right, T.J. This is something I needed to hear," he said when I was done, his face relaxing as he cocked back in his lounger and put his black wingtips on his desk. "But I don't think we need to take it too seriously, and I'll tell you why. There are several reasons, actually, but the main one is from you, something you told me."

"What was that?"

"About Margulis. You said she had a reputation for being ballsy and in-your-face, but there was no way in hell she'd have turned her back on this Harper guy when she was alone in her office at night. Not as humongous as he is and hating her like she knew he did. No way, you said."

"Yes, but I didn't know then that Harper had lied about being with Jennifer Tompkins and had scared her into backing him up. She said it was because he himself was scared, that it was obvious he was."

DiFong shrugged. "Sure he was scared. Being grilled about a homicide like you did him could scare anybody. But whether he was by himself in his apartment or not doesn't change a thing about Margulis. She just wouldn't drop her guard like that. No way. Not with that guy."

Pausing, his eyes never leaving mine, DiFong favored me with another of his disgusting little smirks and said, "I understand where you're coming from, T.J., and I appreciate it. Truly I do. Wagner's your old professor and you want to do what you can for him. But you really do need to back off and relax. Wagner's our man. We've got the earring, the novel with the plan, the opportunity, and the absence of an alibi. And the motive. I'm happy to tell you that we've finally got us a motive."

"What is it?"

"We're looking at a hate crime here. No doubt about it."

His smugness igniting my cheeks, I said, "That's a load of feminist crap. Chuck Wagner was tolerant of everybody. It was part of his gentleman's code."

DiFong shook his head. "I've been in his computer. I spent a half of Friday afternoon in it and there're some things in it you didn't tell me about. Or maybe just didn't see."

"No. I checked everything in that computer. Everything on the hard drive, in the email, everything. It was all in my report."

"Did you check his Favorites?"

"His Favorites?"

"Right. You know, that little list like a speed dial that lets him go straight to his favorite websites?"

"I'm not a cybergeek, Eddie, but I know what Favorites are."

"Sure you do, but did you check out Wagner's?"

"No, I didn't."

"Why didn't you?"

"I didn't think to."

"You didn't think to," DiFong repeated, again smirking as his eyes studied mine.

"That's what I said. I didn't think to. What are you getting at?"

"This is some heavy stuff. Some really heavy stuff," DiFong said, nodding slowly, the certainty in his eyes stoking the fire in my cheeks at the same time that it sent ice up my spine.

***

Mariners Lounge was a hole-in-the-wall bar on the rough side of Savannah, three or four blocks up from the docks on the riverfront. Having worked that precinct during my first two years with the SPD, I knew exactly where to go that Tuesday morning around eleven, but the lounge, like most such dumps, didn't look in the day as it did, or rather had, on those two or three Saturday nights when my partner and I had been sent there to deal with trouble, two stabbings and a pistol-whipping as well as I can remember.

It looked even worse. The neon sign over the entrance, once electric blue, was now pale blue and had lost the o and the u from Lounge as well as the right prong of the little red anchor beneath it. In the unpaved parking area in front were three scruffy looking pickups and an old Mustang that looked right at home, along with another car that didn't—Chuck Wagner's ancient but still immaculate green Mercedes 300-D, Green Girl, he called it.

The bartender, a balding old guy with a huge gut, was watching a game show on a little TV and three construction types as scruffy as the trucks outside were off to the side throwing darts at a board that, because of the dim light, I couldn't at first make out. All four of them eyed me as, having spotted Chuck at a table at the corner farthest from the door, I walked over to him.

He looked awful. His face was sagging and puffy, with several splotches of broken blood vessels, and his dark eyes, instead of having the tragic grandeur of a fallen angel's, now had the lightless gaze of a despondent old man's. He was in a black turtleneck beneath a beige corduroy jacket with leather elbow patches, and in his right hand, which was as massive and powerful looking as ever, was a half-down glass of what I was sure was either a double gin or vodka on the rocks. In his left hand was a Camel and even above the residual stench of such a low-rent bar I could smell a fog of sickly-sweet Certs and cologne hovering about him. His cane dangled from the table by its crook.

"Good to see you, T.J. So very, very good to see you," he said, his voice still deep and dramatic but no longer Darth Vader's as he looked up at me and started to rise.

"Good to see you too, Chuck. Keep your seat. Keep your seat," I said, shaking his hand and giving him a weak little grin.

I sat down in the chair across from him, but almost before "So tell me how you've been" was out of my mouth I saw the bartender coming toward us.

I sensed from his face that he knew Chuck, which did not surprise me. I had heard rumors that Chuck had, or used to have, a taste for rough trade and several times, when I was taking courses under him, he'd come to class with various marks on his face, one of them a badly split lip. Further, when I had called and said I needed to see him, and in a completely safe place, he had immediately specified the Mariners Lounge, which, being on the other side of town, was at least ten miles from his condo.

I was right. After asking me what I'd have and being told a Diet Coke, the bartender looked at Chuck and said, "How about you, Professor? You ready for another one?"

Several minutes later, after setting our drinks on the table, the bartender gave me a lingering look that at first made me think he thought I was Chuck's sweetie or catamite or whatever you call it. Then I remembered having seen such a look countless times before. It said, "Plainclothes or not, you're not fooling me. You're a cop and I know it."

Instead of relieving me, though, my understanding of the look bothered me even more. Even if he didn't watch the local news or read the newspaper, the bartender had to know about Chuck, and here Chuck was, an accused murderer, in a tete-a-tete with a cop. And if the fat old guy'd seen me on the news, which was very possible, he might recognize me as the very cop who'd made the arrest.

Seeming to read my mind, Chuck inclined his head toward the departing bartender and said, "Larry there's a splendid conflation of those three discreet little monkeys, T.J. I'm sure you get my drift."

Nodding, I took a sip of my Diet Coke, then looked him in the eyes and said, "You're not doing well, Chuck. It's getting to you, isn't it?"

"Yes, it is. I confess that it is," he said with a weariness that now seemed bone deep rather than just part of his dramatic persona.

"It was seeing the indictment, wasn't it?"

"Indeed it was. At least mainly. I mean, it's one thing to know that you soon will charged with murder, but it's another thing altogether, as you seem to know, to see it in black and white, in the solemn and official majesty of the printed word. It becomes engraved on your very soul. To wit: On or about January 11 of this year, within the venue of Chatham Country, C. Clarkson Wagner, defendant herein, did commit murder in the first degree in that he did knowingly, intentionally, and with malice aforethought, et cetera, et cetera, et goddamn cetera."

I nodded. "That's how just about everybody reacts when they see their very own name on a murder indictment. I'm sorry, Chuck. I can't tell you how much I wish I'd never laid eyes on that damned earring. Jesus, I wish I hadn't!" I said with a grimace as I shook my head.

"I know, T.J. Believe me I know, but you still shouldn't be meeting me like this or, really, like anything. You could lose your badge and that, I assure you, would make me feel genuinely guilty rather than just very much, and most unconscionably, put upon. You have nothing, absolutely nothing to make amends for. You were merely doing you duty."

"To hell with my badge and my duty. There're some things you and your lawyer need to know now, before DiFong gives them to y'all in the discovery. I had a talk yesterday morning with your colleague, Professor Flanagan."

"Yes, I know," Chuck said, finishing in a single gulp the remainder of his first drink.

"You do?"

"Jack's a good, very loyal friend, and there just may be some merit to his claims about Professor Kerns. I trust, as he said you assured him you'd do, that you passed them on to Mr. C. Edward DiFong, the third of that name?" Chuck asked with a flash of his old wryness.

"Yes, I did. What Flanagan told me and also what I was told by an SUS student named Jennifer Tompkins," I said, filling him on who she was, the lie she had told, and the fears she had about Jason Harper, whom Chuck said he'd never taught but had seen around campus.

"But DiFong dismissed that too," I said with disgust. "He said it didn't matter where Jason Harper was when Margulis was killed. Even if, as was most unlikely, she would let him in her office, she never would've let him get in a position to garrote her from behind."

"I daresay he's right about that, T.J. She was a brassy broad, but she was no fool."

I took a sip of my Diet Coke, then said, "The main reason I wanted to meet with you, though, aside from just wanting to see how you're doing, is to tell you that DiFong's been in your computer."

"Oh!" Chuck said, raising his right eyebrow. "I thought you'd already been there and done that."

"I have, you know I have, but he obviously doesn't trust me and he thought he could find something I didn't put in my report."

"Well, did he?"

"Not in the places I looked, the hard drive and the email."

"I didn't know there was anywhere else. Aside, I mean, from the disks and the little plug-in gizmos."

"He found something in your Favorites."

"My Favorites?"

"Yes. Your list of favorite websites, the ones you listed so you could go straight to them."

Shaking his head and frowning, Chuck, as if it were water, drained his second drink down to rocks, then said, "T.J., with God as my witness, I have never, not even in response to those silly pop up things, accessed a single porn site on that computer. And even on the one at home I have never, again with God as my witness, accessed, or even thought of accessing, a site with child pornography on it. If that DiFong, the third of that loathsome name, says that he found some, then he..."

I shook my head. "He didn't say anything about porn, child or otherwise."

"What is it, then? I don't see how it could be anything else."

"He showed me the list of your favorites--ten or twelve, I don't remember exactly—and all but one or two were for websites that ranged from ultra-conservative to radical, real nut-case right wing. That's what he called them and I'm afraid, after visiting them myself, that I have to agree with him."

Chuck stared into my eyes for five or six slow beats of my heart, then wearily shook his head and with a little grin said, "Forgive me, T.J., but I have to laugh. I really do. I have to laugh."

"This is nothing to laugh about, Chuck. He's dead serious. He's going to claim that you murdered Margulis because of y'all's political differences, she being a Colorado Yankee and to the left and you being a Southerner. He's going to say that you're an un-reconstructed Southerner and to the right, the far right. He's going to call it a hate crime."

"At this point, my good friend, nothing about my lamentable situation would surprise me, but this really is laughable. It really is," Chuck said, grinning again, then breaking into what seemed a laugh of gut-wrenching despair that for a moment caught the attention of the bartender and of the dart players.

***

About twenty minutes later I was outside in the noon glare watching as the vintage old Mercedes, Green Girl, lumbered out of the parking lot and into the traffic, her diesel befouling the air and clattering like a dozen roofers hammering tacks. Although Chuck probably could have blown two or three times the legal limit on a breath test, he showed no signs having drunk even a glass of wine, let alone two vodka or gin doubles on the rocks. Cop or no cop, I didn't question his ability to get safely home.

The last thing he had said to me was, "See you in court, T.J."

Chapter 13

During the jury selection DiFong wanted as many females as he could get, especially if he could identify them as liberal, career-oriented, and non-Southern; and he used all six of his peremptory dismissals on white males who were Southern, blue-collar, and middle-aged.

In his opening statement he strutted and fretted like a pot-bellied little Hamlet in a new blue suit. He said that Mildred Margulis had been a dedicated professional as a teacher, scholar, mentor, and champion of human rights, a struggling single mother from Colorado who had been brutally murdered, martyred for daring to speak out against the glaring injustices of gender, race, and class that so many others pretend not to see. He said that her death was a dark, wicked stain on the city, on the state, on the entire South, and that the "benighted and bigoted although highly educated throwback" who had killed her—and here he pointed angrily at Chuck—was deserving of the contempt and scorn of all decent people for having committed so enormous and dastardly a deed, a hate crime if he'd ever seen one. In short, he did everything he could to hang a halo over Margulis and to pin not just a forked tail but also a swastika and a Confederate Battle Flag on poor Chuck.

I'd been relieved and maybe even a little heartened several days earlier when I'd heard through the grapevine that the judge would be L. Dwayne Peabody, a native white Savannahian of about Chuck's age with a drawl thicker than mine and a reputation of intolerance for grandstanding lawyers. On learning that Judge Peabody would be presiding, DiFong, according to my source, had rolled his eyes and said, "Oh, Jesus, please! Not him!"

Instead of entreaty, however, DiFong no doubt had offered thanks when he got the scoop on Chuck's lawyer. I say "got the scoop on" because the man's name, Luther Jackson, probably had meant even less to him than it had to me. At least I knew that Jackson had been Chuck's student and that Chuck had complete confidence in him, which had led me to assume that he was good and pricey but so low-profile as to be little known outside his circle. After all, Chuck knew what was at stake, despite what some of his antics might suggest, and he was by no means poor, apparently having a comfortable amount of family money in addition to his salary at SUS.

I'm not an eye-roller, but I did shake my head and mutter, at least to myself, after I checked out Jackson's credentials. In the yellow pages of the phone book, in an inconspicuous little 2" by 2" square at the bottom of the page, his ad said LUTHER JACKSON, ATTORNEY-DIVORCE-DUI-WILLS-WORKERS'- COMPENSATION-CRIMINAL LAW, and had a phone number and an address but no picture, website, or email.

I was even more depressed after several phone calls, one to a lawyer friend who'd been a cop and, as luck would have it, had gone to John Marshall Law School at night with Jackson. He said that Jackson had been in practice for about four years and, except for a secretary, worked alone. He'd needed three tries to pass the bar exam and, as his dinky little ad suggested, he was barely eking out a living, almost all of his work being low-fee grunt stuff such as divorces, DUIs, and deadbeat dads. He was a very hard, conscientious worker, though, a good talker, and "a nice guy, a really nice guy." All of my sources asked why I was interested and when I told them had said essentially the same thing: "DiFong'll probably eat him alive."

They'd not needed to tell me, though all of them did, that Luther Jackson, in addition to being black, was also short, balding, obese, soft-spoken, and so incorrigibly disheveled that his suits and ties looked like leftovers from a yard sale. Two of my other informants—Lou called them my courtroom spies—had given me a detailed description of how he had looked and a largely verbatim account of what he had said during his opening statement, both of them fearing that Jackson's sloppy appearance might well be a metaphor for the worse kind of courtroom incompetence.

Nervous, sweating, and asked by Judge Peabody as well as by two jurors to please speak up, Jackson had assured the seven women and five men that the charge of a premeditated hate murder against his client was so circumstantial as to be totally without merit.

"In fact, ladies and gentlemen, what we've got here is a frame-up, a sad miscarriage of justice, and when I'm through, when you fine folks have seen and carefully weighed all of what our learned prosecutor is so bold, so downright desperate as to call evidence, you will agree with me, and will so announce, that Professor C. Clarkson Wagner is the real victim here, completely and totally innocent. Furthermore, you will agree with me that this case should never, and I mean never, have been allowed into this courtroom. Thank you very much," Jackson had said, wiping his shining black brow with a white handkerchief as he bowed slightly toward the jury and then toward Judge Peabody.

DiFong's first witness was Johnnie White, the old janitor who had found the body. He was followed by Sergeant Thomas Baldwin, the SUS cop, and then by Lou. All three cited pretty much the same details in describing the scene and confirmed that what they had seen early that morning in office F-212 of Hampton Hall was exactly what they saw in the five photographs that DiFong showed first to them and then to the jury.

Luther Jackson objected to the photographs, arguing that they were inflammatory, but Judge Peabody let them stand. He apparently agreed with DiFong that the jurors needed to see with their own eyes that, as DiFong said, "Mildred Margulis was not just some abstract victim. She'd been somebody's mother and somebody's daughter. She'd been a woman whose life had been choked out of her and whose body, whose limp and helpless body, had been desecrated. Her right ear, as you can plainly see, was torn when her earring was ripped out and the murder weapon, the purple ribbon on a medal she had won as a runner, was again hung around her neck--a neck no longer warm and living, ladies and gentlemen, as it had been on the day she won the medal, but cold and dead, forever dead."

The old janitor, Sergeant Baldwin, and Lou were followed in the witness chair by DiFong's expert on extremist groups such as the ones bookmarked as Favorites in Chuck's computer. White, lanky, four-eyed, around forty, and from Wisconsin, Dr. James Cox was a history professor at SUS, and although I'd never had him for a class, I knew of his reputation as an outspoken liberal and firebrand basher of the United States, the South in particular.

According to a friend of mine who took him for two classes, he had said not once or twice but regularly, and during lectures no less, that 9/11 was exactly what we in America deserved, our "racist, hegemonic chickens having at last come home to roost." He was also known for deducting points from any assignment in which his student used a capital C on Confederate, Confederacy, or the Confederate States of America, the upper case conferring, he insisted, "a dignity and legitimacy altogether specious and unmerited."

Dr. Cox's characterization of each of Chuck's Favorites was, in substance if not in language, almost identical to my own, the range, as he put it, "extending from the nostalgically conservative to the insanely radical." Contrary to what I would've thought, though, he did not dwell on the one for the Aryan Nation or for any other such group of bona fide nutcases. Nor did he have much to say about the sites for the Sons of Confederate Veterans and the League of the South, even though the League openly advocated another secession of the South from the Union, as I knew from my own visit to its site.

His main target was a book titled 'The South Under Siege', which neither I nor either of my two courtroom sources had ever even heard of. According to Dr. Cox, the book argues and attempts to show that the South continues to be under attack from the North, particularly the politically correct Northeastern Liberal Establishment, which, in a kind of totalitarian culture-cleansing, is using the courts, the schools, the media, and the ballot box to root out and completely expunge all remaining vestiges of traditional Southernisms, from accents and phrasings to Confederate marbles and prayers in public. The book also contends, in an urgent call to arms, that this "cultural genocide" can and should be fought, and devotes its last 66 pages to showing how.

Furthermore, Dr. Cox said, Professor Wagner had in his office a copy of 'The South Under Siege' that was copiously annotated and underlined as well as signed by the author.

"What might that signify, Dr. Cox? I mean, why would someone take the time to mark up or underline passages in a book?" DiFong asked, frowning as if such a matter were a deep mystery.

"For mnemonic reasons, generally," Dr. Cox said.

"Mnemonic reasons?"

"Yes, to help him remember them."

"And he'd want to remember them because he thought they were important?"

"Yes. That's generally the case."

"And maybe too because he agreed with or advocated the ideas in the passages? Is that likely? Or possible? Is that at least possible?"

Luther Jackson rose from his seat beside Chuck and said, this time with enough volume for the entire courtroom to hear, "I object to that, Your Honor. Just because somebody owns a book and marks in it doesn't mean they agree with or advocate what it says. When I was in college I sure didn't agree with or advocate slavery, but I marked up a whole lot of passages about it in my history books."

Before Judge Peabody could reply, DiFong said, "Your Honor, Counselor Jackson's point is well taken, but in this particular instance we have a document that very much supports the connection we're attempting to establish between agreeing with or advocating what's underlined in 'The South Under Siege'. I respectfully request Your Honor's permission to present this document to the court."

"What is this document, Mr. DiFong?" Judge Peabody asked.

"It's a book in manuscript by the defendant, Your Honor. A novel."

"How do you plan to present this novel, Mr. DiFong? Surely you don't plan to read it to us, do you?" Judge Peabody said, peering over his half-lens glasses down at DiFong.

"Oh, no, Your Honor. I just want to show the document to the court and have Dr. Cox answer a few questions about it. He's studied it very closely."

"You may proceed, Mr. DiFong, but you are not to waste the court's time by drifting off into irrelevance. Is that understood?"

Seconds later DiFong held up a manuscript bound with rubber bands that, to judge from its thickness, was around 300 pages.

"This is the manuscript of a novel by the defendant, C. Clarkson Wagner. It was one of five such novels, all of them unpublished I might add, that were found in his office at SUS," DiFong said, pointing to the manuscript. "The title of it is 'Matters of Vision' and it has a subtitle: 'The Beam and the Mote'. I wonder if the court knows the source of that subtitle, what famous book the phrase 'the beam and the mote' comes from?"

One of the jurors, a black man, sixty or so, nodded slowly and waved his hand. "Matthew. The Gospel of Matthew. It come from the Gospel of Matthew," he said.

"Yes, sir, it does and would you mind telling the court what it means? Some of us, and I certainly include myself among the some, might not be as versed in the Good Book as maybe we should be," DiFong said with a self-deprecatory little grin.

"It mean you got faults a whole lot bigger than I got but my faults be the only ones you see and fuss about," the juror said. "Jesus say it's what hypocrites do."

"Thank you, sir. Thank you so very much. I couldn't have put it any better myself," DiFong said, giving the man a smile, then turning from him and going over to the witness chair.

"Dr. Cox, you've studied this novel, have you not?" DiFong said, looking up at his expert as he pointed to the manuscript.

"Yes, I have. At considerable length," Dr. Cox said.

"Tell us, in brief, what it's about, if you would."

"It's about a young, white, highly privileged English professor from the North, fresh out of Harvard, who comes South to teach in a small college in Alabama. The time is 1965 and the main theme is that of initiation—

the rites of passage, that is, or in simplest terms, the lessons that a young person learns when his illusions or preconceptions collide with new experience."

"And what exactly does he learn, this young, white, highly privileged English professor who comes South?" DiFong asked.

"He learns what he perhaps should have already known, which is that the South, far from welcoming, is in fact hostile to strangers, foreigners, intruders, interlopers, Yankees, Damn Yankees—call them what you will. He learns that the South is, in a word, xenophobic. He's characterized as well-meaning but naïve and self-righteous, as an idealistic young fool, really, and is called, among many epithets meant to be insulting, an Academic Freedom Rider."

"An Academic Freedom Rider?" DiFong repeated with a quizzical look up at his expert.

Dr. Cox nodded. "A Northern academic, a college professor, who comes South and attempts to do in the academy—in the colleges and universities, that is—the equivalent to what the other Freedom Riders attempted to do in the body politic. And that, of course, was to protest, to march against, figuratively if not always literally, the many wrongs, especially racial wrongs, so deeply entrenched as to be systemic. To be an agent of change, in other words."

"And you say that this young man, this young Yankee, in his efforts to correct the wrongs he perceives in the academy—specifically in the little Southern school where he comes to teach—is not welcomed?" DiFong asked.

"'Not welcomed' would be an understatement. Met with much resistance and hostility, even hatred, would be more like it," Dr. Cox said.

"By everyone he meets?"

"No, not by everyone. Several of his students become his 'disciples', as the narrator calls them, and the narrator himself, a white Southern male who teaches at the same small college, befriends him and acts as a mentor and guide through what amounts to a kind of social and academic minefield for the young professor."

"And the end result?" DiFong asked. "Does the narrator keep him from getting blown up or what?"

"Yes, he does, for the most part. The narrator has the young man understand that if he's going to stay in the South and perhaps be effective in bringing about reform, he's going to have to change his ways. He's going to have to be careful in what he says and even more careful in how he says it. Specifically, he's going to have to shed his tone of moral arrogance and acquire some manners, Southern manners, in other words. And to do this, he has to understand and acknowledge, as the narrator points out, that he'd be wise to clean up his own back yard before he presumes to go down the street and clean up his neighbor's. This of course is the narrator's way of saying that if he wants to crusade against injustice of any kind, social, racial, academic, whatever, he doesn't need to come South to do it. There's plenty of it in the North. Hence the subtitle: the crusading young Yankee can see what's in the South's eye but not what's in his own, not in the North's."

Nodding as if his own eyes had at last been opened, DiFong said, "It sounds to me, Dr. Cox, as if the defendant's novel is very much like 'The South Under Siege'. I mean, in the way that the young man, the protagonist, tried to bring Northern ways, Yankee ways, to the South, and in the South's resistance, its hostility to those ways. So I ask you, am I correct or am I perhaps stretching or oversimplifying, or maybe even imagining, the parallels between the two books? What would you say?"

Nodding slowly, Dr. Cox said, "I'd say your parallels are obvious and valid. Actually, I'd say you could go further. I think you could say that the defendant's novel, 'Matters of Vision', is in many ways a dramatic particularizing of The South Under Siege. A novelized version of it, if you will."

"And the narrator of this novel, the Southern white male English professor—does he, in his general depiction, resemble or reflect the author, C. Clarkson Wagner?"

"I'd say so, yes. As he's generally represented."

"To the extent, maybe, that we could consider him the author's spokesman or mouthpiece?"

"Certainly. The narrative voice in any written work, novel, history or whatever, is always the author's spokesman or mouthpiece."

"Let me rephrase my question, Dr. Cox," DiFong said with a brisk shake of his head. "What I mean is, do you think that the opinions, thoughts, feelings, attitudes, and so forth of the professor in the novel are the same as, or to a telling extent parallel to, those of C. Clarkson Wagner?"

"I object to that, Your Honor," Luther Jackson said in what for him was a loud voice as he rose from his chair beside Chuck. "Dr. Cox is not even a casual friend of Professor Wagner, let alone a friend close enough to know what goes on inside his head in the way of thoughts and feelings. Furthermore, something I learned way back when I was taking English courses in college was that it's generally a big mistake to think that whoever's telling the story in a novel or poem is the same as the person who wrote it, even when the teller uses I, me, mine, and other such when he refers to himself. My professors said all that was just a mask, just a character the author was pretending to be, same as an actor playing a role in a movie. I'll give you an example of what I'm talking about. The book's kind of old and I don't know if any of you"—he looked toward the jury—"have ever read it, but it's a novel called 'The Confessions of Nat Turner'. The story in it's told by Nat Turner—it's his confessions, like the title says—and he's a slave up in Virginia back before the Civil War. He's the I-me, but he's not the author. The author, the man who actually wrote the book, was not a slave and never had been one. He's not even a black man. He's a white man, a Virginia white man who's still living for all I know. He's no more the Nat Turner, the I / Me in his book than ..."

"I note your objection and I share it, Mr. Jackson," Judge Peabody said, cutting him off, then with an annoyed look turning to DiFong. "Mr. DiFong, would you please tell the court where you're going with all this speculation, this literary second-guessing?"

"Yes, I will, Your Honor," DiFong said. "I'm attempting to establish a connection, a definite link between the hostility and hatred that killed Mildred Margulis and the hostility and hatred in two books that obviously and undeniably are very close to the defendant, C. Clarkson Wagner. He wrote one of them himself and the other one he not only bought and had autographed by the author, but he also marked it up and underlined passages in it the way some people do a textbook or a Bible. The hostility and hatred in both of these books, as Dr. Cox has testified, is what Northerners—Yankees, Damn Yankees, if you will—so often face when they come to the South. Mildred Margulis, although from Colorado, was just such a Yankee in just such a situation. Just about everywhere the poor woman went here in the South but especially, especially in her workplace, which was the English Department at SUS, she was regarded as, and treated as, an annoyance at best and, at worst, as nothing less than an invading and hated enemy. I repeat: as an invading and hated enemy."

***

The next morning DiFong began by calling four witnesses to the stand and asking each of them if they had personal knowledge of any hostility that Mildred Margulis may have faced from her colleagues at SUS in general and in the English Department in particular.

Dr. Julia Kerns said that her memory was all too full of such knowledge. If she had ever felt betrayal from or anything other than professional admiration for and feminist solidarity with Mildred Margulis, she managed to keep it well hidden as she held forth on the many times her dead friend, "so distressed she was close to tears," had told her of feeling "marginalized and demeaned, demonized" from the way she was routinely treated, in department meetings, committee meetings, even in hallway encounters, by most of her colleagues in the English Department, starting with the Head, Dr. Steven Harrison. The reasons for such treatment boiled down to just one thing, Dr. Kerns said: "Dr. Margulis was a strong and outspoken woman in a place where strong and outspoken women are not wanted."

Next was Sandi Haynes, Margulis's student, disciple, and eulogist at the campus memorial service back in January. Unlike Dr. Kerns, Sandi did not remain composed. Her brown hair still as long ala Gloria Steinem as Margulis's had been, and her earrings still as dangly, she again had been torn between rage and grief. Choking back tears, she told of how bravely her mentor had struggled against "the entrenched agents of hatred and fear of anything new and different" who dominated the SUS English Department. She again said, as during her eulogy, that just as the murder of Dr. Martin Luther King, Jr. had been a hate crime, so was the murder of Dr. Mildred Margulis. If looks could kill, Chuck would've died a thousand deaths from the ones Sandi Haynes gave him.

Dr. Nigel Helton, aka Ping Pong, got even more emotional. Identifying himself as "a man who had loved Milly Margulis, who had loved her very deeply for the beauty of her courage and humanity, for her commitment to her ideals," he had, at one point, sobbed so piteously that DiFong, his own face a mask of grief, had handed him a handkerchief and asked if he needed to be excused. Very much in the spirit of his dead love, though, Ping Pong had fought on, wiping his eyes, glaring at Chuck, stopping to catch his breath as he remembered what he'd been told of the slights and exclusions, the ugly looks and low hisses of "FemiNazi" that highly educated people who were supposed to have been her colleagues, her very own colleagues, had regularly inflicted on "poor brave Milly."

Gloria Wills, Margulis's daughter, was the last of the four and, at least in looks, far and away the best for every male in the courtroom. One of my sources for that day, the bailiff in fact, said she was dressed entirely in black and was "one hot number, like Jessica Simpson but not trashy. She was classy, really classy, with brown hair and tall, a lot taller." Gloria said that her mother had never felt completely comfortable in the English Department at SUS, even after eleven years, and at times had felt not just disliked but hated by most of her colleagues and students.

"One of the few I times I ever saw my mother cry," Gloria said, getting close to tears herself, "was when she read what some of her colleagues had written about her when she came up for promotion. They said she was divisive and unprofessional, not a teacher but a propagandist, that she was rude and hated men and Southerners and was just the worst kind of arrogant Yankee bitch. That's an exact quote: 'The worst kind of arrogant Yankee bitch.'"

In his cross-examination of these four, Luther Jackson reminded them that they were under oath to tell the truth, the whole, truth, and nothing but the truth, then asked each of them only one question: "Did Professor Margulis ever tell you of being treated in a hateful, hostile, or even in just a rude or unprofessional manner by the defendant, Professor C. Clarkson Wagner? Yes or no?"

The answers from Kerns, Haynes, and Ping Pong, though reluctantly given, especially by Kerns, were all the same: "No. Not that I can recall."

DiFong, obviously, wasn't happy to hear this, but he was even less happy to hear Gloria Wills say the same thing, then add, "Actually, I can't remember ever hearing my mother say anything really negative about Professor Wagner. Just that he was so Southern and old-fashioned and disagreed with her on a lot of departmental matters. She said he was always polite and professional about it, though."

Shortly after these four stepped down, DiFong called me to the witness stand. This was the first time I'd been actually in the courtroom, having hitherto stayed away so that my testimony couldn't possibly be tainted or to any degree influenced by that of the previous deponents. What I say about the trial from here on is therefore based on what I myself, rather than my spies, saw and heard, which means, among other things, that the speeches I attempt to reproduce are much closer to verbatim.

After I raised my right hand and took the oath, in the seconds before DiFong started on me, I sat with my hands on the arms of the witness chair and glanced around the packed room. Luther Jackson looked every bit as sloppy and un-lawyerly as I'd heard, but Chuck, sitting beside him, didn't look at all as he had when I'd last seen him, which had been six or seven weeks ago in that little rat hole of a bar, the Mariners Lounge. His face was no longer so splotched and puffy and his eyes, those tragically dark and fallen-angel eyes, had much of their old wry shine as, when they met mine, he gave me a grin and a nod so slight, so close to imperceptible that for a moment I thought I'd only imagined them.

That Chuck could again be or maybe just seem so flippant amazed me, even more than before he'd seen his name on the indictment, and I wondered if he'd sunk to a new depth of despair or if maybe, just maybe, Luther Jackson had given him some altogether new and miraculous reason for hope.

In the throng of spectators behind him my eyes moved over some media people I recognized along with several SUS professors I vaguely remembered, then fixed on a face I knew but for a split second couldn't place. Deathly pale and emaciated but still poignantly, hauntingly pretty, it was the face of Mahalia Harrison, the wife of Dr. Steve Harrison. I remembered being told of her computer wizardry, of her drinking and blackouts, of her—and by her own mouth no less—hatred of Mildred Margulis and relief that she was dead, and I myself had observed how touchingly devoted to and protective of each other she and Dr. Harrison were. I also remembered that she and Chuck were good friends. She'd described him as "just the sweetest, gentlest old thing," and I'd never heard him say "Mahalia" without putting "poor" in front of it.

After having me confirm that I was one of the two investigators assigned to the Margulis case, DiFong took from the evidence table and held before me a small clear plastic bag.

"Detective Loomis, have you ever seen the contents of this bag before now?" he asked.

"Yes, sir, I have."

"Would you please tell the court what you see in this bag?"

"I see an earring, an earring with two little gold balls at the ends of two little gold chains."

"Have you ever seen this earring before now?"

"Yes, sir. I have. Several times."

"When was the first time? The very first time you saw it?"

"On Wednesday, January 21 of this year, around two in the afternoon," I said, glancing at Chuck, whose eyes were fixed on me like a pair of gun sights.

"Correct me if I'm wrong, Detective Loomis, but I believe that day, Wednesday, January the 21st of this year, was exactly seven days after Dr. Mildred Margulis was found dead in her office. Am I correct?" DiFong asked, frowning as if he might truly be in doubt.

"Yes, sir. You are. You're correct."

"Now, Detective Loomis, would you please tell the court where you were on that Wednesday when you first saw this earring?"

"I was on the campus of SUS, in Hampton Hall, in the office of Professor C. Clarkson Wagner."

"Where, exactly, was the earring when you saw it?"

"It was on one of the bookshelves behind the professor's desk. On a boxed set of books, in the inch or so of space above the top of the set and the shelf above it."

"What, after you saw the earring, was your reaction?"

"I pointed it out to Professor Wagner and told him not to touch it. Then I took the earring off the book. I used my ballpoint to do it."

"Why the ballpoint, Detective Loomis? Wouldn't it have been simpler just to use your hand?"

"Yes, sir, it would, but I didn't want my fingerprints to be on the earring."

Again frowning, DiFong said, "Because you thought the earring might be evidence of a crime you knew about?"

I nodded. "Yes, sir. I did."

"And what crime might that be?"

"The crime that Detective Sergeant Lou Ackerman and I were investigating. The murder of Professor Mildred Margulis."

"Why? Surely you had some reason for thinking that."

"I was all but sure the earring matched the one that was in Professor Margulis's left ear when Detective Ackerman and I first saw her body."

"Did it? Did it match the other earring?"

"It did. Perfectly."

"How could you be so sure of that? You didn't have the other earring with you, did you?"

"No, sir, but I'd studied it and had a very precise picture of it in my mind. I later put the two earrings side by side. They were identical."

DiFong nodded. "I see. So you're saying that the earring you saw in Professor Wagner's office, being a perfect match of the one you saw in Professor Margulis's ear, was the very same earring that the killer, after strangling the life out of Dr. Margulis, ripped out of her right ear and took as a souvenir? Is that what you're saying?"

I shook my head. "Not exactly. I think, but I don't know for sure, that the killer ripped out the earring. The only thing I know for sure is that the earring I saw in Professor Wagner's office was and is a perfect match of the one I saw in Professor Margulis's ear."

"Very well," DiFong said with a grudging nod. "When you told Professor Wagner not to touch the earring and you yourself handled it with a ballpoint pen, did you tell him why?"

"I did."

"What did you tell him? Exactly what?"

"I told him that I was almost sure that the earring we both were staring at had been ripped out of the right ear of his recently murdered colleague, Professor Mildred Margulis."

"What did he say when you told him that?"

"He said he'd never seen the earring before and had no idea of how it got in his office," I said, glancing down at Chuck, who was leaning over and whispering something to Luther Jackson.

***

Several minutes later I was still up in the witness chair and Luther Jackson, about to begin his cross-examination, was standing slightly below and few feet in front of me, again wiping his brow with a white handkerchief.

Putting the handkerchief back into a side pocket of his jacket, he turned and looked me straight in the eyes. His face was blank, but I could see in his eyes, or at least I thought I could see in his eyes, that he knew I would help Chuck in any way I reasonably could.

"Detective Loomis," he said, his voice soft but loud enough for everyone in the courtroom to hear, "how was it, on Wednesday afternoon the 21st of January, that you came to be in Professor Wagner's office? Did you go there as part of your investigation —to question Professor Wagner, that is—or for some other reason? Would you please tell the court?"

"I went there because Professor Wagner and I chanced into each other in Hampton Hall and he suggested that I stop by and see him."

"What exactly were you doing in Hampton Hall? Pursuing your investigation, I assume?"

"Yes, sir. I was taking another look in Professor Margulis's office."

"When you say 'chanced into' Professor Wagner, I assume you mean that the two of you met entirely by accident, that you, so to speak, 'bumped into' each other? Is that correct?"

"That's correct. I had just come out of Professor Margulis's office and Professor Wagner was on his way to the men's room. We almost literally bumped into each other."

"And you say that he asked you, invited you to stop by his office?"

"Yes, sir, he did. He said if I wasn't too busy, maybe I could stop by and we could visit for a little while."

"The word 'visit,' as you just used it, implies some sort of personal relationship, some degree of friendship, does it not?" Luther Jackson asked.

I nodded. "I'd been Professor Wagner's student back when I was working on my degree at SUS and he'd been my faculty adviser. I'd taken four courses under him and we hadn't seen each other since I graduated last June."

"Are you saying that you knew Professor Wagner pretty well, Detective Loomis? At least well enough to trust him and have no doubts about his integrity?" Luther Jackson asked, tilting his head slightly to the right and frowning.

"I'd say that, yes. I took four courses under him, as I said, and he never gave me any reason not to trust him and take him at his word."

"And you say that after the two of you met in Hampton Hall purely and entirely by chance, almost literally bumped into each other, Professor Wagner invited you to stop by his office? Not that you asked but that he invited you? Professor Wagner invited—I repeat—invited you to stop by and visit? That is correct, is it not?" Luther Jackson said, glancing over at the jury, then turning back to me.

"Yes, sir. That's correct. Professor Wagner invited me to stop by his office and see him," I said.

"Very well. Now, Detective Loomis, you say that while you were visiting with Professor Wagner you saw—spotted is perhaps more like it—the earring Mr. DiFong showed us a few minutes ago. That it was sitting on top of a set of books on one of Professor Wagner's bookshelves? Is that correct?"

"That's correct. It was on top of a boxed edition of Shelby Foote's history of the Civil War."

"Where exactly in Professor Wagner's office was that bookshelf located, Detective Loomis?"

"It was directly behind Professor Wagner's desk. It was the third shelf from the bottom."

"Would that have put the Civil War set on it as high as or higher than the top of Professor Wagner's desk?"

"Slightly higher, by maybe an inch or so."

"And you--where were you sitting when you spotted the earring?"

"I was sitting in a chair directly in front of the desk."

"And Professor Wagner? Where was he at this time? I assume he was sitting in his chair behind his desk? Was he?"

I shook my head. "No, sir, he wasn't. He was sitting in one the two visitors' chairs in front of his desk, in the chair to the left of mine."

"Which gave him the same line of vision that you had? Is that correct?"

"Not exactly the same, no, because he was a foot or so to the left of where I was," I said.

"Even so, he could see everything behind his desk and on his bookshelves that you could see? Is that correct?"

"Yes, sir. It is."

"Including the earring?"

"Including the earring. When I saw it and pointed it out to him, he didn't have to move to see it. He could look over the top of his desk and see it just as clearly as I could."

"But what about Professor Wagner's desk chair, the one he sat in when he was behind his desk? That chair, at least the back of it, would've been in the way and kept you, and then Professor Wagner, from seeing the earring, wouldn't it?"

I nodded. "Yes, sir, it would if it had been where it was when Professor Wagner sits in it. But it wasn't there. It was pushed a few feet over to the right of the middle of the desk."

Taking his handkerchief of his pocket and this time not merely wiping but mopping his sweating brow with it, Luther Jackson shook his head and gave me a look that could've passed for confused.

"Let me see if I understand this, Detective Loomis," he said, replacing his handkerchief in his jacket pocket. "You say that you first and then Professor Wagner saw Professor Margulis's earring on a bookshelf directly behind Professor Wagner's desk and at a height of an inch of so above the top of the desk? Is that correct?"

"Yes, sir. That's correct."

"And then you said that the location of the earring on the bookshelf behind Professor Wagner's desk put it directly behind where Professor Wagner's desk chair would've been if he'd been sitting in it?"

"Yes, sir, I did."

"But you made it clear that Professor Wagner was not sitting in his desk chair behind his desk. You made it clear that he was sitting in front of his desk, in the chair to the left of the one you were sitting in, and that he could easily see whatever you could see, including the earring? That is correct, is it not?"

"Yes, sir. It is."

"That would mean, then, that if Professor Wagner had been sitting in his chair behind his desk, where he generally sat, his body would've blocked your view of the earring and you wouldn't have seen it. Is that correct?"

"Yes, sir. That's correct. I never would have seen it."

"I have to object, Your Honor," DiFong said in the weary manner of a man whose patience and good will had been sorely tried. "Mr. Jackson, almost from the start of his cross-examination, has been indulging in questions that have little or no bearing on the case. Detective Loomis has clearly established that he saw Professor Margulis's earring in Professor Wagner's office and seized it as evidence. Where he was sitting at the time, along with where Professor Wagner was sitting at the time, is utterly and totally irrelevant."

"I must beg to differ with you on that, Mr. DiFong," Luther Jackson said with a seemingly shy little smile. "Where these men were sitting, especially Professor Wagner, at the time Detective Loomis spotted the earring is highly relevant because of the inference that any rational person would quite naturally and logically draw from it. It has inferential relevance, Your Honor, a great amount, a compelling amount of inferential relevance."

Peering over his half-lens glasses down at Luther Jackson, Judge Peabody said, "Mr. Jackson, you need to clarify for the ladies and gentleman of the jury, as well as for me, what you mean by 'inferential relevance.'"

"I'll be happy to, Your Honor," Luther Jackson said, turning to face the jury. "It's really quite simple, ladies and gentlemen. If Professor Wagner had killed Professor Margulis and known that her earring was in his office on such conspicuous display, he wouldn't have wanted it seen, especially by the detective investigating the case. So, first of all, when he chanced, almost literally bumped into Detective Loomis, he wouldn't have invited the detective to stop by his office and visit. Second, if he were guilty as charged but for some reason had invited his former student to stop by, he would've sat in his usual place behind his desk and thereby kept the earring out of Detective Loomis's sight. But Professor Wagner didn't sit in his chair behind his desk. He sat in a chair in front of his desk, right beside Detective Loomis, thereby putting the earring directly in Detective Loomis's line of vision. Therefore, ladies and gentlemen, we must infer that Professor Wagner was completely ignorant of the earring, which, incidentally, is perfectly in keeping with Detective Loomis's testimony."

"Your Honor," DiFong said, standing up and raising his hand like a schoolboy. "I need to clarify something for Mr. Jackson. May I do so?"

"Yes, Mr. DiFong. You may," Judge Peabody said.

Turning to Luther Jackson, DiFong said, "Detective Loomis did not testify that Professor Wagner was ignorant of the earring. He testified that Professor Wagner only said he was ignorant of the earring, that he had never seen it before and had no idea of how it got in his office." Turning to me, DiFong said, "That is correct, is it not, Detective Loomis?"

"Yes, sir. It is. That's what Professor Wagner said," I said, glancing down at Chuck.

Walking from the jury over toward me, Luther Jackson said, "Detective Loomis, do you think that Professor Wagner was telling the truth when he said that? In other words, was he surprised when you explained the significance of the earring?"

"Yes, sir. He was. He was very surprised."

"I object, Your Honor. Detective Loomis knows only what Professor Wagner said. He has no way of knowing whether Professor Wagner was really and truly surprised or not," DiFong said.

"I'll re-phrase my question, Your Honor," Luther Jackson said.

Judge Peabody nodded.

"Detective Loomis," Luther Jackson said, "did you, and do you, think that Professor Wagner was telling the truth when you told him about the earring?"

"Yes, sir, I do. I thought it then and I think it now."

"That's your professional opinion?"

"It is."

"You have a good bit of experience in questioning suspects, do you not?" Luther Jackson asked.

"Yes, sir. I do. I haven't been a detective for long, but I've been a police officer for seven years."

"Would you say, then, that you've become pretty good, if not an expert, in being able to tell when a suspect is or is not telling the truth?"

"Yes, sir. I'd say that."

"And I believe you said that after taking four courses under Professor Wagner and having him as your faculty adviser that you'd gotten to know him pretty well and had no reason to question his integrity? You did say that, did you not?"

"Yes, sir. I said that."

"And of course, Detective Loomis, I don't need to remind you that you are a sworn police officer as well as a witness under oath to tell the truth, the whole truth, and nothing but the truth, irrespective of how you may or may not feel about the defendant?"

"No, sir. You don't need to remind me of that."

"I have no further questions, Your Honor," Luther Jackson said with a conclusive and very confident shaking of his head.

***

I hadn't seen or talked to David Allen since that day in his pastor's study back in January, but the little guy, except for being in a nicely cut gray suit this time, looked exactly as he had then—blond and delicate, almost pretty, and so troubled by his dilemma that he seemed close to trembling. He was DiFong's last witness, obviously his star, and the tension in the courtroom, already high, rose another notch.

After David had been sworn in, DiFong, with an altogether new gentleness in his voice and manner, asked questions that David answered in such a way as to make clear the he had been Chuck's student, literary protégé, and close friend.

"Mr. Allen, those three relationships that you say you had with Professor Wagner—are they all in the past? That is, did they all end when you graduated and left SUS?"

David shook his head. "No, sir. They didn't. Professor Wagner and I remain good friends."

"Being here in this courtroom, then, and seeing your close friend and former teacher and mentor accused of felony murder, and of course being a witness for the prosecution—all of this has to be very painful for you, Mr. Allen, does it not?" DiFong asked, his face a study of concern.

"Yes, sir. It is. It's extremely painful," David said, his nervous blue eyes closing for a moment as he nodded.

"I understand, Mr. Allen. Believe me. I understand," DiFong said, with a sympathetic, downright woeful shaking of his head.

After giving himself a moment to recover, DiFong said, "Mr. Allen, would you please tell the court if you know of anything Professor Wagner may have said, done, or perhaps have written, he being a professor and a writer, a novelist, that you think might bear on the murder of his colleague, Dr. Mildred Margulis?"

Looking as if he'd rather be in hell itself rather than where he now was, David said, "Yes, sir. I do. I'm afraid I do know of something."

"What might that be something be, Mr. Allen?"

"A scene in a novel that Professor Wagner was writing. It was on his computer and he let me read it."

"A scene in a novel he was writing?" DiFong repeated with a perplexed frown.

"Yes, sir. A murder scene. A murder scene similar to, if not identical to, what the media reported as happening to Professor Margulis."

The courtroom, as the cliché has it, emitted a collective gasp and I, in my aisle seat in the rear, felt my pulse quicken.

After a long moment, DiFong said, "Mr. Allen, would you please tell the court exactly what you mean when you say 'similar to if not identical to'? In other words, what are the specific parallels or similarities between the murder scene you read on Professor Wagner's computer and the real-life murder of Professor Margulis, at least as you know of that murder from the accounts of it in the media?"

David glanced in the direction of Chuck and Luther Jackson, then quickly looked away. Swallowing hard, he said, "In the scene I read the person who is murdered is a female English professor at a small university. The university is in Savannah and the professor is from the North and a feminist, a radical feminist."

"Was Dr. Margulis from the North and a radical feminist? Are those two of the parallels or similarities, Mr. Allen?"

"She was from Colorado, but, yes sir, she was a radical feminist."

"How do you know those things about her? They weren't in the media, were they?"

"No, sir, but I knew Professor Margulis. I had her for two classes when I was at SUS."

Nodding, DiFong said, "I see. Please go on."

"The media said that Professor Margulis was in her office, sitting at her desk, and was strangled. She was strangled from behind."

"And the radical feminist professor in the scene you read--is that what happened to her?"

"Yes, sir. It is. She was in her office one night, sitting at her desk, and was strangled from behind."

Again frowning, DiFong said, "Correct me if I'm wrong, Mr. Allen, but didn't you say that what happened in the scene you read on Professor's Wagner's computer and what the media reported as happening in reality to Professor Margulis were similar if not identical? Didn't you say that?"

"Yes, sir. I did."

"Why just 'similar?' I mean, from what you said, they didn't sound just similar. They sounded identical, completely identical."

David grimaced as he shook his head. "I said 'similar' because that's all they were, at least as far as I know. In the scene I read on Professor Wagner's computer, the professor, while she sat at her desk in her office, was strangled from behind with the ribbon on a medal she'd won in a race and the ribbon was hung around her neck, like an award. But in reality Dr. Margulis, again as far as I know, was..."

"Was the medal, the one in the scene you read, by any chance a bronze medal, Mr. Allen? A third-place bronze medal?" DiFong interrupted.

"Yes, sir. I think it was. I think it was a bronze medal."

"And the ribbon on it—was that ribbon by any chance purple?"

For a long moment David just stared at Difong. Then he said, "Yes, sir. It was. It was purple."

"Do you have any idea of how I know the ribbon was purple, Mr. Allen?"

"I would think it's because you've read the scene."

"Oh, yes. I've read the scene all right. I've read it on a disk, on a hardcopy, and, at least the crucial parts of it, on a fax sent to me by Professor Wagner's literary agent. Actually, though, I wasn't referring just to that medal, Mr. Allen, the one in Professor Wagner's novel. I got a little ahead of myself and I apologize for it, to the ladies and gentleman of the jury as well as to you," DiFong said with a frown and a prolonged, regretful shaking of his head.

With a waiting, perplexed look on his face, David stared at DiFong and the courtroom suddenly got so quiet I could hear, or thought I could hear, the way my heart was starting to hammer, even though I knew exactly what was coming.

Glancing at Judge Peabody, then turning to ensure that he had the complete attention of the jury, DiFong looked at David and said, "What I'm getting at, Mr. Allen, are some things about the actual murder scene, as opposed to the fictional murder scene, that you don't know about because they were withheld from the media. I think if you'd known these things, these specific details from the actual crime scene, I don't think you would've used the words 'similar to if not identical to' when you were comparing the two scenes. I think you would've used the same words I would've used and that I use now. Can you guess what those words are, Mr. Allen?"

His face reddening, David said, "Identical to?"

"Exactly, Mr. Allen. Identical to," DiFong said with a slow nod as the courtroom emitted another gasp. "Dr. Mildred Margulis was murdered in reality in the same exact way that the radical feminist English professor from the North was murdered in Professor Wagner's novel—strangled from behind, cruelly garroted with the purple ribbon on her own third-place bronze runner's medal while she sat at her desk in her office. The medal was then hung around her neck, as you said, like an award."

Pausing for a moment to let the gasp subside, DiFong said, "In point of fact, Mr. Allen, the two murders, the fictional and the real, weren't quite identical. In the novel the murdered professor's earrings, although dangly, are left in her ears, whereas, as you and the court know, the one in Dr. Margulis's right ear, in desecration of her body, was ripped out and taken as a souvenir. That earring, as you also know, is the very same earring that Detective Loomis testified that he found in Professor Wagner's office and that, along with its twin, I am again going to show you."

Going over to the evidence table, DiFong took the little clear plastic bag and, like Vanna White with a number card, held it up for David, then for the audience, then for the jury. "Here. In this bag. Behold the earring that was once in the warm, living ear of Dr. Mildred Margulis."

Replacing the bag on the table, DiFong walked back over the witness box and looked up at David.

"Mr. Allen, I have only one more question. It's a question, unless I'm badly mistaken, that the ladies and gentlemen of the jury have been wanting to ask almost from the start of your testimony."

"Yes, sir?" David said, waiting.

"The murder of Dr. Mildred Margulis occurred sometime between 8:30 and ten on Tuesday night, the 20th of January 2008. That has been clearly established, has it not?"

David nodded. "Yes, sir."

"Now, Mr. Allen, would please tell the jury when you read on Professor Wagner's computer the murder scene in his novel? Please be as accurate as you can about the time—that is, of the day, the hour, the month, and so forth."

Again looking as if he'd rather be in hell itself, David said, "I can't remember what day of the week it was, but it was when Professor Wagner was in class, which would have been in the morning, sometime in the morning. And it was during my junior year when I was taking him for American Literature I. That would've been in the fall of 2005."

"You're sure about the year, Mr. Allen? 2005?"

"Yes, sir. I am."

"So the murder of the radical feminist English professor in Professor Wagner's novel preceded, anticipated, prefigured--came before, in other words—the actual murder of Dr. Mildred Margulis by almost three years?"

"Yes, sir. It did. At least I read it almost three years before she was killed."

"Would you please repeat that, Mr. Allen?"

"What I just said or what you just said?"

"What you just said about the time line, that you read the murder scene in Professor Wagner's novel almost three years before Dr. Mildred Margulis was murdered."

Swallowing hard, David said, "I read the murder scene in Professor Wagner's novel almost three years before Dr. Mildred Margulis was murdered."

"Thank you, Mr. Allen. That's all I have, Your Honor," DiFong said with a very respectful nod toward Judge Peabody.

Chapter 14

Luther Jackson declined to cross-examine David Allen. If their mutterings were any indication, this surprised the rest of the spectators as much, at least at first, as it did me. I'd expected Luther, having no doubt been fully informed of it by Chuck, to dig into the "close friend" relationship that David said he still had with Chuck. With such tabloid-worthy dirt on the table, the jury, like the rest of the courtroom, probably would be inclined to reconsider David's testimony and maybe discount some or even a lot of it as the vengeful bitterness of the dumped lover.

But the more I thought about it the better I understood Luther's restraint. Although Chuck's account of the relationship differed markedly from David's and I believed Chuck rather than David, I nevertheless didn't doubt the truth of anything else David had revealed, first in the rectory study and then in the witness chair. Nor had I ever doubted the pain and Judas-like sense of betrayal that his coming forward had cost him and, sensitive soul that he was, most likely would continue to cost him even if Chuck were exonerated.

What I mean is that if I, as skeptical about such things as I generally am, could be convinced of David's sincerity as a witness against a man whom he obviously still cared deeply for, then there was a very good chance that the rest of the courtroom, the jury included, could too. Therefore Luther, apparently believing as I did, had curried favor with the jury by taking the moral high road and sparing David what, unless I'm badly mistaken, the entire court knew would've been a great deal more pain, none of it really necessary.

Luther's next move, however, didn't surprise me a bit.

He called to the witness chair three female professors in the SUS English Department, each of whom I knew from having taken a course under her. One was in her late twenties and the other two in their mid to late forties, but all three were white and all three were from the North, one from Detroit, one from Boston, and one, the young one, from somewhere in New Jersey. They also, as even an idiot soon could see, were seriously if not militantly liberal and feminist, the Bostonian in particular.

Their answers to Luther's questions about the South and SUS, although differing in detail, were for the most part identical in substance. All three continued to have mixed feelings about the South but had found more in it to like than not to like and had little or no desire to return to the North, unless maybe some school up there offered them not just a better job but a much better job than the one they had at SUS. Such an offer, the two older ones said, was not likely, the SUS English Department, all things considered, being a good place to work. Their students on the whole were no better or worse than those they'd taught in the North, Dr. Steve Harrison was a good Department Head, and most of their colleagues, in the department as well as elsewhere on campus, were almost always pleasant as well as supportive and collegial.

What Luther managed to get them to say about their late colleague, however, was even better and in fact almost as good as what he got out of them about Chuck.

They all said that Mildred Margulis had been a dedicated and fine, maybe even brilliant teacher and scholar, with fierce energy and very high and laudable social and political ideals; but, perhaps like many professionals of such rare gifts, she sometimes could be a bit overbearing and difficult to work with. On the other hand Chuck Wagner could hardly have been any easier or more pleasant not only to work with but just to be around. The two older professors said that he was always a perfect gentleman, never more so than when he and they were on opposite sides of heated departmental issues. The young one, with a little grin as she glanced down at Chuck, said that he "really was just a sweet old teddy bear."

In responding to the last question that Luther asked each of them, all three, though in different words, could hardly have been any clearer or more emphatic. They all said no, absolutely not, that they'd never personally seen or heard of any hostility or even unpleasantness on the part of Professor Wagner toward Dr. Mildred Margulis. Dr. Carr, the one from Detroit, went on to say that Chuck was perhaps the only member of the English Department of whom she could make such a statement.

Immediately after the last of these three, the young one from New Jersey, stepped down, Luther called another SUS English professor to the stand. In her mid to late thirties, this one was also a female from the North, but she wasn't white. She was black. I'd never had her for a class, but I'd seen her in Hampton Hall and knew that her name was Dr. Elyse Rainey and that her specialty was African–American literature. Tall and very athletic looking, obviously something of a fitness nut, she was in a beautifully fitting charcoal pants suit and reminded me, especially with her pretty face and unflappable poise, of Condolezza Rice.

After having her sworn in, Luther again used his white handkerchief to mop the sweat off his face, then said, "Professor Rainey, you've from the North, are you not?"

"I am. I was born and grew up in Dayton, Ohio."

"Did you go to college up there too?"

"Yes, I did. I went to the University of Dayton as an undergraduate and to Ohio State for my Ph.D."

"What about your teaching experience, your college teaching experience? Before you came down here, that is? Was it up in the North too?"

"Yes, except for two years at Mars Hill, in North Carolina, which was right before I came to SUS."

"When was that? When you came to SUS?"

"In the fall of 2007. This is just my second year."

"So you're still kind of the new kid on the block then, aren't you?" Luther said with a little grin.

"I suppose you could say that," Professor Rainey said with a little grin of her own.

His grin fading into a frown, Luther said, "Wouldn't I be more accurate, though, Professor Rainey, if I said that you're an outsider? Doubly an outsider in fact?"

"I'm not sure I know what you mean."

"Well, first of all, you're black, the only black in the SUS English Department. That is correct, is it not?"

"Yes, that's correct."

"Second, you're from the North, a Yankee, an outsider, one of only six—six before Professor Margulis was killed, that is---in a department of twenty-three. Of your seventeen other colleagues, one is from California, one is from Boston, one is from Vermont, and the other fifteen are from the South. In other words, you're a black, a Yankee black, a female Yankee black at that, in a department dominated, at least numerically, by white Southerners, most of them male. Is that correct or are my numbers amiss?"

"They're correct about race and gender. I don't know about the other."

"Where your colleagues came from, you mean?"

"Yes. I know about some but not all."

"Do you mean to tell me, Professor Rainey, that you, a black female professional from the North, took a job at a historically white university in the Deep South without researching the backgrounds of your prospective colleagues? Is that what you're telling the court?" Luther demanded, raising his voice and scowling as if in disbelief.

"Mr. Jackson," she said calmly, "I looked at the SUS catalog and at the SUS English Department website and saw where each of my prospective colleagues went to school and what his or her field of special expertise was. I also saw—I couldn't help but see—if they were male or female or black or white or whatever because their pictures were on the website. But where they were born and raised was not in the catalog or on the website and I didn't research them."

"Those things didn't matter to you? Is that what you're saying?"

"Essentially, yes."

"What do you mean 'essentially'?"

"As a matter of personal pride, Mr. Jackson, I try very hard not to let my judgment of people be influenced by their place of 'nativity and nurture,' as one of my professors used to put it. Or by their gender, race, age, or socioeconomic class either, for that matter."

"Do you always succeed?"

"No. I'm afraid I don't, but I have to say that in most cases it's because other people won't let me. That sounds self-righteous, I know, but it's true. There are just some people who won't let me be neutral."

"What about your colleagues in the SUS English Department? Will they let you be neutral about their 'nativity and nurture,' as your professor put it?"

"Most of the time they will, yes."

"But not all of the time?"

She smiled. "During baseball season, when the Red Sox are winning, Professor Flanagan, knowing I'm a Yankee fan, never lets me, or anyone else for that matter, forget that he was born and bred in Boston. 'Old Beantown' he calls it."

Luther returned her smile for a moment, then said, "But what about you? Do you ever give your white, mostly male Southern colleagues any reason for not judging you entirely, or at least as much as is humanly possible, on the quality of your character and work rather than in big or even small part on what color you are or where you were born and raised? On the things that make you an outsider, in other words?"

"I don't ask for or expect any special consideration, if that's what you mean."

"You may not ask for or expect any, but do you get any? Yes or no?"

"Yes. I think I get some. I'm not sure how much, though."

"You get it because you're a black and a female, twice a minority? Is that correct?"

"Maybe. Maybe not."

"What other reason there could there be, Professor? I don't understand," Luther said, again acting dumbfounded.

"I'm still new in the department, Mr. Jackson, still 'kind of the new kid on the block,' as you put it, and my colleagues on the whole are very nice people. They want me to feel included and welcome," she said as if to a very dense student.

"So what have they done, Professor? The court would like to hear just exactly what these all white and mostly Southern colleagues have done to make you feel, as you put it, 'included and welcome'?" Luther asked, acting skeptical now rather than dumbfounded.

"A variety of things. They helped me move into my office. They invited me out, and continue to invite me out, to lunch and for coffee or drinks. I've been given my choice of committee assignments. Dr. Harrison had a little reception for me when I first came here. One colleague, when I was looking for somewhere to live, spent two entire days helping me find something. He drove me all over town and showed me where he shops for groceries and takes his laundry and gets his car serviced, things like that. In every way he was just as thoughtful and as welcoming and gracious as anyone could be. I don't know what I would've done without him."

"I don't suppose this 'welcoming and gracious' colleague is by any chance in this courtroom today, is he?" Luther asked, still seeming skeptical.

"He's right over there," Professor Rainey said, looking behind Luther as she raised her right hand and pointed with her index finger.

Slowly, dramatically turning and with his own eyes following her eyes and the aim of her finger over to Chuck, Luther said, "The defendant? My client? You mean to tell us that this Southern male, Professor C. Clarkson Wagner, went so far out of his way—spent two whole days in fact—to help you, a black female Yankee newcomer, find a place to live and get settled? And was so welcoming and gracious about it? Is that what you're saying, Professor?"

"Yes. That's what I'm saying," she said with a quick nod. "And I'd like to add, for what it may be worth, that in the entire time I've been at SUS, a little over two years, Professor Wagner has never been anything but welcoming and gracious to me. He's a gentleman. He's one of my best friends in the department."

Pausing for a very long moment to let her point take root, Luther wiped his brow yet again, then said, "These best friends that you have in the SUS English Department, Professor Rainey—was Professor Mildred Margulis ever one of them?"

"At one time she was, yes. At least I thought she was."

"When was that, Professor?"

"The first several months I was here, at SUS."

"You say 'thought she was'. Do you mean that you and Professor Margulis got off to a good start as friends then had a falling out?"

"Yes."

"This falling out—what was it about?"

"Politics. Department politics, mostly."

"You mean personality clashes, power struggles, turf battles? Stuff like that?"

She nodded. "Yes. Stuff like that."

Shaking his head and again looking dumbfounded, but this time apologetically so, Luther said, "I'm sorry to be so naïve or maybe just plain ignorant, Professor, but I've always been under the impression that you college professors were just too educated and high-minded for all that petty, ego stuff. But y'all aren't? Is that what you're saying?"

"Yes, Mr. Jackson, it is. Unfortunately, that's what I'm saying."

Luther nodded in a way that made me think of an old computer struggling to process a long document, then said, "So you and Professor Margulis, after a good start as friends, had a falling out over something in your department, some issue? Some professional issue? Is that correct?"

"Yes, but the issue wasn't entirely professional. Some of it, maybe a great deal of it, was personal. At least it seemed that way to me."

"What was it, Professor? Tell us what it was. Tell us. Please," Luther said, moving a step closer to her and looking eager to hear.

"I think the essence of it is that Professor Margulis assumed certain things about me because I was a black female from the North and a specialist in African-American literature. She had in her mind a rigid preconception of me, a stereotype in other words, and assumed that she could automatically count on me to support her on all departmental issues."

"But you surprised her? Is that what you're saying?"

"Yes, on one such issue I surprised her and betrayed her. That was the way she saw it."

"What kind of departmental issue could you be talking about, Professor? I mean, it must've been really serious if Professor Margulis could feel not just surprised but betrayed by the way you voted on it," Luther said.

"It was a serious issue. It was the women's studies program that Professor Margulis was pushing—that is, trying to develop and put in place at SUS."

"'Women's studies,' you say? I'm not sure I know what you mean by 'women's studies,'" Luther said, again giving her a look of deep perplexity.

"Women's studies, Mr. Jackson, is a curriculum that focuses on and highlights the roles that women have played in, and the contributions that they have made to, all fields of human endeavor but mainly literature, history, and the social sciences," Professor Rainey said as carefully as if to students taking notes.

"I see," Luther said with a nod. "And Professor Margulis wanted SUS to have a women's studies program?"

"Yes, she did. She was ready to take her proposal to the university curriculum committee, which is a committee that decides what courses and programs the university can offer. But before she could do that, she had to have the support of her own department, the English Department. In a special meeting she put the proposal before us, we discussed it, and then we voted on it."

"Did it pass?"

"Yes, it did. Twenty-three to two."

"You, I assume, were one of the two?"

"I was."

Luther looked at her for a very long moment, then shook his head and said, "Once again I hate to seem so naïve about such things, Professor, but I was under the impression that the kind of voting you're talking about, really serious voting, was always done anonymously, like political voting, with secret ballots and all."

"We voted anonymously that day. We always vote anonymously on such matters."

"How, then, did Professor Margulis know that you voted against her? That you betrayed her?"

"I spoke out during the discussion."

"Against her proposal, obviously?"

"Yes. I was opposed to it."

"Are you a feminist, Professor Rainey?"

"Yes, I am, if by feminist you mean a person who advocates and works for the empowerment of women to the point of equality with men."

"How could you then, as a feminist, oppose a women's studies program? I don't understand," Luther said, giving her another look of bewilderment.

"I believe, Mr. Jackson, that if women are ever going to be able to compete successfully with men, especially in the workplace, then they need to study the same things that men study—math, science, medicine, law, economics, history in general, not mainly female history. Ask successful women, any women with real power, from CEO's to lawyers to high-ranking military officers, what their major was in college and I can all but guarantee you they won't say women's studies."

"Did you say these things to Professor Margulis?" Luther asked.

"Yes, I did. I said them to the entire department during our discussion, right before we voted."

"Did she respond?"

"Not then, no. She knew she didn't need to, the department at that point having made its support obvious, close to unanimous."

"What about after the meeting?"

"She got in my face and said I was a traitor, that I had betrayed her, our gender, the whole women's movement. From then on—and that was over a year ago-- she never said another word to me except strictly in the line of duty, when she had no choice."

"All because you didn't think her way was the best way to reach a goal that both of you, as feminists, were committed to reaching?" Luther asked, seeming more perplexed than ever.

"Yes. That's why I said earlier that the issue that ended our friendship wasn't entirely professional, that much of it was purely personal."

"Professor, once again I have to apologize for being so naïve or maybe just plain dumb about these things, but I understood that diversity—all kinds of diversity, racial, religious, ethnic, sexual, political, cultural, you name it— was a kind of Holy Gospel in colleges and universities these days. And I understood also that the main preachers of it, the Apostle Pauls of it, so to speak, were liberal professors, especially in areas like English and history and sociology. Was I wrong?"

"No. Not in general. Diversity, or at least lip service to it, has indeed become, as you put it, 'a kind of Holy Gospel' in contemporary academe."

Frowning, Luther said, "'Lip service'? You mean there are professors who preach one thing and do another? That they're hypocrites? Is that what you're saying?"

DiFong had begun glaring at Luther and rolling his eyes right after Dr. Rainey spoke so well of Chuck, but I'd hoped—and I think the rest of the audience had too—that he wouldn't object until she'd more or less finished her revelations about the SUS English Department, which for most of us were an altogether new and fascinating kind of dirty laundry. But he didn't.

"Your Honor," he said, reminding me of a fat little jack-in-the-box in the way he sprang up from his chair, "Mr. Jackson is once again, in flagrant defiance of your explicit instructions, indulging in a line of questioning that is completely and totally irrelevant. A woman was murdered, Your Honor, strangled to death in her own office, and nothing she could have said or done to or against her colleagues, personally or professionally, could ever, ever, ever excuse or justify that. I repeat, Your Honor. Nothing."

Again peering over his half-lens glasses down at Luther, Judge Peabody said, "Mr. Jackson, I'm inclined to sustain Mr. DiFong's objection, but before I do, I'm going to give you a chance to connect your dots, if you can."

"Thank you, You Honor," Luther said respectfully. "What I've been trying to do with all of my four witnesses so far, but particularly with Dr. Rainey, is to show three things. First of all, that the SUS English Department, which consists mostly of Southerners, white male Southerners at that, is not at all hostile to newcomers, outsiders, Yankees-- call them what you will--on any kind of per se basis. On the contrary, my four witnesses, Dr. Rainey with specific examples, indicate exactly the opposite—that the SUS English Department is in fact a very welcoming and inclusive workplace."

Pausing for a moment and again wiping his sweaty forehead, Luther said, "Second, I'm attempting to show— and I think I have in fact shown—not just with my witnesses but with Mr. DiFong's as well, that my client, Professor C. Clarkson Wagner, has never been other than professional and gentlemanly in his interactions with all of his colleagues, including so-called outsiders such as Professor Margulis. None of these witnesses, not even Mr. DiFong's hostile witnesses, I beg to remind Your Honor, has ever observed or even heard of any unpleasantness, let alone any hostility, on the part of my client toward Professor Margulis. On the contrary for this too. Professor Margulis herself, according to her own daughter, said that Professor Wagner was never other than professional and polite in all of his dealing with her. Her daughter told us this, Your Honor. Her very own daughter."

Again pausing, this time not to use his handkerchief but to let his point sink in, Luther said, "Your Honor, my third point takes us back to that 'beam and the mote' business Mr. DiFong enlightened us about earlier when he was talking about one of my defendant's novels. I'm sure the court remembers. It's what Jesus said about hypocrites being able to see the little bitty speck in somebody else's eye but not the big old log in their own."

"Yes, Mr. Jackson, I remember," Judge Peabody said.

"Well, Your Honor, the testimony we've had from Professor Rainey more than suggests—it clearly indicates that it was not the SUS English Department in general, and certainly not my client in particular, who is, or was, resistant to, if not downright set against, personal and professional differences—who was against diversity, in other words. It was Professor Margulis."

Looking as if he simply could not believe such low tactics, DiFong angrily shook his head and said, "Your Honor, Mr. Jackson is again implying, this time very strongly, that Mildred Margulis, in having the very life so cruelly choked out of her, got no less than she deserved. That she deserved to die, to be murdered."

Turning to DiFong, Luther was about to respond, but Judge Peabody said, "Mr. Jackson, I'm going to sustain Mr. DiFong's objection. Professor Margulis's personality, no matter what it was, has never been the concern of this court."

After glancing at the jury, Luther nodded respectfully at Judge Peabody and said, "I understand, Your Honor, and I beg the court's pardon."

After another wiping of his glistening forehead, Luther turned back to his witness and said, "Professor Rainey, you said that your department voted twenty-three to two in favor of Professor's Margulis's proposal for a women's studies program. Is that correct?"

"Yes, it is."

"Did your department head, Dr. Steven Harrison, vote on it?"

She nodded. "He did."

"Did he vote against it?"

"No, he didn't. He voted for it."

"How do you know that? Did he speak in favor of it during the discussion or what?"

"No. In our discussion of proposals it's Dr. Harrison's policy to limit his role to that of the moderator. He doesn't want to risk letting his authority influence us. He does vote, though, as I said."

"How then do you know that he voted in favor of Professor Margulis's proposal?" Luther asked, again pretending to be confused. "I mean, you said the voting was anonymous, didn't you?"

"Yes, it was anonymous. It's always anonymous. I know how Dr. Harrison voted because I know who, aside from myself, voted against it, the one other person."

"How do you know that?"

"Because he joined me in speaking out against it during our discussion."

"Joined you, you say?"

"Yes. And afterwards he made a little joke about it."

"What kind of joke?"

Professor Rainey permitted herself a little grin. "He said he'd never before made common cause with a Yankee fan but he supposed there's a first time for everything."

"That sounds like...What was his name? That colleague you said was such a big Red Sox fan?" Luther asked with a frown.

"Flanagan. Professor Jack Flanagan."

"Yes, Professor Flanagan. And you say he was the other one---the only other one aside from yourself—who voted against Professor Margulis's program? Is that correct?"

"Yes. That's correct."

"Are you sure now, absolutely sure, that it was not the defendant, Professor Wagner, who voted against Professor Margulis's program? Absolutely sure?"

Dr. Rainey nodded. "Yes, I am. I'm absolutely sure. During our discussion Professor Wagner spoke in favor of it, but when the meeting was over and we were in his office talking, he told me that after hearing my argument he probably would've voted with me if he hadn't already promised his support to Professor Margulis."

"Professor C. Clarkson Wagner promised his support to Professor Margulis," Luther said very slowly, glancing at the jury, then turning toward DiFong and with a perceptibly triumphant little grin saying, "Mr. DiFong, I'm sure you have a few questions for my witness, do you not?"

Returning Luther's grin with another of his glares, DiFong said, "No, Mr. Jackson, I don't. I have no questions for your witness."

I don't think this surprised anyone in the courtroom. Certainly it didn't surprise me. Professor Rainey had been as good a witness as I could imagine, far too solid a rock of conviction and good sense for DiFong to attack, perhaps also in part, maybe in big part, because he was a white man and she was a black woman. This subtle playing of the race and gender card, if that's what it really was, may or may not have been one of Luther's tactics—I tend to think that it was—but if I'd been in his place it most definitely would've been one of mine.

***

The next morning Luther called Dr. Steve Harrison to the stand. Chuck's unvarying congeniality, along of course with Mildred Margulis's almost equally unvarying fractiousness, having been well established by this point, I had no idea of how Luther could use Dr. Harrison to add any further to Chuck's defense.

As Dr. Harrison was being sworn in, I was at first struck by how different he and Luther looked. Dr. Harrison was in his fifties, white, and had a full head of hair whereas Luther was in his thirties, black, and almost bald. Furthermore, their suits, although both were navy blue, were otherwise as different as could be, Luther's looking slept in and Dr. Harrison's looking new or just back from the cleaners.

Eventually, though, I was struck even more by their similarities. Both men were grossly, morbidly overweight but still handsome in the face, or close to it. Each had a soft voice that carried well, and each had a look of patience and gentleness, or maybe it was just fatigue, in and around the eyes. What struck me most of all was that Dr. Harrison seemed every bit Luther's equal, if not his superior, in the amount of sweat that glistened on his forehead, coursed down his cheeks, and kept him mopping with his handkerchief.

After situating his bulk in the witness chair, Dr. Harrison began surveying the audience, his head oscillating like a fan as his gentle gray eyes moved over person after person until they finally found and fixed on frail little Mahalia, who on that day was sitting three seats over from me. The way he looked at her and returned her smile and nod reminded me of a little boy in a school play who knows he need not panic now that he's seen his mother.

"Dr. Harrison," Luther said as he approached the chair, "in addition to being a professor and the head of the English Department at SUS, you're a poet too, are you not?"

Dr. Harrison nodded. "Yes, I am."

"How many poems have you published?"

"I'm not exactly sure. Five–hundred, maybe more."

Putting on a look of awe, Luther said, "Five-hundred poems! You've published five-hundred poems? Why, that's more than Shakespeare!"

"In the number of individual poems, yes, it is, but not in the number of lines if you include the plays."

"Are your poems as good as his, do you think?"

"No. Of course not. They're not even close."

"How do you know?"

"I've been a serious reader for most of my life and a serious student of literature, in my efforts to teach it as well as to write it, for over thirty years. I've written two widely respected textbooks on poetry. I've also been the editor of three different literary magazines and I currently am a consultant for two more," Dr. Harrison said, his voice low and mellow but still very audible.

Luther thought for a moment, then said, "I guess when you read a novel or a poem or something like that you can see a lot of things the rest of us can't see, symbols and things that don't mean what they look like they mean?"

"I'm a reasonably perceptive reader," Dr. Harrison said.

"I understand that you and Professor Wagner regularly get together and talk about y'all's writing and try to help each other with it? Is that correct?"

"Yes. We've been each other's critic and sounding board for thirteen years, for almost as long as I've been at SUS."

"So you've read Professor Wagner's novels? His unpublished novels?"

"Not all of them, no. I haven't read his mystery novel, 'Murder in Savannah'."

"But you've read the other ones?"

"Yes. The other five."

"Including 'Matters of Vision'?"

"Yes. I've read 'Matters of Vision'."

"Mr. DiFong had one of his witnesses, a SUS history professor, Dr. James Cox, tell us about it. He said it was about a young, white English professor from the North, from Harvard, who comes down to Alabama to teach in a little college and gets his eyes opened when he runs up against a lot of Southerners who don't like his notions about the South. He said the novel's mainly an attack on Northerners, on self-righteous Yankees, who come down South and try to change things. Would you agree with Dr. Cox that that's what it's about?"

"Yes, I would, because it is about that, but that's not all it's about. Far from it," Dr. Harrison said, frowning as he shook his head one brisk, emphatic time. "The narrator of the novel..."

"Dr. Cox said that he's the author's mouthpiece," Luther cut in. "He said that the narrator's view of things, his opinions and all, are a close reflection of Professor Wagner's? Are they? I mean, as well as you know Professor Wagner, you should be able to tell us."

"I can and I will," Dr. Harrison said with an impatient little wave of his hand. "But first let me get back to what I was going to say about what the novel is about."

"Yes, of course. Please do," Luther said.

"The narrator of the novel, the Southern professor, is the key. He's intelligent and highly educated but extremely full of himself. He's capable of a great deal of clarity and insight when it comes to seeing other people but of very little, if any, when it comes to seeing himself. This is most evident when he's fretting and fuming about the shortcomings of the young professor and of the North. He doesn't know it, but he's revealing the same or even worse things about himself and the South. He doesn't know he's doing this, I repeat, but the reader does, and this of course is the great irony of the novel and the reason for the title and the subtitle. They refer much more to the narrator's skewed vision, to the beam in his own eye, than to what the young professor from the North can or cannot see," Dr. Harrison said with a slight shrug as he used his handkerchief on his forehead and, again as if for reassurance, looked at Mahalia.

From where I sat I couldn't tell about his breathing, but I feared that if it wasn't yet labored, it soon would be. I mean, if he could come close to gasping just from teaching a class or talking with me in his office, then he might well lose his breath altogether from being a witness in the murder trial of such a close friend as Chuck was.

Again looking puzzled, Luther said, "So what you're saying, Professor Harrison, is that Dr. Cox didn't understand the narrator of 'Matters of Vision' and therefore didn't see that the novel is really a lot more critical of the South than of the North? That is what you said, is it not? In effect?"

"Yes, it is. In effect," Dr. Harrison said.

With a look of infinite disgust on his face, DiFong rose from his chair and said, "Your Honor, we're not talking about a problem in addition or subtraction here, where there's only one right answer. We're talking about a novel. We're talking about an entity as subjective as one of those Rorschach ink blots psychologists use. We're talking about something in which no two people are ever going to see the same things."

Judge Peabody, again peering over his half-lens glasses, turned from DiFong to Luther and said, "Mr. DiFong's point is well-taken, Mr. Jackson. How a reader interprets a piece of imaginative writing such as a novel is indeed a highly subjective matter. So I must ask you why you would have the court believe that Dr. Harrison's reading of the defendant's novel is the right one and that Dr. Cox's is the wrong one. No, Dr. Cox is not a poet or an English professor, but he is a highly educated, highly literate man."

"Oh, there can be no doubt of that Your Honor!" Luther said quickly. "Dr. Cox is truly a highly educated and highly literate man. We've had ample, abundant evidence of that. But he's a professor of history, Your Honor, a scholar, and as the reader of a novel he might..."

"May I speak to that, Your Honor, Mr. Jackson?" Dr. Harrison said, raising his right hand several inches off his knee and waving it.

Luther stared at Dr. Harrison for a moment, then turned to Judge Peabody and said, "May he, Your Honor?"

"Yes, Mr. Jackson, your client may 'speak to that'," Judge Peabody said, obviously amused by the phrasing.

Wiping his forehead as he took a deep breath, Dr. Harrison glanced yet again at Mahalia, then said, "Dr. Cox, in failing to see the self-damning irony in the narrator of 'Matters of Vision', is in some pretty good company. Five literary agents, four in New York and one in Chicago, read the novel pretty much as he did—as a defense of the South and an attack on Northerners who come South in hopes of making changes, humane and long overdue changes, especially in race relations. All five of the agents liked the novel's evocation of time and place, most of its characters, and the high quality of the writing itself. But they all rejected it, and for the same reason. They said the narrator was totally unsympathetic, a hidebound Southern chauvinist of the worst kind. They said that no reputable publisher would even look at such a novel, and one of them was personally offended and took Professor Wagner to task for even sending it to her."

"How do you know all this, Dr. Harrison? Did Professor Wagner tell you about it or what?" Luther asked.

"He did more than tell me. He showed me. He showed me the agents' letters."

"What was his reaction? To the letters, I mean. He wasn't happy, I'm sure."

"No, he wasn't. No writer is ever happy with rejection. But it wasn't just, or even mainly, I don't think, the rejection in and of itself that make him so unhappy, that in fact hurt him very deeply. It was the reason for the rejection. He'd worked so hard on his narrator and on the irony, as I said before, that the more the old Southern professor railed about the shortcomings of the young professor and of the North, the more he revealed similar or even worse things about himself and the South."

"So what you've saying, Dr. Harrison, is that Professor Wagner, in 'Matters of Vision', tried very hard to write a novel, and thought he had in fact written a novel, that was, shall we say, politically correct in its intentions? Is that what you're saying?" Luther asked.

"Yes, because I myself have no doubt that that's what he did. 'Matters of Vision' is indeed politically correct in its good intentions, but it takes a perceptive reader to see that."

Pausing as he took two short, obviously labored breaths, Dr. Harrison said, "It takes a perceptive reader to see that about the novel just as, I might add, it takes a perceptive person to see the same kind of sensibility in Professor Wagner. In other words, both the novel and the man who wrote it have a depth of gentleness, humanity, and abiding good will that, unfortunately, not everyone can see and appreciate."

Nodding, Luther said, "I think you just answered the question I asked you earlier and that you said you'd get back to."

"What question was that?"

"I asked you if you could tell us, knowing Professor Wagner as well as you do, if his narrator is a close reflection of him, kind of an alter ego, so to speak, as Dr. Cox thinks is the case."

Giving Luther a searching look, Dr. Harrison said, "I think that what you're asking is if I think Professor Wagner's personal views on the North and the South and so on are the same as, or at least very similar to, those of his narrator."

"Yes. That's exactly what I'm asking," Luther said with a pleased nod. "Do you think they are?"

"I don't have to think, Mr. Jackson, because I know. I know beyond any doubt whatsoever that the personal views of the narrator in 'Matters of Vision' are by no means even close to those of his creator, Professor Wagner. Of that I am certain, absolutely certain," Dr. Harrison said with such grimness that his jowls quivered.

Nodding, his eyes lingering on his witness, Luther thought for a moment, then said, "What you just said, Dr. Harrison, makes me wonder about something else."

"What's that?"

"Professor Wagner's apparent interest in very conservative to radical right wing politics. I'm referring to some of the bookmarked websites on his office computer and, also in his office, to a book advocating another secession of the South from the union. I mean, if Professor Wagner is at heart as much of a liberal as you say he is, then why would he be looking at such stuff?"

With a slight shrug, Dr. Harrison said, "Professor Wagner is a long-time student of the American scene, both as a novelist and as a professor with a specialty in American literature. Obviously he needs to stay abreast of what's going on in this country, the bad as well as the good."

"But he's not a right-winger himself or even a crypto right winger or fellow traveler? Is that what you're saying? What you're sure of?"

"Yes, it is. That's what I'm sure of. That's what I am absolutely sure of," Dr. Harrison said, nodding solemnly as he glanced at the jury and then at Mahalia.

Luther had no more questions and DiFong again declined to cross-examine, so Dr. Harrison stepped down. By then, even though the courtroom was closer to chilly than to warm, he was sweating profusely, even more than Luther was, and he looked in much pain as he limped away from the stand, his bad knee or worse back or maybe both apparently undergoing a flare-up from his having had to sit for so long.

Even sadder was that after he took three or four steps his breathing became more than merely labored. It became so hard that I could see, even from where I sat, the look of absolute terror that a man gets in his eyes when he can't catch his breath.

Somehow, though, he managed to catch it, or at least enough of it to look over at Chuck as he passed the table where Chuck was sitting. From my seat in the rear I couldn't see Chuck's face, but the back of his neck and head looked confident and I have an idea that he gave Dr. Harrison the same kind of grin that he'd given me when I'd stepped down. It was the wryly amused old Chuck-grin from our many chats in his office except that there now was something almost cocky about it. This of course had made me wonder even more than I had earlier about how a man on trial for his life could in general look so upbeat if not downright flippant.

***

By the time the bailiff closed the doors behind Dr. Harrison I was somewhat less baffled by Chuck's cockiness, if that's what it was. Shortly before Luther had finished with the three white female professors from the North and begun on the black one, Dr. Rainey, I'd begun to sense in my gut something that should've reached my brain a lot earlier but hadn't. I saw that the mood of the courtroom had undergone another shift, this time in Chuck's favor. There were no oohs and ahhs or collective gasps or anything like that, but I could see, or surely thought I could see, distinct changes in the faces of the people sitting near me and in those of the jury—a new intentness maybe or a softening in the eyes or around the mouth, something, I can't say exactly what.

If I needed any proof that this was not just wishful thinking on my part, I had only to look at DiFong as he sat at his table and alternated between glaring daggers at Luther and scribbling furiously on a legal pad. Borrowing from Hamlet, I gloated to myself, "Desperation, thy name is DiFong."

Despite this seeming shift in Chuck's favor, however, I was getting a little tired of lecture-like testimonies from witnesses so much enamored of their own voices, so I was relieved--as well as very curious--to see that Luther's next witness was not another SUS professor. He was a geek from The Geek Shop, the little computer repair place for which Mahalia Harrison did special jobs and where, early in the investigation, I'd gone to enquire about her.

In appearance Ethan Anderson wasn't the neat-freak, nerdy kind of computer geek who carried his pens in a plastic pocket protector. On the contrary, he was a studiously grungey, in-your-face slob. In his mid-twenties, he was short, pasty-faced, pony-tailed, and, although slight of build, so pudgy as to look downright mushy. Beneath his wrinkled old brown suit coat was a new-looking black Widespread Panic t-shirt, and hanging above his scuffed, once-white Reeboks was a pair of baggy khaki pants cluttered with loops, flaps, and pockets. He had a ruby stud in his left ear and a screw-top bottle of water in the pocket beside his right knee.

Once he opened his mouth, though, I forgot—and I think the rest of the courtroom did too—all about his looks. His voice wasn't strong, but everything else—his delivery, his poise, his knowledge of his subject—seemed every bit as good as that of any of the professors who'd preceded him. So much for looks, I again reminded myself.

After having him identify himself and his line of work, Luther said, "Mr. Anderson, when it comes to your area of professional expertise, I'm not a complete idiot, but I'm close. I can type, surf the net, and do email, but that's about it. And I doubt if I'm the only one here today in such a fix." He grinned at the jury and several of the older members grinned back and nodded. "So, I'm going to have to ask you to be patient with me and not to get any more technical, with special computer terms and all, than you have to. Use as much simple layman's language as you can, in other words."

"I'll do my best," Ethan said with a slight nod.

"Mr. Anderson, you've examined the contents of the computer in Professor Wagner's office out at SUS, have you not?"

"No, sir. Not all of the contents. Just the items you specified."

"What were those items? Please refresh me."

"You wanted me to look at the email, saved and deleted, and at the website favorites, which are the website addresses that are saved for quick access."

"Yes, I remember now," Luther said, nodding and trying to look as if he had indeed forgotten. "Start with the email. I believe I asked you to find out if Professor Wagner had ever received any email from any kind of political organization, including any kind of extremist fringe group. That is what I specified, isn't it?"

"It is."

"And were you able to do it?"

"Yes, sir. I was."

"Even items that had been deleted? I thought that when you hit Delete you completely and irrevocably erased the item. That's not what happens?"

"No, sir. Not the first time you hit Delete. That merely moves the item from what I'll call the 'saved active file'–that's the file that shows up whenever you open your email—and puts the item in what I'll call the 'saved inactive file', which is where it will stay until you delete it from there too."

"How do you do that? Just hit Delete again or what?"

"No, sir. It requires more than that. You first have to access the inactive saved file, which you do by pointing to Deleted Items and clicking your mouse. Then you scroll down to the item you want and hit Delete again. That'll give you a yes-or-no popup asking if you want to completely delete the item. If you do, you point to Yes and click. If you don't, you point to No and click."

"So it's basically a five-step procedure to get rid of an email altogether?"

"Yes, sir, it is. It's basically a five-step procedure."

"That is totally new to me, Mr. Anderson. I had no idea that an inactive saved file even existed. Now that you mention it, though, I do remember seeing a Deleted Items on my screen, but I didn't think anything about it. I mean, I always thought that when you hit Delete, that was it, that the item was gone, completely erased. I guess I'm even more of a computer idiot that I thought I was," Luther said with a self-deprecating little grin.

With an indulgent but slightly smug little grin of his own, Ethan said, "If you are, Mr. Jackson, you're far from alone. I'd say that well over half of my clients, even though they've been using a computer for years, don't know any more than you do about deleting."

"Are you serious? That many?"

"Yes, sir. I'm serious. That many. At least that many."

Continuing to shake his head, Luther said, "But back to Professor Wagner's email. In what you call the 'active saved file', did you find any items that you knew, or maybe just thought, were of a political nature?"

"No, sir, I didn't."

"None at all?"

"No, sir. None at all."

"What about in the Deleted Items, the 'saved inactive file'? Did you find any there?"

"I'm not sure how political it is, but I found one from The Sons of Confederate Veterans, about the renewal of Professor Wagner's membership."

"That's all? Just one? Are you sure you looked thoroughly? Really thoroughly?" Luther asked, his forehead very much in need of his handkerchief.

With another smug little grin, Ethan said, "Mr. Jackson, if you'll look closely at the invoice I'm going to send you, you'll see that I spent six hours and forty-five minutes just on Professor Wagner's email."

"Six hours and forty-five minutes! Just on his email?" Luther said, aghast.

"Yes, sir. Three or four minutes on the active file, which had twelve items on it, and the rest on the inactive file, the Deleted Items file, which had approximately 16,000 items on it."

Luther's jaw didn't literally drop but he gawked as if in utter disbelief at his witness.

"Actually, Mr. Jackson, that number of saved emails isn't all that unusual," Ethan said after a moment. "Most people—if they know about the Deleted Items file, that is—periodically go through it and get rid of spam and other items they don't think they'll ever need. But if they don't know about Deleted Items, then every single email they've ever received, starting with the very first one, will be stored. Professor Wagner's first one is an ad for fake Rolex watches, from back in August of 1996, which is probably when his computer was first installed. It's a Hewlett-Packard Model 603, which was new then but is pretty much of a museum piece now."

"Let me see if I understand you, Mr. Anderson," Luther said, wiping his forehead for at least the fiftieth time. "You're saying that the computer in Professor Wagner's office had approximately 16,000 emails on it and that the first one, about the fake Rolexes, dates back to August of 2000, about eight years ago. Is that correct?"

"Yes, sir. That's correct."

"And you also said that it's not really all that unusual for a computer to have so many emails in what you call the 'inactive file'?"

"No, sir, it's not. In fact, it's often the case with people who have relatively old computers and don't know about Deleted Items."

Looking up at Judge Peabody, Luther said, "I know that Mr. DiFong's going to object to this question, Your Honor, but I'm going to ask it anyway and I hope you'll let Mr. Anderson answer it because it's very important."

"Ask it and we'll see, Mr. Jackson," Judge Peabody said.

Turing back to Ethan, Luther said, "Mr. Anderson, in the case of Professor Wagner, do you think that he knows, or knew, about the Deleted Items option on his computer?"

"Oh, I do object, Your Honor! I object most strenuously," DiFong said, springing up from his chair but with maybe a little less vigor this time. "Mr. Anderson has no way of knowing if Professor Wagner knows or knew about Deleted Items or not. Anything he could say about this would be pure speculation, pure conjecture. Furthermore, Mr. Jackson has again drifted off into utter irrelevance in questioning a witness. Whether Professor Wagner's computer has 50,000 or 16,000 undeleted emails on it, or only one, it has no bearing whatsoever on the murder, the cold blooded murder, of Dr. Mildred Margulis. None whatsoever!"

Peering over his half-lenses down at Luther, Judge Peabody said, "We need to hear what you have to say about this, Mr. Jackson."

"I have several things to say about it, Your Honor," Luther said, with a brisk nod. "First of all, I want to 'connect my dots', as Your Honor so nicely put it a little while ago. My client has been charged with a hate crime, and Mr. DiFong has time and again attempted to connect that charge with some very conservative and far right wing political groups that my client has shown a more than passing interest in—if, that is, we are to judge from a novel he wrote and a book he read as well as from twelve websites bookmarked on his computer. So, in having Mr. Anderson go through Professor Wagner's computer, I'm attempting to show that although Professor Wagner may have received a great deal of snail mail from these groups, he did not receive, not in over six years, mind you, a single item, not one single, solitary item of email from any of them, unless of course you consider one from the Sons of Confederate Veterans, which I don't."

"We don't know that, Your Honor," DiFong said, still standing and frowning furiously. "Professor Wagner could well have deleted everything he got from those groups the minute after he read it."

"Which brings me to my second point, Your Honor," Luther said, seeming to ignore DiFong. "When I asked Mr. Anderson if he thought Professor Wagner knows, or knew, about the Deleted Items on his computer, I was asking for an opinion, a professional opinion, based on what he knows from his work with computers in general and from what he found and didn't find on Professor Wagner's. And I'll ask that question again, with Your Honor's permission."

"You may ask it, Mr. Jackson," Judge Peabody said.

"Thank you, Your Honor," Luther said before turning to Ethan and saying, "Is it your opinion, Mr. Andrews, your professional opinion, that Professor Wagner happens to have eight years' worth of emails on his computer, 16,000 of them, only because, being ignorant of the Deleted Items option, he thought he'd deleted them completely and permanently when he'd pushed the regular Delete button?"

"Yes, sir, it is. I can't think of any other reason why someone would have such a huge file, most of it pure spam."

Nodding slowly, Luther looked from Ethan over to DiFong, then to the jury, then back to Judge Peabody.

"There's another point I'd like make, Your Honor," he said.

Judge Peabody nodded. "Go ahead."

"Let's say, just as something to think about," Luther said, wiping his forehead again, "that Professor Wagner did two things that the facts strongly suggest, if they don't conclusively prove, that he didn't do. The first is that he knew all about the Deleted Items option. The second is that he regularly received email from the Aryan Nation and the eleven other hate or fringe groups but was always careful to delete it completely and permanently right after he'd read it, as Mr. DiFong thinks could well be the case. If we accept these two possibilities, then we have no choice but to ask this question: If Professor Wagner took the time to delete all of the email from these hate groups, why didn't he also take the time to delete the groups themselves from his Favorites?"

Turning back to Ethan, Luther said, "What about you, Mr. Anderson. Do you know the answer to that question?"

"No, sir, I don't know, but I can give you my opinion if you want that," Ethan said, pulling out his water bottle, unscrewing the cap, and taking a swig.

"Yes, I do. I surely do want your opinion, Mr. Anderson, your professional opinion, and I'm sure the rest of the court does too," Luther said, eyeing the water and looking as if he himself would like some.

"Saved website addresses are a lot different from saved email," Ethan said, screwing the cap back on and replacing the bottle in its pocket. "Most people, when they turn on their computer, go first to their email, which shows a list of every item they haven't deleted. They see their email a lot, almost automatically, in other words."

"But not their Favorites?"

"No, sir. They never see their Favorites unless they're looking specifically for them."

Luther thought for a moment, then said, "Out of sight, out of mind, maybe?"

"That's possible, unless the Favorites are used regularly."

"But I thought 'used regularly' was the whole point of Favorites," Luther said with a look of perplexity. "I mean, people aren't going to bother to save them if they aren't going to keep on using them, are they?"

"Ordinarily I'd say no, but not in this case."

"Why not in this case? What makes it different?"

"Mr. Jackson," Ethan said, seeming to take even more than his usual care in being precise, "on the computer in Professor Wagner's office there are twenty-one bookmarked websites on Favorites. Twelve of these are the right-wing/hate sites you wanted me to look for. The other nine are for publishers and literary agencies. The earliest of these nine sites was bookmarked in August of 2000, which, as I said about the emails, is apparently when Professor Wagner got the computer."

"You mean you can tell that? When the sites were bookmarked? Are you serious?" Luther asked, once again seeming to be utterly dumbfounded.

"Yes, unless a computer crashes and totally kills the hard drive. Except when that happens, nothing, or almost nothing, is ever completely lost. Some things'll be clear and not hard to find. Other things won't. They'll be very dim and shadowy, kind of like fingerprints in an ancient tomb, but most of the time they're there and you generally can find them if you have the right equipment and look hard enough."

"That is amazing, just amazing," Luther said.

"You generally can also tell, if you do enough digging, when and how many times these websites have been visited."

"You can do that too?"

"Yes, sir. You generally can do that too."

"Could you on Professor Wagner's computer?"

Ethan nodded. "Yes, sir, I could. I made a list."

"A list?"

"Yes, sir. Of when each of the twenty-one sites was bookmarked and how many times and when each has been visited. Would you like to see it?" Ethan asked, taking from his coat pocket a neatly folded sheet of white paper.

Luther stared at the paper for a moment, then said, "What I'd really like for you to do, Mr. Anderson, if you can, that is, is just to summarize what's on your list. Can you do that for us, you think?"

"Yes, sir, I can. I can do that from memory."

"Do it for us then. Please do it," Luther said, glancing over at the jury, all twelve of whom seem to lean forward in their seats.

"The nine sites for publishers and literary agents, if we've looking at the oldest one, date back to August of 2000, as I said earlier. Each of these nine sites has been visited, but not much, three or four times at the most, and not a single one has been visited after March of 2006."

Nodding, sweating, Luther said, "And the others? The twelve for hate groups? What about them?"

Ethan shook his head. "Not even that much. Every one of them was bookmarked the same week, in June of 2002, and none of them was visited more than three times, the last time being in July of 2002."

Cupping his left ear with his hand as he moved a step closer to Ethan and leaned forward, Luther said, "Did I hear you correctly, Mr. Anderson? Did you just say that not a single one of the twelve hate sites bookmarked on Professor Wagner's computer has been visited more than a total of three times? And that not a single one of those hate sites has been visited even a single time since July of 2002, over six years ago? Is that what I heard you say?"

"Yes, sir, it is. I can show you my list if you like," Ethan said, holding up the little square of paper.

Luther shook his head and for a long, forehead-wiping moment seemed deep in thought. Then he said, "I believe you said that March of 2006 was the last time any of those nine sites for publishers and literary agents was visited. Is that correct?"

"Yes, sir, it is. March of 2006."

"In order to visit those sites, Professor Wagner would've had to click on Favorites and see the whole list, the list of all twenty-one, before he could scroll to the one he wanted. That is correct, is it not?"

"Yes, sir, it is."

"So he would've seen the names of the hate sites, wouldn't he?"

Ethan nodded. "They were on the list. They still are."

"I've already asked you this once, Mr. Anderson, but I'm going to ask you again. Why didn't he delete them?

I mean, he hadn't visited a single one of them in over six years."

"That's a question I can't answer with any degree of certainty," Ethan said with a slow, solemn shake of his head.

"Yes, and also once again Mr. DiFong is going to object when I ask for your professional opinion. But tell me why, in your opinion, didn't Professor Wagner delete from his Favorites those twelve sites, those twelve hate sites he hadn't visited a single time in over six years? I mean, he completely deleted, as far as he knew, all of the emails he didn't want to keep, didn't he?"

DiFong, to my surprise and apparently to Luther's too, didn't object. He just continued to sit at his table and glower at Luther.

"Do you think maybe he didn't delete those hate sites because he didn't know how?" Luther continued.

"That's possible," Ethan said.

Nodding, Luther said "There's something else I'm curious about and I know the rest of the court is too. And that's the dates when Professor Wagner bookmarked and visited the hate sites. All of that was in a period of only one month. From June of 2002 to July of 2002? Is that correct?"

"Yes, sir. It is. That's correct."

"All right. Consider this. Professor Wagner had finished writing a novel called 'Matters of Vision' no later than 2004, according to the date on the manuscript. This novel, expert testimony tells is, is about the same kind of regional conflicts in this country—the North versus the South, that is—and the related racial and political conflicts that the hate sites on his computer deal with. All twelve of these sites were earmarked in the very same week of June 2002, as your expertise indicates, and not a single one of them, as your expertise also indicates, was ever again used after July of 2002. Now, what this one month, this single, solitary month of hate-site activity suggests to me, Mr. Anderson, along with the long time it takes to write a novel, is that Professor Wagner used these sites when he began writing 'Matters of Vision'. He used them for research, for only one month, and after that he never used them again, not even once in a period of over six years. I repeat: not even once in a period of over six years. What do you think? Could I be correct? In your professional opinion, of course."

The last word was hardly out of Luther's mouth before DiFong was again on his feet.

"I object, Your Honor!" he said, looking and sounding more aggrieved than ever. "Mr. Jackson once again is subjecting the court to the worst kind of witness leading and conjecture. Beyond his own imagination he has no basis whatsoever for having the court believe that Professor Wagner used these hate sites only as research for his novel. He is doing what Your Honor termed 'literary 'second guessing.' And he is pressuring Mr. Anderson to do the same thing. Mr. Anderson is an expert with computers, but he couldn't answer such a question even if he were the greatest literary scholar in the world. Nobody could."

I was all but sure from the look on his face that Judge Peabody was going to sustain DiFong's objection, but before he could even open his mouth Luther woefully shook his head and said, "I withdraw the question, Your Honor, and I sincerely apologize for it and for leading the witness. I got a little carried away." Turning to the jury, he added, "You good folks be sure not to remember what I just said because it was really and truly irrelevant and I just don't know how in the world I could've said it. So delete it with your delete button, your permanent delete button."

This tactic of guaranteeing that the jury would remember something by urging them to forget it was of course too much of a courtroom cliche for anybody not to see. Even worse, at least in terms of transparent phoniness, was the face of abject contrition that Luther wore during Judge Peabody's rebuke and that he continued to wear when he turned and apologized to DiFong.

Even so, I knew in my gut that Luther still had the jury with him, maybe even more than before, and that he knew it as well as I did. When he glanced over at Chuck, sweat was pouring from his woebegone face but his eyes gleamed, and a minute or so later, when he thanked Ethan Anderson and called his next and last witness, his body English and overall manner, his voice in particular, bespoke the euphoria that comes with assured and imminent triumph.

Chapter 15

Marguerite Wilcox was a spry little white woman of at least seventy-five. She had the blue-rinse hair and fastidious look of one of the well-to-do church ladies back in my home town of Thornhurst, except for one thing. She wasn't wearing a dress. She was wearing a charcoal pants suit, nicely fitting and, at least to me, very stylish and expensive looking. She was also wearing a pair of trifocals in some very stylish, expensive looking frames.

After she was sworn in and seated, Luther gave her a little smile and said, "Ms. Wilcox..."

"Mrs., please," she said quickly but not at all snappishly.

Luther smiled again. "Yes, ma'am. Mrs. Wilcox, would you please tell the court if you know the defendant, Professor C. Clarkson Wagner?"

"Of course I know Professor Wagner, Clarkson Wagner. I know Clarkson very well," she said, glancing over at Chuck, who gave her a little nod and maybe even a little wink too.

"How do you know him?"

"He's my neighbor."

"Your close neighbor? In terms of distance, I mean? Does he live close to you?"

"Yes. The Anchorage is next door."

"The Anchorage?"

"That's what Clarkson calls his condo. The Anchorage."

"Do you live alone, Mrs. Wilcox?"

"No. I have David."

"I assume David's your husband or significant other?"

"David's my dog, Mr. Jackson. My red mini dachshund."

The audience emitted a titter or two and Luther smiled, then said. "You said that you know Professor Wagner very well. How long have you known him?"

"Ever since he and Sammy—Sammy's his friend—moved into The Anchorage. That was almost six years ago. I remember, because it was the same week I got David."

"Do you see much of Professor Wagner? Every day, maybe?"

"No, not every day, but I see him. Every Wednesday afternoon, when he gets in from the college, he drives me to the Kroger. Wednesday's senior citizens' day at the Kroger, you know. And whenever I need a light bulb changed or anything, I call him or Sammy. They have me over for dinner at least once a month and on my last birthday...."

"Professor Wagner's a very good neighbor. Is that what you're saying?"

"Clarkson Wagner is a very good neighbor. He's a kind man, a very kind and gentle man."

Nodding, Luther let her words linger for a moment, then said, "Mrs. Wilcox, can you possibly recall where you were and what you were doing between 7:30 and 10 on Tuesday night, the 21st of January?"

"Yes. I can. I can tell you exactly."

"But that was over three months ago. How can you be so sure?" Luther said with a doubtful little smile. "I mean, most of us have trouble remembering what we were doing even just a week ago. I know I do."

"Yes, but I have a very good reason to remember that night."

"What reason is that, ma'am?" Luther asked, moving a step closer to her and putting on his most intent face.

"It was in the paper the next morning, on the front page, and I remember thinking to myself 'Why, that poor thing taught with Clarkson. She was his colleague. He's going to be so-o-o upset'."

"I assume you're referring to Professor Mildred Margulis, the SUS English professor who was murdered in her office the night before?"

"Yes, and do you know what else I was thinking when I was reading about her?"

"No, ma'am, I don't. Please tell me."

"I was thinking about what I was doing at the very time that poor woman was being strangled to death. It was around 8:30, the paper said."

"What were you doing, Mrs. Wilcox?"

"I was in my living room. David was in my lap and we were watching 'Dallas' on a DVD. Bobby had just been shot, as it turned out, by Pam's half-sister, that awful Katherine Wentworth. I didn't remember that she did it, but I never did like that woman and I wasn't a bit surprised."

Luther smiled for a moment. "What about Professor Wagner? Do you have any idea where he was and what he was doing at the time?"

"Probably reading. That's what he does most of the time, that and writing. He was at home, though. That I know."

"Did you see him or what?"

"No, but I know."

"How? How do you know he was at home? Please be specific."

"David never fails to let me know when anybody comes or goes."

"He barks, you mean?"

"Yes, and I'll tell you, Mr. Jackson, it can be very annoying sometimes. He knows Clarkson and Sammy and our other neighbors as well as I do, but they can't even so much as step out of their front door without setting him off. He carries on about them the same way he does about the UPS man and the bug man, so I always have to get up and look out the window. But I don't fuss at him. Not much anyway. I mean, I'd rather have him bark about everybody than not bark about anybody."

"But that Tuesday night, the 21st of January, when you were watching 'Dallas', he didn't bark? Is that what you're saying?"

"Oh, no. He barked. He got in a frenzy when Sammy went out to his car and drove off."

"What time was that?"

"Around seven."

"Was Sammy alone or was Professor Wagner with him?"

"He was alone. He went to the picture show, Clarkson told me later, to see 'The Dukes of Hazard', and when he got back he set David off again, worse than before."

"What time was that?"

"That was about 9:30."

"You got up from watching 'Dallas' to see?"

"Yes. I could see his car and then him when he got out. He has a Buick, a silver Buick."

"But after that? Did David bark anymore?"

"No. He didn't say another word until six o'clock the next morning, Wednesday morning, when he got me up to take him out."

Nodding thoughtfully, Luther said, "Let me see if I understand you correctly now, Mrs. Wilcox. You said that you have a clear memory of where you were and what you were doing on Tuesday night, the 21st of January, because of your friendship with Professor Wagner. You were in the living room of your condo, which is next door to, actually contiguous to, Professor Wagner's condo. Your Dachshund David was in your lap and you were watching 'Dallas' on DVD. How long did you watch 'Dallas'? From what time to what time? Did you say?"

"From about 8 until a little after Sammy got back. I watched three episodes, so it must've been close to 10. Quarter till, maybe."

"You said too that David hears the least little sound outside, that nobody anywhere near your condo can come or go without 'setting him off.' Is that correct?"

"It is. It's very correct. Sometime I wish it wasn't," she said with a rueful little smile.

Luther returned her smile. "And you said that Sammy, Professor Wagner's friend, set him off twice that Tuesday night—once around seven and again around 9:30?"

"Yes."

"But you said that David was quiet—that he didn't say a single word the rest of the night?"

"Yes. Not a single word."

"Are you sure you would've heard if he had?"

"Oh, yes. I'm a light sleeper and my hearing, thank heaven, is still good."

"So, because of David's failure to bark, except when Sammy left and again when he came back, you're sure that Professor Wagner didn't leave or even step out the door of his condo at any time that night--the night of Tuesday, the 21st of January of this year, the night Professor Mildred Margulis was killed?"

"I didn't hear Green Girl either."

"Green Girl? Who is Green Girl, Mrs. Wilcox?"

"She's Clarkson's car, his old green Mercedes-Benz that has some kind of diesel motor in it that's the loudest thing I ever heard. Why, when he first starts it up, it makes more racket than the garbage truck and it smokes up everything and smells awful, just awful."

"It's that loud? So loud you can hear it above your TV?"

"Oh, yes, and even if I couldn't, David surely could."

"But neither of you heard it that Tuesday night, not a single time?"

"We heard it in the afternoon when Clarkson came home from the college. That was around 2:30, when I was watching 'As the World Turns' and my other shows. But we didn't hear it again until Wednesday morning when Clarkson left to go back to the college. That was around 6:30 and I was having my coffee and reading about poor Professor Margulis. I was going to hurry out and tell Clarkson, because I knew he didn't know. I mean, he and Sammy get the paper, but Sammy sleeps late and Clarkson doesn't read it until in the afternoon when he gets home. So I was going to tell him, but he got away too fast and I couldn't."

Wiping his forehead for about the hundredth time, Luther took a dramatically deep breath, the look in his eyes reminding me of a marathon runner getting ready for a final kick.

"Mrs. Wilcox," he said, solemnly, "you know of course what the charges against Professor Wagner are. This is why we need to be sure, just as sure as we possibly can be, that on Tuesday, the 21st of January, Professor Wagner remained inside his condo, not coming out even once, from about 2:30 in the afternoon, when he got in from work, until around 6:30 the next morning, Wednesday, when he left to go back to work. You're sure of that now? Absolutely sure?"

"Yes, Mr. Jackson. I'm sure of that. I didn't hear Green Girl and David didn't hear Clarkson's door open or any other little sound that always sets him off."

"You don't think it's possible, just possible, that during 'Dallas', maybe when the music got loud, that professor Wagner could've slipped very quietly, almost noiselessly, out of his condo without David hearing him? Just possible?"

"I guess he could. I guess it's possible," Mrs. Wilcox conceded, obviously annoyed.

"Wouldn't it also have been possible for Professor Wagner, after he slipped out of his condo, to have walked the three miles to the SUS campus, murdered Professor Mildred Margulis, and then walked back to his condo in time to be there when his friend Sammy got back from seeing 'The Dukes of Hazard'? Isn't it possible, just possible he could've done that?"

Shaking her blue-rinse head as she glared at him, Mrs. Wilcox said, "Mr. Jackson, Clarkson Wagner walks with a cane and you know it. He doesn't have any cartilage in his right knee and he can't even keep up with me at the Kroger. Why, the other day he hurt so bad he had to stop and lean on his buggy. And you're asking me if he could've walked six miles? I simply cannot believe that you could ask such a stupid, stupid, stupid question!"

***

At that point I knew it was over, and I think that everybody else did too. Several minutes later DiFong cross-examined Mrs. Wilcox at considerable length, but his heart obviously wasn't in it and I have the feeling that he did it for much the same reason that a shamefully routed team doesn't just quit and walk off the field.

He was, if anything, even worse the next afternoon during his summation. He was in fact so bumbling that I came close to feeling sorry for him. Rambling on and on about his evidence, he conceded that it all was circumstantial, then repeatedly insisted, twice to the point of shouting, that the murder in the defendant's novel and the appearance of the stolen earring in his office could mean only one thing: that Professor C. Clarkson Wagner, deliberately and with malice aforethought, had murdered Professor Mildred Margulis.

From my customary seat in back I saw that it was more than just the certainty of defeat that had put DiFong in such a fret. It was also the presence of his boss, the DA himself. James C. "Jimmy" Franklin may or may not have been there before—I hadn't seen him—but he definitely was there now, in an aisle seat near the front, and when I say that he didn't look happy, I'm understating the scowl on his bourbon-hued old face.

When Luther mounted the stage for his finale, his white shirt and the back of his dark blue coat looked as soggy as his handkerchief. Further, he moved with the dragging, underwater sluggishness of a fat and badly out of shape man who was also completely exhausted. His eyes gleamed even more than before, though, and as he spoke to the jury, in a tone relaxed and understanding, he sounded to me as if he were reminiscing with old friends who had been through the same sad ordeal that he had.

Instead of rambling on and on with simplistic repetition, he reminded the jury of what he called "the circumstantial precariousness" of DiFong's case, then of the specific ways in which the testimony of each of DiFong's witnesses had been either called into question or completely discredited by the testimony of each of his own witnesses— five English professors, a computer geek, and an elderly lady whom Professor Wagner, despite the pain in his bone-on-bone knee, always took to the grocery store on senior citizens' day.

Standing only a few feet from the jury and, of course, continuing to daub at his forehead, Luther said, "Ladies and gentleman, before you folks retire to consider your verdict I'd like to call your attention just one last, sad time to what our learned prosecutor has been trying to offer up as evidence. He would have us believe that Professor C.

Clarkson Wagner is a man full of hate and is violently, downright murderously intolerant of diversity. Mr. DiFong would also have us believe that Professor Wagner is so stupid that he would commit a murder almost exactly like a murder he wrote about in a novel he hoped would be published and read by thousands of people. Even stupider, far, far stupider is the notion that Professor Wagner would keep the earring of his victim on virtual display in his office and then invite a detective, the very detective who's investigating the case, mind you, to stop by for a visit! That Mr. DiFong could think that anybody in their right mind could believe this is incredible! Just plain incredible!"

Shaking his head, Luther held up both hands as if he were truly and sadly amazed that any prosecutor could offer such an insult to a jury's intelligence.

Then he said, "When Mr. Anderson, our expert from The Geek Shop, was on the stand, one of the things he made clear is that there is no such thing as a completely secure computer, not even at the Pentagon. He also said, as I'm sure I don't need to remind you folks, that it would've been a piece of cake for even just a middling good hacker to have hacked into a computer at SUS State University. I'm convinced, ladies and gentlemen, that this is what happened. Somebody broke into Professor Wagner's computer, read the murder scene, strangled Professor Margulis per the scene, then somehow without Professor Wagner's knowledge managed to put the ripped-off earring on display on the bookshelf in his office. The killer did this, I say, because he knew that sooner or later somebody would spot the earring and a full blown investigation of Professor Wagner, including the contents of his computer, would follow. This, as you know, is exactly what happened. Exactly."

Luther was silent as he looked at each juror in turn and slowly, grimly shook his head. Then he said, "In other words, ladies and gentlemen, what we have here is a frame-up, a frame-up with Professor Wagner as the victim. I said this at the beginning of the trial. I said it then and I say it again now, at the end, because I don't have any doubts that it's true. I don't believe you folks have any doubts either."

The only thing that came even close to surprising me about the verdict was that the jury was allowed to retire and decide it. The state, in the person of DiFong, having so miserably failed to meet the burden of proof, I'd more than halfway expected Judge Peabody to say that the case should never have come to trial, to express his regrets to the jury, and then, after a profuse apology, to declare Chuck a free man.

But he didn't. Instead of exercising his prerogative and directing the verdict, he let the jury decide, maybe because he thought that what they would do would burn DiFong a lot more than anything he himself could've done. He was right too. He definitely was right.

First of all, the jury was out for less than an hour. Second, and far more humiliating for DiFong, was what happened a moment after Judge Peabody announced that Chuck had been found not guilty. At least half of the spectators began clapping, actually clapping, and within seconds were on their feet and looking as if they expected Chuck and Luther to face them, join hands, and take a deep bow.

However happy I was for Chuck—and believe me, I was very, very happy—I was too much of a cop, and maybe just too much of an old-fashioned guy, not to be bothered by such an outburst. We were, after all, in a courtroom, not on Oprah or at a tractor-pull, and I kept waiting for Judge Peabody to rap his gavel and call for order so that he could declare the trial over and Chuck a free man.

I don't think even a full minute passed before he did just that, but it was a long minute for me and, I have no doubt, a far longer minute for DiFong, probably the longest in his life thus far. He sat rigidly at his table and stared straight ahead, seeming not to hear, directly behind him, the crowd celebrating his defeat or to see, only a few feet to his left, the joyous hug that Chuck and Luther were giving each other.

I was sitting too far in the rear to be sure about Luther, but I know that Chuck was not just crying but boohooing. His mouth was quivering like a little child's and his eyes, those dark, fallen-angel eyes, were overflowing

with tears that gleamed like liquid glass as they slid down
his face.

Chapter 16

I could've predicted most of the aftermath. All three of the local channels had it on the evening news, with footage of Chuck being interviewed on the courthouse steps, his tears gone and his Darth Vader voice back in full as he expressed his gratitude to Luther and his relief that the ordeal was over. Neither DiFong nor the DA could be reached for comment, the newscasters said.

The next morning, in fonts again almost as big as for 9/11, SUS PROFESSOR FOUND INNOCENT was splashed across the front page of the Savannah Morning News. The story, which ran three columns on page one and two more on page four, quoted both Chuck and Luther at length but didn't have a single word from either DiFong or Jimmy Franklin. Unlike on TV, though, DiFong wasn't completely out of the picture—the literal picture, that is, beneath the headline. Taken only seconds after the verdict came in, it shows Chuck and Luther in the foreground hugging and DiFong in the background sitting alone at his table and looking as grim as if he himself had just been found guilty and sentenced.

Three days after the trial, in the Sunday edition of the paper, the lead editorial began with two paragraphs blasting DiFong for general incompetence. Then, as Lou put it, "they stopped pussyfooting around and got down to reaming Jimmy a nice big new one." The paper, which tended to be Republican, had always had it in for Jimmy, who was a Democrat, and used the occasion to reprise his many shortcomings. "Not the worst, just the latest" of them was the Wagner case, which, with such "flimsy evidence," should never have come to trial. That it had, and that had been handled so poorly, "was an embarrassment to the county, a waste to the taxpayers, and some of the best proof yet of our need for a change."

DiFong, at least the few times within the next month or so when I chanced into him, seemed to have shrugged off his funk and to be as full of himself as ever, but I knew otherwise. According to my sources, mainly Lou and two other cops, one of them married to Jimmy's secretary, the pudgy little careerist spent almost an hour in Jimmy's office around noon on the Friday before the editorial. When the door finally opened and he emerged, his face was red and he practically ran down the hall and into his office, slamming the door and not coming out or taking any calls for the rest of the day. A week later, according to my source, he fired off his dossier to four firms in Atlanta, four in Charleston, and three in Augusta.

Almost as predictable, at least for me, was the phone call that I got from Caroline Curry, whom I'd not seen or heard from since we'd had lunch together that day shortly after the media circus of Chuck's arrest. I'd been with three or four girls since then, but Caroline sometimes still played in my head, kind of like the Neil Diamond song on an oldies station with the volume on low.

She said she was happy for Chuck and knew that I was too. Having read that the case had been reopened, she asked if I were back on it and said she was glad when I said no, that neither Lou nor I was, the Chief wanting a fresh start. In response to my question, she said she was still with the group of orthopedists and doing fine, then asked about me and got an equally bland answer. She didn't say if she was seeing anybody or ask if I was, and she didn't invite me to lunch or sound other than polite when she said she'd stay in touch.

After we hung up, I began to wonder even more about her call than I had during it. Having always been able to read her voice, I knew, first of all, that I was now as completely out of her heart as I'd been out of her life for the past two years. I knew too that her concern for Chuck and her curiosity about the case, although genuine, were not even close to being the real reason for her call. So what was? Why had she even bothered?

The only thing I could come up with was that she may from time to time have had a tender memory of me and therefore a need to hear my voice to reassure herself once again that I was really and truly just some guy she used to know.

In any case, by the next day I was both surprised and relieved to realize, not just in my head but also down deep in my gut, that I was every bit as over Caroline as she was me. Probably the best measure of this is that about the only thing from her call that continued to buzz in my head was my answer to a question she'd asked. She'd wanted to know if I really believed that Chuck was innocent and I, shrugging to myself, had said, "Doesn't matter what I believe. It's what the jury believes that matters."

***

Down at The Other End, where I still moonlighted once or twice a week, Peterson continued with his interrogations and general gaff. Now as during the proceedings, which he'd followed on TV and in the Morning News, he persisted in his belief that Chuck should never have been arrested, let alone brought to trial. He didn't blame Lou and me for that, he said, because he knew that we'd gone as easy as possible on my friend and old professor.

What he did blame us for, me especially, was our failure, as he put it, "to stick enough screws to Ping Pong's ass," Ping Pong of course being Nigel Helton, the SUS biology professor whom Mildred Margulis had been obliging with a ping pong paddle and then had dumped. I told him, as much to shut him up as for any other reason, that the new crew probably would be taking another and much closer look at Ping Pong.

And of course I heard from Chuck.

***

The first time he called, which was late one afternoon a week or so after the trial, he sounded very upbeat and a little drunk. He asked how I was, thanked me for having always been so unwavering in my support, and, after a very theatrical pause, indulged in a pontification that

I'd heard him make at least a dozen times in the classes I'd had under him.

Sounding like a cross between Sir Laurence Olivier and Darth Vader, he said, "For human beings, life has always had and always will have only three guarantees: change, death, and, alas, irony. You do know that, do you not, T.J.?"

"Yes, Chuck, I do. I surely do," I said, knowing that more was on the way.

"In this case the irony to which I am about to refer calls into serious question the biblical adage that a corrupt tree cannot bring forth anything save corrupt fruit."

"Are you about to tell me that something good's come out of your ordeal?"

"Yes, I am. That is precisely what I'm about to tell you."

"Tell me."

"'The National Enquirer'—you of course are familiar with that rag, are you not?"

"More or less. At the grocery store I'll thumb through it every now and then."

"What about the one for last week? You didn't thumb through it, did you?"

"I can't remember. I might have. Why?"

"Well, somebody on the Savannah scene—some local stringer no doubt—sent the 'Enquirer' an account of the trial, along with pictures, no less. The two of me, incidentally, are really quite flattering. Poor Mildred, though! She would be so mortified by the one of her. I don't know where they got it, but it makes her look so-o-o butch. You need to see it. The whole piece, I mean. You really do."

With a low chuckle he paused for a moment, then said, "But making the pages of the 'Enquirer', although they do provide me with a national stage—indeed an international stage—is hardly what I'd consider good fruit. I haven't yet sunk—and I pray I never do sink—to such depths as to think that."

"What is it, Chuck? Tell me," I said.

"My literary agent—Doris Wilcox, the one in Atlanta who sent Mr. Edward DiFong the third of that

loathsome name--a fax of the murder scene in my novel?
I'm sure you remember her?"

"I remember."

"Yes, well, she called me this morning to tell me
that the editor at Doubleday, a man named Joseph Carr, to
whom she'd sent my manuscript and who'd been hanging
fire on it for the past three months, heard about the story in
the 'Enquirer' and..."

"Wants to publish 'Murder in Savannah'?"

"Exactly. In fact, at this point Doris says it's just a
question of the amount. His first offer, of the advance and
all, was fine with me, but she says no way. And..."

For the next five or so minutes that seemed at least
an hour, I had to endure an update of my old professor's
standard jeremiad on the state of book publishing in
America. It wasn't about art or literary merit or anything
evenly remotely high-minded, he said, not even at the so-
called elite houses such as Random House and Little
Brown. It was about money and money alone, of which the
circumstances of 'Murder in Savannah' were absolute proof.
That publishers could routinely reject the five novels that he
had put his heart and soul into but could accept the little
piece of brainless fluff that he was almost ashamed to put
his real name on—and then would do so only because its
author had made a splash in 'The National Enquirer'—well,
it was enough to make the angels weep, etc.

He was not at all upbeat the next time he called,
which was about a month later and only two days after I
read in the Savannah Morning News an obituary that
shocked me without the least bit surprising me.

It said that Dr. Steven C. Harrison, age 56, had died
of a heart attack at his home. A native of Newport News,
VA, he was the author of over 500 poems and two textbooks
and had been the Head of the English Department at SUS.
He was survived by his wife Mahalia and by two sons, two
daughters-in-law, and three grandchildren. There would be
no funeral but remembrances could be sent to a favorite
charity or to the Chatham County Humane Society.

"Yes, Chuck, I saw it in the paper and I'm so sorry.
He was a good guy and I liked him. I liked him a lot," I said.

"Yes, T.J., and he liked you, which is why I'm calling. Sunday afternoon, from three until six, Mahalia is having a little gathering and she said she knew he'd want you to be invited. It'd mean a lot to her if you could make it, the poor little thing," Chuck said, his voice deep and resonant but his manner, for once, solemn without in any way being theatrical.

"I'll be there," I quickly assured him.

Chapter 17

As I slowed the Crown Vick and turned into the Sherwood Forest subdivision, I suddenly realized that it was D-Day, the 6th of June, the anniversary of the Normandy Invasion. Naturally I thought of my old unit, the 82nd Airborne, and of the legendary courage it had shown during that terrible time, but I no longer was filled with my old ambivalence about having missed combat. As a cop I'd seen enough of the civilian equivalent, and thereby learned enough about my manhood, to be only thankful that I'd been spared both of our wars in Iraq, the first one because I'd been too young and the second and current one because I'd mustered out and become a cop before the shooting could again get serious.

I'm exaggerating of course, but at that particular moment, Sunday, 4:02 p.m., I think I would've been almost as grateful if I'd been on my way to just about anywhere other than the gathering for Dr. Harrison. Being at heart such a sentimental slob, I've always hated such occasions and, whenever possible, have lied or in some other way weaseled out of them.

I couldn't get out of this one. I'd given Chuck my word and at my back, with the force of time itself, was the grief that I imagined in the face of poor little Mahalia. I was also, I have to admit, curious about whether certain members of the SUS English department would show up and, if they did, how they would behave.

Of the dozen or so cars in the driveway and out by the curb on either side of the street, the only ones I recognized were the only ones I'd expected to recognize--- Dr. Harrison's silver Buick and Chuck's noisy old diesel Mercedes, Green Girl.

In the house, however, I could identify most of the crowd, at least by face. In twos, threes, and fours they clustered about in the den and living room and around the table of food and drinks in the dining room, most of the women in nice dresses or pants suits and most of the men, as I was, in a coat and tie. Dean Thomas and his wife and the SUS president and his wife were there, as were most of the English Department and their spouses or significant others, including Dr. Elyse Rainey, the only black in the department and at the gathering. When I first saw her, she was talking to Sammy Ray, Chuck's friend, at the same time that she was leaning down and petting the Harrison's black lab, Sabilio, who was sporting a royal blue scarf and looking every bit as gentle as his late master had been.

I didn't see, and hadn't expected to see, Dr. Julia Kerns and Professor Jack Flanagan, who no doubt continued to be in hateful discord on everything other than their abiding contempt for Dr. Harrison. For a moment I thought of their absence as a boycott and a final statement of that contempt, then reconsidered and tried to give them the benefit of the doubt when it occurred to me that Mahalia would never have allowed them in her house, let alone have invited them.

From their pictures on the mantle I recognized Dr. Harrison's two sons, to whom, along with their wives, Chuck introduced me. In their early thirties, both men closely resembled their father in being of medium height, handsome, and very kind-looking in the eyes and around the mouth. Neither, though, was even fat, let alone obese, and the younger of the two had the semi-sunken face of a fitness nut.

Also on the mantle were the wedding picture of Dr. Harrison and Mahalia, the striking portrait of a young Mahalia as a Nicolette Sheridan look-a-like, and a picture that hadn't been there when I'd stopped by and questioned Mahalia back in January. In a 10" by 12" frame and bigger than all of the others, it was a black-and-white of Dr. Harrison at twenty-fire or thirty or maybe even older but well before obesity had descended on his lean good looks like Vesuvius on Pompeii.

Mahalia was still frog-belly pale and Dachau-scrawny, and her eyes still had the strained, squinty look I've come to associate with computer geeks, but she was far from the vessel of grief I'd expected. On the contrary, the black of her dress and the bright red of her lips made me think of both a black widow and a merry widow as she segued among her guests, patting an arm here, giving a hug there, and several times actually laughing at some of the anecdotes being told about Dr. Harrison. When she'd hugged me at the door, I'd not smelled anything suspicious, not even Listerine, and I knew for a fact, having seen her pour it, that the clear drink in her hand was only ginger ale.

"Is she really that strong, Chuck, or what?" I asked.

"No, my dear T.J, she's not. The poor little thing somehow managed for Steve's sake to get herself together for this, but I don't know. I just don't know what'll happen when everybody's gone and she's again alone," he said with a mournful, barely perceptible shake of his head.

Only once that afternoon did I see Mahalia's grief break through. This was when she was telling Dean Thomas and his wife of how, around two a.m., she'd gotten up to get some water and on her way back to bed had stopped by the computer room to check on Dr. Harrison. She'd found him lying face down on the hardwood floor, his eyes open and his lips smeared with blood the exact color of raspberry Jello, a little puddle of which, no larger than a half-dollar, had formed on the floor beside his cheek. On the computer screen in front of the empty chair were three stanzas of the poem he'd been writing, the fourth stanza ending abruptly at the beginning of the second line with "Memories, so corrosive and lasting...." The word "lasting" was the last word on the screen and the last one Dr. Harrison would ever write.

Even more than about Mahalia I was concerned about Chuck. I can't say that he didn't seem himself, because I didn't know him well enough to know what his real self was. Plus, he'd just lost his closest friend, after Sammy Ray that is, and what I thought I was seeing could've been nothing but the way he dealt with grief. He was, after all, a very theatrical man much given to irony, especially in the forms of under-statement and flippancy.

In any case, something seemed to be on his mind, "sitting on brood," as in 'Hamlet'. More to the point, but unlike in 'Hamlet', that something didn't seem to depress him. On the contrary, it—whatever it was—seemed to lighten the great load he'd been bearing in the months since that day in his office when I'd spotted the earring. As I watched him mingle with the other guests, leaning on his cane as he sipped from a double gin-and-tonic, I thought I could see in those dark, fallen angel eyes the kind of deep relief and gratitude that a man might feel in response to a biopsy that had come back negative.

I didn't merely think, however—I knew beyond doubt—that there had been something upbeat in his voice right after Mahalia greeted me and Chuck, as he shook my hand, leaned close to me and all but whispered, "I need to have a little word with you before you go, T. J."

After my obligatory half-hour, I found Mahalia, again expressed my condolences, and said goodbye, her fleshless little body feeling like a packet of sticks as she hugged me and thanked me for coming. She said she'd walk me out to my car but Chuck, who'd been talking with her and two other women, said she needed to stay with her guests, that he'd see me out.

My curiosity, already acute, became even more so when we were outside and Chuck said, "I think you need to be sitting down, T.J."

I knew even more from his eyes than from his low, solemn voice that he was not being theatrical.

"How about my car?" I said, gesturing toward the unmarked white Crown Vick on the other side of the street.

He gave me an abrupt nod, then began limping on his cane beside me, his face, as always, seeming to register the pain of every step.

With my remote clicker I unlocked the doors of the Crown Vick and we got in, he at shotgun and I behind the wheel. I started the engine and switched on the air conditioner, then turned toward him.

Sitting completely erect, he was studying the car's interior, a quizzical look on his face as his dark eyes took in the police radio, the steering wheel, the back seat. "This is the one, is it not?"

"One what?" I asked.

"The cruiser in which you and the fell sergeant gave me that unprecedented and, I truly hope, never to be repeated ride down town on that day of infamy?"

"No, I don't think so. I think that was Lou's," I said.

"Yes, well," he said, still studying the interior.

I waited several long seconds, then said, "So what is it, Chuck, that you think I need to be sitting down for?"

"All right then," he snapped, raising his eyes from the dash and staring out over the hood. "Yesterday morning around ten, poor little Mahalia came out to The Anchorage to give me something. I wasn't there, so she gave it to Samuel. It was a padded manila envelope, taped shut, with my name on it. It was from Steve and I assumed, quite naturally, that it was just some more poems he wanted me to look at. Anyway, late last night, after Samuel had gone to bed and I was just sitting around staring at the walls and being morbid, I took the envelope off the bookcase and opened it. It was a good thing I was sitting down. Truly. Otherwise I would've been floored, perhaps quite literally," Chuck said, turning to me and looking me in the eye.

"What was in it?" I asked.

"Two things. This is one of them," he said, reaching into the inside pocket of his blue blazer and taking out a letter-size white envelope, unmarked and unsealed but so stuffed as to be rounded on both sides. "See what you make of that."

Taking the envelope and opening the flap, I saw a block at least an inch thick of crisp new money bound by three red rubber bands.

"They're hundred-dollar bills, T.J., two-hundred of them, $20,000," Chuck said as I took out the block and stared at the picture of Ben Franklin on top.

"What in the world, Chuck?"

Reaching back into his jacket, he took out another letter-size white envelope, also unmarked and unsealed but almost flat on both sides, which he extended toward me.

I replaced the hundreds in their envelope, then gave it back to Chuck and took the second envelope.

"Read what's in it. Read it very carefully," he said as I opened the flap and saw inside, neatly folded, what looked like three, maybe four white pages.

Taking the pages out and opening them, I saw that they were typed, single-spaced, and addressed to Chuck.

"This is from Dr. Harrison?" I asked, riffling to the last page and seeing "Steve" handwritten in blue ink at the same time that Chuck said, "Yes, God rest his soul."

Returning to the opening page, I was at first more mindful of Chuck's eyes on me and of the hum of the Crown Vick's air conditioner than I was of what I read. Gradually, as if on a dimmer switch, everything on the periphery faded into a gray blur and Dr. Harrison's words were all I could see. This is what they said.

May 27

Chuck,

Read this carefully and please believe me when I say that I feel totally, unforgivably, damnably rotten about involving you in what I did.

On that afternoon I left school around 5:30, drove home, walked Sabilio, got cleaned up, and took Mahalia for our Tuesday evening dinner at Luigi's. Despite my pleas she once again drank to the point of falling asleep and Brad (the manager) once again had to help me get her out to the car.

On the way home I remembered that I hadn't emailed to my home computer and hadn't brought a hard copy of a poem I wanted to work on, so I stopped by school. This was around 8:15, right before the 6-8:20 classes let out, and I had to park in the big parking lot because some student's pickup was in my slot. I thought of calling security and getting it ticketed but I wouldn't be but a minute and I knew that Mahalia, still dead to the world, would be fine. As dark as it was, nobody would even see her, so I cracked a window, locked the car, and went to my office.

When I got there, I emailed the poem to myself at home, then turned off my computer and was about to leave when, with its sudden urgency, my bladder began screaming at the very same moment that I noticed on my desk the folder of new poems I'd been wanting you to see. Taking the folder, I turned out the light, locked my door, and hurried down the hall and up the stairs. By the third or fourth step I was sweating, breathing hard, and fearing I was about to pee in my pants, so I was glad classes were not yet out and nobody was around to see me.

I was in the men's room for maybe ten minutes, not peeing—that went fast—but leaning against the sink as I waited for my heart to calm down. Classes let out and I could hear the sounds of doors opening, people walking, talking, etc. When I finally felt okay, I washed my hands and came out. By then the hall was empty, quiet in the ghostly way of all school buildings without students in them.

As I turned out of the hall and started down your cul-de-sac, I saw that Mildred M's door was open and her light was on. Your office being directly across from hers, I could hardly slide the poems under your door without her seeing me, so I choked down my Mildred-nausea and made myself be polite.

Seated at her desk, she responded to my greeting by looking up from what she was reading and for a moment glaring at me with pure and undisguised loathing. Then her own hypocrisy kicked in and with more smirk than smile she motioned for me to come in. "You need to see this, Steve. You really do," she said, stabbing her pen at what looked like a student's essay.

Having so seldom been in her office, I self-consciously noted the wall of books, the mugs and a coffee maker, the framed pictures of feminists, the ultra thin computer monitor with a color portrait of a very young Sylvia Plath as a screen saver. As in the past, only the running medals on the coat rack really struck me, and the reason for this is something I've long been ashamed of and need to explain.

For almost two years now, thanks to Mahalia, I've had complete access to every computer in the SUS system, from the president's all the way down to the ones in groundskeeping. This has enabled me to see anything anybody on campus has sent, received, saved, etc., including the outpourings of viciousness that my enemies, chiefly Mildred M. and Julia K, have directed at me and several times at Mahalia as well. More to the point, it enabled me to read the hundred or so pages that you thus far had written on your work in progress, later titled 'Murder in Savannah'.

I was so profoundly impressed by your murder scene that I returned to it and re-read it at least once a week for several months, and in several of our early morning chats came perilously close to confessing my sneakiness so that I could congratulate you on such a fine piece of writing. It had the effect on me of some really good pornography in the way it kept me coming back to it and visualizing it and at times wishing to a scary degree that I could actually do the forbidden things it so beautifully described.

At this point I have little doubt that you can guess the rest of the story. I killed Mildred Margulis. I killed her exactly, or almost exactly, as her counterpart in your novel is killed. I know how literary and phony this sounds, but I had the spooky sense of being outside myself and watching myself as I did it. I watched myself enter her office and again be struck by the medals hanging from the coat rack behind her desk. I watched myself stand behind her and look over her shoulder and pretend to be interested in the very bad student essay she began reading aloud. I watched myself carefully remove from the coat rack one of the medals and wrap the ends of the purple ribbon around my hands. Then I watched myself suddenly slip the ribbon around her neck and yank back on it with all of my weight and strength at the same time that I jammed my right knee into the back of her chair and pushed forward as hard as I could.

She took what I have no doubt seemed to her a very long time to die, maybe ten or twelve terrible minutes, but it was nowhere near long enough for me. Even after she stropped gagging and flailing and went limp, I continued pulling on the ribbon and pushing on the chair, and watching myself as I did it. For probably the first time in my life, my adult life anyway, I was living completely in the moment, with no fear of the hours and days and years to come and regretting only two things: 1) that, being behind her, I hadn't been able to watch her face, and 2) that, during her agony, I hadn't thought to lean down and whisper, "This is for Mahalia, you miserable creature."

And it indeed was, or mostly was, for Mahalia that I did it, so much so that for a kind of condign parallelism I wanted to lug the body to the men's room, then situate it so that she would be found dead on a toilet rather than just passed out, as poor Mahalia had been that time at the restaurant and about which, as I know you remember, Mildred M. had informed the entire SUS community in that gloating, vicious, evil email. But I didn't do it or even try, mainly because, the way my heart was acting up, I was afraid I might drop dead and be found in the hall with that miserable woman's body beside me or even on top of me, which was too awful to risk.

I wasn't aware of it at the time, but I now also think I probably was subconsciously aware that I couldn't move the body from behind the desk without departing from the script, i.e., the scene in your novel. That this could be the case eats like acid into my soul because it strongly suggests that my attempt to make you the main suspect was not the mere mindless impulse I've been trying to convince myself that it was. So does something else that I did. I used my handkerchief to wipe my fingerprints off the ribbon; then, just as you did in your novel, I awarded her with the medal by hanging it around her neck.

Even so, as I was taking my last look at the terror in her bugged-out eyes and sagging mouth, my demons again seized me and I watched myself depart from my hitherto exact enactment of the script by grabbing her left ear and ripping out the dangly earring with the little golden balls on it, halfway hoping, however irrational it may seem, that she would cry out or at least wince from the pain.

I left the light on and eased the door to behind me, then wiped my prints off the knob and made my way out of the cul-de-sac, down the stairs, and out of the building. I know how silly it sounds, but I thought of myself as Wiley E. Coyote sneaking up on the Road Runner as I slipped out, my heart crazy with fear that I would be seen by some student or faculty member still in the building. As far as I knew, my luck held then and in the parking lot, which still had enough cars in it to keep mine from being alone and conspicuous. Mahalia, bless her heart, was still slumped against the door, dead to the world.

I don't think I came completely out of that trance-like state of being both actor and audience until, after getting Mahalia to bed, I fixed myself a drink and accessed the email of the poem I'd sent. Then it all came back with such force and immediacy that I began to gasp and sweat and my hand shook so badly that I had to put my drink down. It was only chance, pure chance, that there hadn't been anybody in the halls to have seen me enter or leave Hampton or, with the door wide open, to have heard Mildred M.'s gagging and flailing and caught me in the act. What was worse was that, far from feeling any remorse, I felt only the kind of simple, uncomplicated, self-congratulatory relief—but a great deal more of it—that I'd once felt in a high school baseball game when, after striking out three straight times, I'd singled in the winning run in the bottom of the ninth.

This sudden and dreadful knowledge of the kind of man I really am remained the main source of my agony, even more than my fear of getting caught, until early that Friday morning in your office, two days after the murder. You may remember that in the midst of our talk about the investigation you excused yourself to go to the men's room and left me alone, in the chair in front of your desk. It was then that I did something that, instead of being the mere mindless impulse I wish I could believe it was, probably was part of the truly evil scheme that in my subconscious I could well have begun hatching shortly after hacking into your computer and being so impressed by your murder scene.

Getting up from my chair and going around behind your desk, I took from my jacket pocket the earring I had yanked out of Mildred M.'s ear, wiped it clean with my handkerchief, then carefully placed it so that it would be visible on top of a set of books that was on a shelf about the same height as your desk. Insane or not, I had been carrying the earring around in my jacket pocket and, ala Captain Queeg in The Caine Mutiny, had regularly fondled the little golden balls on it as a way of re-living, and re-enjoying, my crime. If you had finished in the men's room only a minute earlier, you would have caught me wiping off the balls instead of, as you did, standing behind your desk and pretending to wipe my nose and to be interested in one of your books.

As much to my horror and guilt as to my surprise and relief, the scheme worked out exactly, or almost exactly, as my subconscious apparently had hoped or maybe even had foreseen that it would. Detective Loomis—our mutual former student no less—chanced to see the earring; soon thereafter, the scene in your novel was revealed, first by another of our mutual former students, David Allen, then by your literary agent. Your indictment soon followed and I gave thanks that I was off the hook, home free, etc.

But I wasn't. On the contrary, I felt even more rotten than before. I knew I was not only the kind of man who could take pleasure in murdering a fellow human being; I was also the kind of man who, to spare his own sweet, guilty-as-hell ass, could scheme to stick the blame on, and make no end of trouble for, someone who had never been other than a great and good friend to me.

More than ever I played the role of Tolstoy's "Kutuzov the Imperturbable," as you used to call me, and thereby, as far as I could tell, succeeded in covering my agony from everyone except Mahalia. For once she was only half correct in her reading of me. She knew I was eaten up with guilt, but she thought it was from my being as glad as she herself was that Mildred M. was dead. Over and over she assured me that my feelings were perfectly normal, and over and over I would want to confess everything to her even though I knew I would rather be burned alive than have her know, or even suspect, that I was not the poetically sensitive, hyper-gentle soul that she so proudly and lovingly believed that I was.

Chuck, I'm not exaggerating—and you know me well enough to know I'm not exaggerating—when I say that I've not passed a single waking hour since this whole mess began without fearing I would go completely insane if I didn't come forward and confess my guilt both to you and to the police. But I didn't because I was afraid, just plain chickenshit, and I over and over reassured myself that the evidence was too weak for you to even go to trial, let alone be convicted. Had you been convicted—and you have to believe me when I say this, you simply have to--I would've gone to DiFong and made a full confession. Even I, coward though I am, was not so low and despicable that I could've seen you go to prison and know that I and I alone was the reason for it.

But you weren't convicted, thank God or something, and I'm gone from this world, or will be if you're reading this, so I'm making the confession I wish I'd had the guts to make when I could've looked you in the eye and felt the lash that your stare would've been and that my poor guilty soul so richly craves and deserves. I'm not asking you to forgive me—I can't ask it and you can't and shouldn't even try to do it—but I'm begging with all of my poor sick heart that you try to understand how desperately sorry I am that my hatred and weakness caused you such grief.

Steve

"Good Lord! This is amazing. Just flat out amazing," I said when I finally looked up from the last sheet and over at Chuck.

"The murder itself is, T.J. It is indeed amazing," Chuck said, easing the four sheets out of my hands and, after re-folding them, slipping them back into their envelope. "I knew of course that Steve loathed Mildred, and for good reason too. But I never, not even in my most lurid fantasies, would've thought him capable of killing her, especially by strangulation, which is so up close and intensely personal. Nor would I ever, ever, ever have thought him capable of scheming to dump the blame on me, or anyone else for that matter. I thought him altogether too kind and decent for that."

"So did I," I said.

"The rest is Steve, pure, quintessential Steve," Chuck said, mournfully shaking his head and turning from me to stare though the windshield at the sky or the hood ornament or maybe just at some sad picture in his head.

"You mean in his need to tell you and have you hate him? Hate his memory?" I asked.

Chuck nodded. "Like some poor agonizing character in Dostoyevsky craving to be punished. And he has indeed been punished, ever since that day in my office when he left the earring. God knows the poor man's been punished. He's been in the worst kind of hell, the absolute worst."

"Yes, the one inside his head. The one that's always there," I said. "I don't wonder about that, but I do wonder about something. I mean, I can understand why he couldn't face you but didn't want to die without knowing you'd know. But he said he'd rather be burned alive than have Mahalia know and yet he tells you."

"Of course he does. What's to wonder about that?" Chuck asked, raising his left eyebrow as if at a slow student.

"Mahalia's what's to wonder. Did he think you wouldn't tell her?"

"No. He knew. He knew I'd never, never do such a thing to her. Never," Chuck said, grimacing as if he'd bitten into something rotten.

"But the money? Won't she miss the money?" I asked, eyeing the envelopes in his hands.

"Steve kept a stash of cash, his 'secret emergency fund', he called it, in a hollowed out book or some such place, and he said Mahalia didn't know a thing about it. It was mostly royalties from those two textbooks he wrote."

"He didn't mention it in the letter, though. Why?"

"I have no idea."

"But you're sure, you say, that it's not hush money?"

"Absolutely. Steve knew me too well for that."

"Maybe he meant it for your legal fees and just forgot to mention it?"

"If he did, it's far more than enough. Luther gave me a generous discount, a former-student discount so generous in fact that I had to make him take more, bless his heart."

After waiting for a long moment, I said, "So, Chuck, what are you going to do?"

"With these, I assume you mean?" Chuck asked, indicating the two envelopes.

I nodded. "Yes. What?"

"This, first," Chuck said, replacing both the envelopes in the inside pocket of his blazer.

"Then what?"

"Then I'm going to start putting the cash in the bank, in a succession of deposits too small to attract any attention of course. Unless, that is, you need some of it."

For a very long moment I studied his face and those fallen angel eyes, which remained steady on mine. Then with a weak little smile I said, "You're not offering to buy my silence by any chance, are you, Chuck?"

"Heavens no. I know I no more need to buy yours than Steve did mine. Otherwise, I never would've shown you the document. Which, incidentally, figures in the second thing I'm going to do. I'm going to reduce it to ashes just as soon as I return to The Anchorage this afternoon."

Still studying his face, I said, "So, if you and I keep silent, Mahalia's golden image of Dr. Harrison will remain untarnished and the Margulis case will eventually join the ranks of The Unsolved. And that'll be that, right?"

Again as if to a slow student, Chuck raised his left eyebrow and said, "In this case, my dear T.J., the truth is not going to help anyone. It can only make an already miserable woman even more miserable. Follow your professional conscience and that's what we'll have. Is that what you want?"

"You know it's not."

"I certainly don't, so that is indeed that. Is it not?"

"Yes, as far as I'm concerned," I said with a nod. A second or so later I said, "There is one more thing I need to know, though."

"Oh?"

"Yes. You say you know me well enough to know you weren't risking anything, but there still was no reason for you to tell me all this. You could've kept it to yourself and..."

"No, T.J., there was a reason. An irresistibly compelling reason."

This time it was I who said, "Oh?"

"Yes, and I'm surprised you don't know or can't guess what it is."

"Well, I don't and can't, so tell me."

"You're a very dear friend, T.J., and I dare say I value your good opinion of me almost as much as poor Steve did Mahalia's of him."

"So?"

"Throughout this whole sorry ordeal you've been as loyal and supportive to me as any man, let alone one in your official position, could possibly be. I am grateful. Believe me, I am more grateful than I can ever tell you. You're a fine, decent man, T.J. A good man. A really good man, too good to be a cop."

"But?"

"But I know—and you need not deny it—that you've had doubts about me ever since that morning in my office when you saw that earring. I needed to remove those doubts, and to show you the confession was the only way I could do it. In short, I needed for you to know beyond any question that your old teacher and friend, C. Clarkson Wagner, did not murder Professor Mildred Margulis. That and that alone is why you had to know the terrible truth about poor Steve."

***

A few minutes later, as I headed the Crown Vick out of Sherwood Forest and back toward downtown, I still had a sharp after-image of Chuck leaning on his cane in front of the Harrisons' house and looking every inch the English professor as he grinned and, with his free hand, bade me goodbye with a military salute in extreme slow motion. I was again awash in ambivalence, much as I'd been about one thing or another ever since early that cold Wednesday morning back in January when I'd first seen Mildred Margulis blank-eyed and dead behind her desk.

This time my inner conflicts were limited entirely to Chuck. On the one hand I resented him for putting me in a position where I had to choose between my duty to the law and my pity for a sweet and altogether innocent little widow. On the other hand I was touched that anybody, let alone my former and all-time favorite professor, could care so much about easing my doubts and regaining my high opinion.

The more I thought about it, the more it seemed to me that both of us had done the right thing, Chuck in showing me the confession and I in promising to keep my mouth shut about it. Even if only the two of us were aware of it, Justice had been served, the murderer having paid for his crime with his suffering and death; a grieving little woman could still believe the best about her dead husband; and a crippled, lonely old English professor had been restored to grace in the eyes of his friend and former student.

For these good things, though, as for all good things, there was a price. I would have on my professional conscience the additional time and money the Savannah Police Department would continue to waste until the case was marked Unsolved.

It was a price I was willing to pay.

~*~*~*~

Meet our Author

William Breedlove Martin

William Breedlove Martin is a veteran of the U.S. Air Force
and a graduate of Armstrong State College and of Duke

University. He and his wife live in Savannah and have two daughters, three grandchildren, and one Dachshund. His other novels are IN ANOTHER TIME—A Southern Family During the Great War, 1914-1918, and DON'T ASK FOREVER—A Love Story of 1968, both available on online at Amazon and the latter also at www.a-argusbooks.com.

Printed in Great Britain
by Amazon